THE SCOOPER AND DOG PLAYER

CRAIG CAUDILL

Characters

<u>Sutherland Tailoring Harrodsburg, Kentucky</u>

Marcel Sutherland, CEO

Brock Skinner, Investor

<u>Vigneron Winery Hazard, Kentucky</u>

Maude Skinner, Proprietor

Truman, German Shepherd Guard Dog

<u>Real Buy Louvers Lawrenceburg, Kentucky</u>

Elijah Ashby, President

Marilyn McDonald, Vice President

<u>Gibbous Metals Danville, Kentucky</u>

Cheryl Welch, President

<u>Woodford County High School Classmates Versailles, Kentucky</u>

Kyle Becker, Professional Gambler

Penny Gaines, Horse Farm Office Employee

Esther Rice, Thoroughbred Exercise Rider

<u>Laurel Mechanical Harlan, Kentucky</u>

George Pelham, Owner

<u>Retirees Jacksonville, Florida</u>

Mindy McDonald

Peter McDonald

Bonnie Pratt

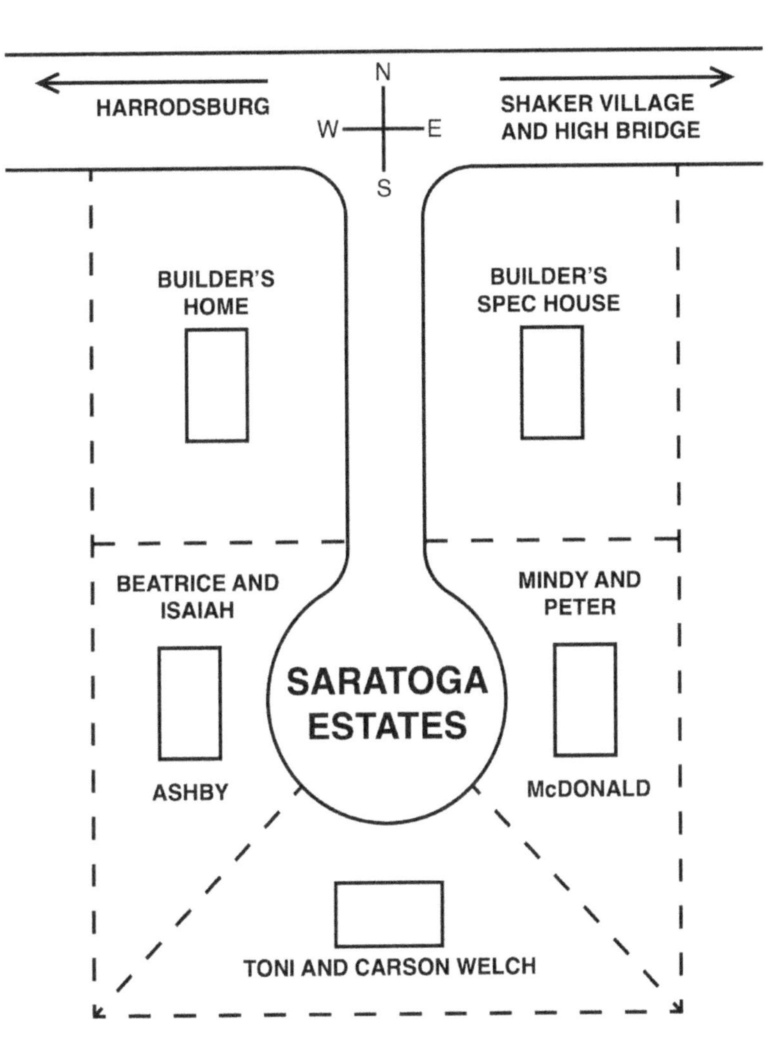

N
W E
S
HARRODSBURG
SHAKER VILLAGE
AND HIGH BRIDGE
BUILDER'S
HOME
BUILDER'S
SPEC HOUSE
BEATRICE AND
ISAIAH
MINDY AND
PETER
SARATOGA
ESTATES
ASHBY
McDONALD
TONI AND CARSON WELCH

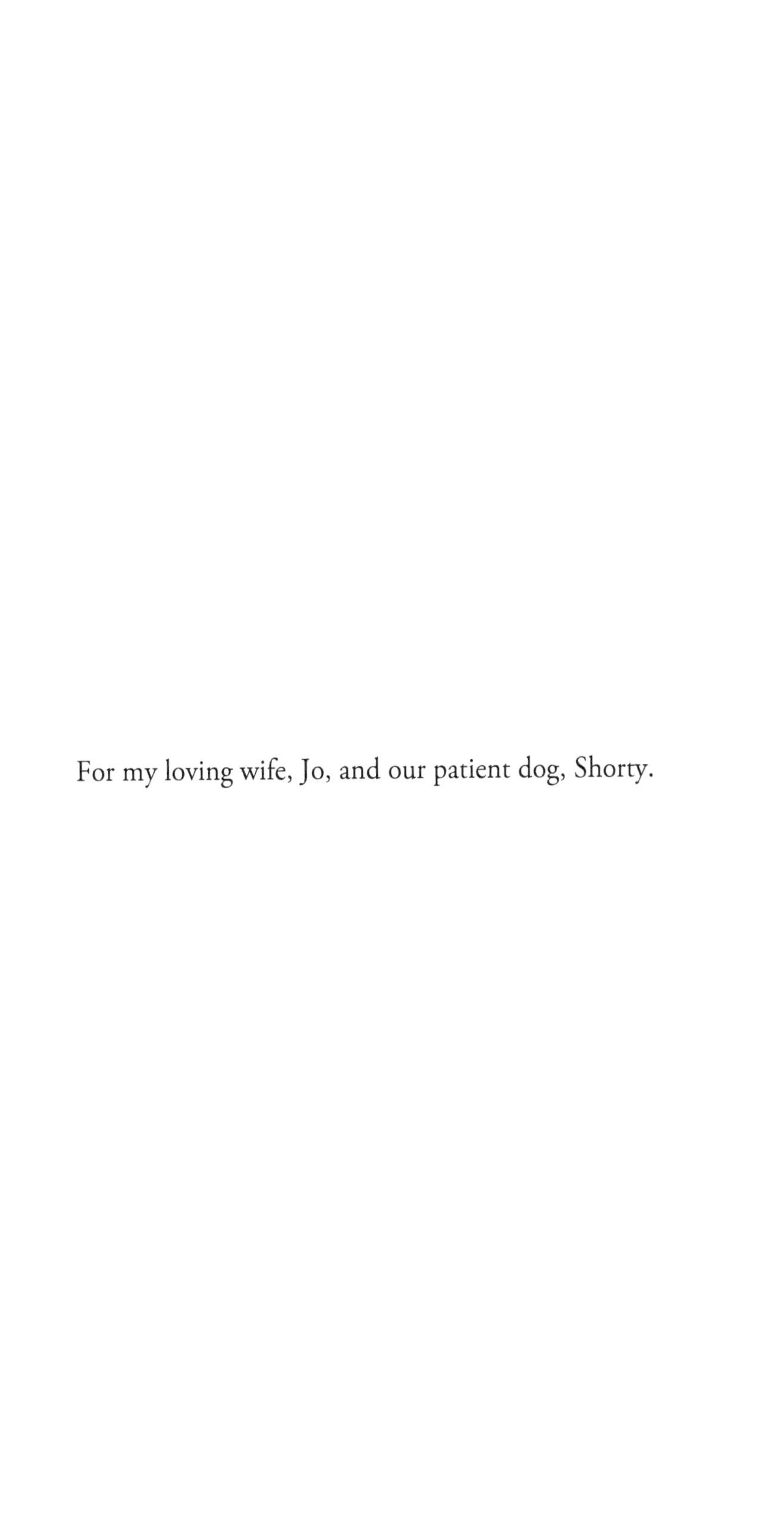

For my loving wife, Jo, and our patient dog, Shorty.

CHAPTER 1

Wintertime proved tolerable for the Skinners because of their fondness for Kentucky culture. They learned to face the oft-gray days from December to March with a cheerful attitude. The couple possessed the wherewithal to avail themselves of the comforts that made the freezing temperatures seem nothing more than a minor nuisance, and they leveraged those means when the weather got bad. Brock Skinner was no wimp, though, always willing to take on exasperating inclement weather for the sport of it. During the wintry weeks, he refused to morph into some cloistered creature with lousy posture and soft hands. His wife, Maude, knew of this proclivity before they married. However, she was not aware of his propensity for getting into scrapes and rooting out mischief no one else suspected.

Brock grew up in Lexington on a small horse farm off Athens Boonesboro Road. He had a fair grasp of horse racing, enough to know that wholesale betting on Thoroughbreds was a losing proposition, and the type of people deep into it were never as smart as they thought they were. His grandmother left him $250,000 when she died. It landed in his bank account right after he graduated from high school, feathering his nest before he ever set foot in a classroom at the University of Kentucky.

When he got to college, Brock made friends with Marcel Sutherland, a bright young student from the innocuous village of Campton, Kentucky, near Red River Gorge. Brock had a chance to meet Marcel's younger sister, Maude, on several occasions. Every time he saw her, she seemed more beautiful, both inside and out. It wasn't until he visited her years later in Hazard, Kentucky, at the picturesque winery she built with Marcel's backing, that he fell hopelessly in love.

Skinner invested his inheritance in Marcel's scheme of digitized, Internet tailoring outlets after college. The first years were lean, and then the cash started pouring in. They were both multimillionaires before age thirty. The first thing Brock did with his money, before Maude figured into his life, was buy a condo in downtown Lexington near the boxing gym he frequented. He took up the sweet science to stay in shape, always wearing headgear, padded gloves, and a kidney belt when he stepped into the ring. Brock eschewed any actual fights for fear of winding up punch drunk. Even so, he was the most feared sparring partner in the country. Ranked fighters paid him to come and train with them. He didn't need the money. He just had an itch to knock a cocky boxer on his rear end. Boxing honed his skills for bringing rotten people down a peg or two.

Skinner reeked of boredom when he wasn't sleighing dragons. Maude recognized the signs; listlessness, like the Energizer Bunny, batteries flagging. She suggested, "Let's run over to Lexington before I open the winery on St. Patty's Day."

"You beat me to it. Marcel called a few minutes ago and asked if we could meet him there for dinner tonight. He said he had something to spring on me."

"Outstanding. Shall we take Truman?"

"He'd be lonesome without us." The overly intelligent, white German shepherd heard every word, wagging his tail in anticipation.

Maude had had trouble at Vigneron Winery a couple of years back when Marcel asked Skinner to drive into Hazard to find out what it was about. Brock cleaned up the mess, and in the process, was astute enough to pick up on the fact that Maude had put her tap root down in the mountain town, and if he was going to woo her, he'd have to tiptoe carefully into her sphere, keeping his big mouth shut. The masterstroke came when he bought a gigantic log cabin behind the vineyard and announced his intention to refurbish it. Maude's fairy-tale betrothal came together with panache when she took up residence with her swashbuckling husband. He unapologetically drove a gaudy blue-green Lamborghini, and everybody in the county knew who he was.

The family piled into Maude's SUV, Truman on a blanket in the back seat, and Brock behind the wheel. The late-winter, cold gusts blew the vehicle to-and-fro as it rolled up onto I-75 north. They had made the trip between their two homes many times, going in and out of Appalachia with ease. "Did Marcel tell you any more about what he wanted to spring on you?"

"He said it had something to do with a neighbor by the name of Elijah Ashby."

"Which house does he live in?" Maude tried not to envision some perilous adventure where Brock would get strung up by his thumbs.

"I'm not sure. His neighborhood only has five houses in it." He changed the subject. "How many bottles do you have in the cellar at the winery?"

"Oh, probably enough to make it until Memorial Day. I'll have to dump more barrels in May to gear up for the summer onslaught."

Brock looked in the rearview mirror to see what the dog was doing. "Truman, you've only got another week before you'll have to get back to work." The dog's job was to keep the varmints away from the grapes. He raised up and stuck his head between the front seats, expecting to be petted. The impressive-looking animal was one of the rarest German shepherds in the world. He had a bright-white coat and red markings on his head and feet, so unusual that kennel clubs barred him from being entered in any competitions.

The Skinners thought their condominium—near Sayre School, Gratz Park, and Transylvania University—stood at the center of the universe. The United States, greatest nation on earth, widely acknowledged as the world's Promised Land, was arguably where a new Jerusalem could emerge. Kentucky shared borders with seven states, more than any other in the country, or the world for that matter. Lexington, at the western edge of Appalachia, and the eastern edge of the western frontier, would be the axis if the state map were a propeller. The Hunt-Morgan Home, a block away, had been a bulwark against Rebels advancing north in the Civil War. Ashland, former estate of Henry Clay, the great compromiser, was still intact a mile up Richmond Road. The roof patio of the Skinner condo felt like a vortex—Union to the north, Confederacy to the south, rugged mountains to the east, and pastoral rolling hills westward.

The Sutherlands grew up in Appalachia, believing America was full of beautiful places, like those in abundance in Kentucky, which, of course, it wasn't. The forty-five square miles of Red River Gorge, sixty miles east of Lexington, teeming with flora and fauna, were breathtaking. There was also Shaker Village beyond High Bridge, an ethereal gem on a bucolic hill west of the Kentucky River. Marcel Sutherland's tailoring business was headquartered in the historic city of Harrodsburg, six miles west of Shaker Village. He lived in a charming development called Saratoga Estates, halfway between the two places.

Finally, Keeneland Racecourse, next to the famous Calumet Farm, right outside Lexington's beltline, opened more than eighty-five years ago, across the street from Bluegrass Field. Three weeks during spring and fall, people flew into town and walked across the highway to complete the twice-yearly haj to the horse-racing mecca.

Maude called her brother to discuss dinner plans after settling in the condo. Both believed the Monday night crowd would be light, so they decided on Jeff Ruby's at six o'clock. The Skinners fed Truman, took him out, put on heavier jackets, and began the short, windy walk over to the restaurant on Vine Street.

Marcel had already been seated at a high-top in the bar area. Maude saw him and cleared the way for her and her husband to join him. Marcel hugged his sister warmly and shook Brock's hand with verve. "Ah, to be where the action is," he stated enthusiastically, over the chatter of the madding crowd. Maude's brother was a slight man, medium height, with curly blond hair. He wore rimless glasses and had the physique of a jogger. Being rather bookish, he was an unlikely friend for the rough-and-tumble Brock Skinner, who looked like a stevedore searching for another cargo ship to unload.

"I think I can get into a fight in here," Brock commented comically. The restaurant was an angstrom away from being big-city mafioso, featuring not-so-subtle shades of deep red décor all around. Since the help and patrons were wholesome looking, the establishment came across as being legitimate.

"Can't you see he's bored, Marcel? I hope you've found some good, clean fun to keep him occupied," Maude said with a pleading expression on her face.

Marcel began sharing what he'd gotten caught up in with his neighbor. "Elijah Ashby owns the house next to mine to the west. It's that big, dark, Tudor-style ranch. He told me his parents built the place forty years ago, when all the other homes in the development went up."

"Did he buy it from them?"

"I'm not sure. He was living there when I bought my house nine years ago."

"What kind of cat is he?"

"Normal. A bit gregarious. Sharp dresser."

"Like my wife and your sister here," Brock muttered, adding levity.

"Doesn't sound anything like you, though," Maude replied.

"To the quick," Brock rebuffed. "So, what happened?"

"He invited me over one evening and asked if I could recommend two trustworthy people, not in his industry, whom he could put on the board of his company. I told him you and me."

Brock frowned. "What did he say to that?"

"He wants to interview us."

Maude stiffened, and said, "Oh, boy, down the rabbit hole we go."

Marcel continued, "He kept questioning me, trying to figure out if we had the pedigree to bring any value."

"What brought this on?"

"It seems to me something's afoot he needs help with."

"That's pretty obvious. Most executives ask their lawyers and accountants for board recommendations. They like to keep everything in the club. What's the name of his company, anyway?"

"Real Buy Louvers."

"Rather plebeian. How big is it?"

"From what I've looked up, it's in the range of one hundred million in sales. We've never talked business. Well, actually, we haven't talked about anything over the years. He's never been in my house. The vice president of his company, Marilyn McDonald, lives on the other side of me. She's a looker, and a bit of a flirt, but has never spoken of the business either."

"Ashby seems to have an affinity for keeping things in the neighborhood."

After the server tugged away the near-empty plate that Marcel had his hand on, sopping up gravy with his last bite of bread, the three of them ordered espresso. Brock asked Marcel about his girlfriend, Valerie Goddard. She had just left to return to Roswell, New Mexico, where she lived and worked. Then, the men probed Maude about the winery, to make sure everything was going well. She assured them it was and pulled the conversation back to Elijah Ashby. "When does he want to meet with you guys?"

"Tomorrow at ten o'clock, in his office."

"Where's that?" Brock asked.

"The factory is between Harrodsburg and Lawrenceburg, behind a farm implement dealership."

"I can meet you there. What are you going to wear?"

"I say we put on sport coats and power ties," Marcel suggested.

"Suits me. Did you find out much else about the business on the Internet?"

"I looked at their website to see what products they make. All different kinds of louvers. The news feed said the company had its tenth anniversary at the first of the year."

"Do you know who else is on the board?"

Marcel looked at his sister with trepidation, fearing she'd not like the next bit of information. "Besides Marilyn McDonald, a woman by the name of Cheryl Welch."

"Do you know anything about her?"

"Yeah. She sold me the home I live in. Apparently, she grew up there and inherited it when her parents died. She must have had bad feelings about the house or something."

Brock said, "That might mean Elijah Ashby, Cheryl Welch, and Marilyn McDonald go way back."

"Well, if they do, it looks to me like they may be setting you suckers up for a fall," Maude said dryly.

"Now I'm getting interested." Brock sat up in his chair and smiled. Marcel had just put new batteries in the Energizer Bunny. Maude was already worrying. He said, "I'll meet you in Real Buy's parking lot at 9:50 a.m."

Walking on the heaved sidewalks leading up the gentle hill to the condo, Maude said to Brock, "I guess it won't do any good to ask you to watch your step."

"I don't like trouble any more than you do, and I'm certainly not looking for any," he said.

"But it seems to find you. That's what worries me."

"No sense getting worked up beforehand. Let me see what the guy wants. I promise I'll keep you informed." He kissed her softly on the neck as they stepped into the condo. Truman could tell Maude was disturbed about something. He meandered over and gave her the *Is-everything-okay?* look.

Maude said with resignation, "Well, you've made it this far without getting killed. I don't suppose it'll be any different this time." She hesitated for a moment and then headed off to take a hot shower.

Brock thought it mighty peculiar that a man would consider someone he knew marginally, and a *buddy*, to be on the board of his company. He keyed in the computer password and began researching Real Buy Louvers.

Chapter 2

Kyle Becker, at a young age, knew he never wanted to work for anyone but himself. He wasn't interested in sucking up to power brokers, playing politics, or toiling away on the clock for small money. He wanted it fast and easy, using his brain, and expected to produce nothing in life. His good fortune would be at the expense of lazy people throwing money around unless something went wrong, which it occasionally did.

He came from a haphazard family in Versailles, Kentucky. His father was a rounder who practiced the sins that were easy for a Kentucky man to fall into: smoking, drinking, cussing, gambling, and chasing women. Old man Becker was handsome, had wavy white hair, wore high-collared shirts, khaki pants, and slip-on, canvas deck shoes when he went out to shopworn bars featuring cheap booze, rustic bands, dance floors, and women with miles on them.

Kyle's mother had thrown in the towel. She had decided not to leave Kyle's father, figuring nobody wanted to support her at her age. She retreated to diversionary hobbies of reading and quilting. Kyle was partial to his mother. She made him feel loved, at least by her, if not by his father. Kyle responded to his frustrating home life by being a terrific student. He was salutatorian of his graduating class at Woodford County High, having received a B in Phys Ed, the only blemish on his record.

The modern era of Woodford County began in 1963, when the new high school was built on US 60, northeast of downtown

Versailles. Frankfort was twenty minutes north, and Lexington twenty minutes east. Incredible horse farms lined US 60, and if the high school represented home plate on a baseball diamond, center field would be the town of Paris, with hundreds of equine operations on the field of play. Keeneland happened to be at first base, and every owner of a racehorse aspired to get a hit.

The Woodford County High School campus had the feel of a brooding, brown-brick monolith. Kyle took advanced classes the whole way through, which meant he was with the same smart kids all day long. His classes consisted of seventeen girls and four boys. The odds were good for getting a date to the prom. Problem was, all but three of the girls were down the scale in the beauty department, leaving one of the four boys without a chair when the music stopped. Kyle was it. He enjoyed the company of less-than-radiant females, and all fourteen of them knew it. He was smart enough to treat them equally, forging pleasant relationships with each. Those friendships, alive and well among the women still in the area, were levers he pulled to successfully ply his trade. A few of the girls were connected to horse racing in some way, and that was how Becker made his living.

Betting on horses followed the same pattern as all gambling. It began with low-odds bets and progressed to ones with higher odds and bigger payoffs. Kyle worked his way up from win, place, and show to the exotics, and finally, pick-six races. He had dialed it back to the superfecta in recent years, which was picking the order of finish of the first four horses in a race. In high school, he frequented the Red Mile, a track for trotters and pacers near downtown Lexington, where he caught the bug. He hit a trifecta one night with an ALL-with-ALL-with-7 ticket that paid over $17,000. The winning horse went off at 99-to-1. The second-place finisher was 67-to-1, and the favorite, at 3-to-1, finished third. Kyle shared the pool with one other ticket holder.

Becker went on to the University of Kentucky, completing a degree in mathematics in three years. He performed elaborate statistical analyses on racing data to formulate algorithms for betting strategies during that time. The system worked well, but not well enough to win any serious money. The variables impossible to bake in were declining form of a Thoroughbred on a given day, decisions made by the jockey, darkening of a horse, and the trajectory of an improving animal. He found his sweet spot, concentrating on horses likely to improve and spring upsets, along with ones ready to fire after being darkened. The best betting opportunities came when two such horses were in the same race. If he picked them, which he did several times a year, the payoffs were huge.

Horse racing, generally, had been declining since Secretariat won the triple crown in 1973. That was because small farms couldn't compete anymore with the corporations and big money taking over the industry. Many conventions of twentieth-century American life began their decline at that time like country clubs, heavyweight boxing, contract bridge, auto racing, jazz, coin collecting, pulp fiction, muscle cars, true rock and roll, and ballroom dancing. Bourbon drifted into obscurity but had a remarkable resurgence in the twenty-first century, making Kentucky relevant again. The whiskey business, like horse racing, had also been swallowed up and corrupted by big corporations.

A horse-track's take on straight wagering was 17 percent, with another point added for breakage when payoffs were rounded down to the nearest dime. Twenty-five percent got taken out of the exotic pools. When the industry threatened to increase the take on exotics to 27 percent several years back, professional gamblers stopped placing bets to send the signal they'd not put up with such a move. The theory at work held that half the betting public was uneducated, placing wagers for ridiculous reasons like a horse's name or colors, which meant that group lost its betting capital and *enjoyed* doing it. Serious horseplayers and the Thoroughbred racing industry preyed on those people.

Quasi-educated horseplayers also lost money but kept coming back since ciphering worked out occasionally. There was nothing as satisfying as figuring how horses would finish, and see it play out that way. A bit of knowledge was a dangerous thing. A lot of data could be studied to unlock the secrets of a race, such as pace, speed, class, past performances, distance, jockeys, number of horses, and track conditions. The bottom line remained—part-time gamblers, not quite smart enough for their own good, helped finance the industry too.

Then, there were the professionals at the end of the bell curve who made money at the betting window. They studied long and hard, wagered sparingly, and had access to inside information. People like Kyle Becker. He was what was known as a "dog player," a person who bet on the kind of horses affectionately referred to as dogs. That's where the big payoffs were.

~ ~ ~

"Penny, it's Kyle. How are you?"

"I'm doing good." Penny Gaines had known Kyle since the ninth grade. They'd been on a few dates over the years. She was terribly low-waisted, had a young grandmotherly face, and worked in the office of a prosperous horse farm in Bourbon County.

"What did the trainer say about Warp Card?" The horse was running in the sixth race at Turfway Park, a track in northern Kentucky, south of Cincinnati. Racing happened somewhere in the state most days of the year. Turfway closed when Keeneland opened for three weeks in April. Churchill Downs started up in May and ran through the fall.

"He's sure the horse will fire."

"When I win today, I'll scoop you up at six thirty for a steak dinner at Malone's. I've got a reservation."

"You better keep that date. I'm already hungry."

"Count on it." Becker had female pipelines to inside information, as well as dozens of male acquaintances he kept in touch with nominally. He was aloof with the men but worked the women more familiarly, trying not to lead them on. His crowd of women enjoyed having a well-dressed, prosperous man escort them around from time to time.

The sixth race had nine horses in it, which meant the wager would be twelve bets. Warp Card, darkened by his connections, and Doorclob, an improving horse ready to move up, would be first and second, Kyle figured. The favorite was good enough to hold off the rest of the field for third. Fourth place was anybody's guess. He went to the betting machine at the OTB and punched in the ten-dollar superfecta bet of 3,5-with-3,5-with-2-with-ALL, which cost him $120.

A long-odds horse came in fourth, driving the payoff up to $2,874 on a one-dollar ticket. Kyle had it ten times. The manager at the OTB knew Kyle well and wished he'd find another spot to place his bets since he was why the location occasionally ran a cash deficit. Becker took the money, less the 20 percent for Uncle Sam, and walked out. He called Penny to report the good news.

Kyle happily paid for the succulent beef and side dishes they enjoyed leisurely at a cozy, corner table in Malone's Steakhouse. He put ten, crisp one-hundred-dollar bills under Penny's purse when she went to the restroom. Upon returning, she saw the bills, tucked them away, and grinned.

~ ~ ~

A few days later, Esther Rice, another lady friend of Becker's, called him to pass on valuable information. She was an exercise rider for several of the prominent Thoroughbred trainers in the area. "Hi, Kyle. I've been invited to a shindig at a big farm on Saturday night. How 'bout you escorting me to it?"

"I'll wear cowboy boots and a big hat," he said.

"I want you to go out and buy a new expensive outfit. Everybody needs to know I have impressive friends."

"I'm not sure that's in the budget, Esther."

"It will be. A horse by the name of Reachy Amici is running in the seventh race at Turfway on Saturday. I've been riding him the last six weeks. His improvement has been ridiculous. He's ready to steal one."

Becker spent the next two days researching the other six horses in the race. He concluded that three of them had no chance of finishing in the top four. The ticket he bought read 5-with-1,4,7-with-1,4,7-with-1,4,7. The five-horse ran clear at 33-to-1. It was a blanket finish among the next three, which didn't matter. He had them in all combinations for second, third, and fourth. The manager of the OTB saw Kyle get up from his seat. He knew the look and wondered how much the man had won this time.

~ ~ ~

Esther Rice saw Becker ease his car up just outside her apartment building, letting out a horse laugh when she saw him get out. He had on a black hat, white shirt, black vest, bolo tie, and creased blue jeans. His boots were highly polished burgundy. "What a dude you are!"

"You told me to get some fancy duds," Kyle said, defending his attire.

"I love it. Your ship must have come in."

"Just this once. You look very nice. I'll have to keep my head on a swivel to fight off the men."

"You won't be upset if I run off with one of them, will you?" she asked.

"No. But if you do, I'm going to return these clothes and get my money back. How much were the tickets to this party, anyway?"

"Five hundred dollars." The tickets had cost her nothing. Kyle pulled five bills out of his wallet and handed them to her. He thought it a fair price to pay for the information Esther had shared with him.

The March weather was calmer than usual on the Saturday night Kyle and Esther walked from his car to the party barn. After sauntering in, they saw food stations had been set up in the four corners. The two of them sampled a little of each, and between mouthfuls, politely made small talk with the folks milling around. A seven-piece string band on the raised stage pounded out bluegrass music across from the partially rolled-open barn doors. The busy parquet dance floor took up the center one-third of the floor space.

"Oh, there's someone I want you to meet." Esther drug Kyle by the sleeve back to the Mexican food stand. The man he got introduced to talked about a horse that was on the move up. As the drinking increased, the boisterous talking and honky-tonk dancing did too.

For the next two hours, Esther Rice made sure Kyle Becker met the people there who knew important things. Two people told him the track secretary at Keeneland had just set the racing card for Thursday, April 10. A couple of "dogs" were running in the tenth race, the kind Kyle liked to bet on.

When they got back to Esther's apartment, she said, "I want to ask you for one more favor."

Kyle got worried. "What's that?"

"I would like you to go to church with me in the morning. My brother's getting baptized. I need to be there for him."

"Sure. Can I meet you there?"

"Yes. Thanks, Kyle, for being a good friend."

"Well, we've known each other for a long time. You know I'm not the marrying type. Is there anybody you're interested in these days?"

She looked at him sheepishly. "Yeah. He goes to my brother's church. I want you to meet him tomorrow. I value your opinion, and I'm thinking of going after the guy. I'd like to get your impression of him."

Kyle Becker was walking a fine line with his lady friends.

The man he met the next day at church, whom Esther had set her sights on, was a bad choice. Kyle would have to figure out how to break the news to her. All he could think of was what his father had done to his mother. He couldn't bear the thought of that happening to his good friend Esther.

Chapter 3

A real estate developer from Danville bought a ten-acre parcel forty years ago on the south side of the highway that connected Shaker Village to Harrodsburg. He chopped it into five two-acre lots, put in a road and utilities, and named the development Saratoga Estates. Two lots were on either side of the street, with the pie-shaped connector lot at the end of the cul-de-sac. As a home builder, the developer constructed a house for himself on one lot closest to the main road and then put up a spec house across from the home he built. The three nicest parcels were offered as build-to-suit opportunities.

The first takers were Toni and Carson Welch. They picked the choice spot at the end of the cul-de-sac to have a sprawling, white-brick ranch erected. The roof, shutters, and entrance doors featured three different honey-brown tones that complemented each other. People who came in the house over the years commented that the design was considerably ahead of its time. The rooms were huge and wide open, and tall windows illuminated the whole house naturally. A fireplace in the great room, made from craggy limestone slabs, had the look of a slave fence. Cherry hardwood floors throughout were set off by putty-colored walls. An office by the front door had a wet bar built in for entertaining. When Marcel bought the house thirty years after it was built, he updated everything, replacing the bar with a home office loaded with computer equipment.

With ease, Carson Welch could sell ice to an Eskimo. After graduating from Centre College, he took a sales job with an inglorious company by the name of Gibbous Metals that made industrial aluminum parts. The owner wanted to retire, so Carson put together the financing to buy the place when he was in his late twenties. By his early thirties, company sales had tripled, and he was making enough money to build an ostentatious house in Saratoga Estates. Not long after, the lots on either side of the Welch place sold, and houses were built on each—Mindy and Peter McDonald on one side, Beatrice and Isaiah Ashby on the other. By request, the builder put the same fireproof wall safe and hard-wired security system in each of the houses.

The three neighbors in the rear of Saratoga Estates socialized little with each other because they were extremely different folks. Peter McDonald had an administrative job with the Harrodsburg police, and his wife, Mindy, worked at a prestigious law firm on the town square. Isaiah Ashby held a position at a megachurch in Lawrenceburg. His wife, Beatrice, taught third grade at the elementary school. The Welches were hard drinkers, and the abstemious Ashbys steered clear of them. The McDonalds didn't like the cut of the jib of either couple. As fate would have it, the three women got pregnant right after the first of the year in the Estates, thirty-six years ago. It had to be more than something in the water.

Elijah Ashby came into the world first, followed by Marilyn McDonald, and then Cheryl Welch. Even though the children's parents rarely spoke to each other, the three youngsters became fast friends at a young age. Their home lives were radically different. The McDonalds were poor communicators and considered Marilyn a mild aggravation. The Ashbys were "perfect" parents, raising Elijah in the church. They taught him good morals and manners and to be respectful of other people. Cheryl Welch had a tough time. Her parents were bona fide drunks.

Carson Welch crawled in the bottle when Cheryl was ten. By then, he'd turned the management of his company over to professionals so he could drink full time. His health woes started with pancreatitis and moved to sclerosis, and then his liver turned hard as rock salt. He croaked just before Cheryl's fourteenth birthday. That didn't seem to deter his wife, Toni. She went back to pounding vodka the afternoon of Carson's burial.

The three young friends in Saratoga Estates graduated from high school the same year. They attended Transylvania together, drifting apart when on campus, always reconnecting back home during breaks. Right before Thanksgiving their senior year, Cheryl Welch called Elijah, and said, "I've already spoken to Marilyn. Now, I want to ask you the same favor."

"What can I do for you?" Elijah asked.

"I need you and Marilyn to come in the house with me when I get home this afternoon. I talked to Mother right after lunch, and she's probably already soused. I don't know if I can control her when I get there. It's getting bad. Why she hasn't drunk herself to death by now is beyond me."

"Sure. I'm sorry she's in such a state. Is there any way we can get her into rehab?"

"I've tried. Maybe she'll listen to you."

"What time are you going to head for home?"

"Four o'clock."

"We'll leave a few minutes before that. Have Marilyn watch for you. We can walk over when your car pulls in at your house."

~ ~ ~

"Mom, I'm home," Cheryl hollered out.

Toni stumbled into the family room, and said, "Oh, you've got your friends with you." She had on a floral moo-moo and was slurring her words.

Elijah said, "Hi, Mrs. Welch." He could tell she'd imbibed way beyond the limit.

Toni's eyes opened and closed slowly. "Hello, Elijah." A little of the drink she held in her hand sloshed onto the floor. She swayed and turned her head. "Marilyn."

"Would you like to sit down? It looks like you've had too much to drink," Elijah said politely.

"What's it to ya?"

"Well, we're all worried about you. We'd like for you to get some help."

Toni became angry. "For what?"

"We're worried about your health. You know, the drinking."

"You'd drink too if you had a worthless daughter like mine, and your husband was dead. I'm stuck here alone." She raised her shoulders and thrust her elbows back. More liquid escaped from the glass.

Marilyn was looking at the smartphone in her hand. She commented, "That's your choice, a bad one."

"Why, you little whore," Toni spat.

Three minutes later, Cheryl Welch called 911 in a panic. "Please send an ambulance to Saratoga Estates! My mother has fallen and hit her head."

Before she got to the hospital, Toni Carson died from the crack she put in her skull. Her blood-alcohol measured .21. With no fuss, she was cremated per instructions in her will. No one offered condolences.

Toni's house and Gibbous Metals, her husband's company that she'd inherited worth ten million dollars, now belonged to her daughter. When Cheryl graduated from college the next spring, she went to work at Gibbous, and put her friend, Marilyn McDonald, on the payroll. The two young girls quickly learned the business, and after a couple of years, installed themselves as president and vice president, with the help of existing management.

Peter and Mindy McDonald built a plantation-style house when they bought into the neighborhood. The structure seemed freakishly out of character for the beautiful Kentucky countryside. That was one of several reasons they didn't get along with the Welches and Ashbys. The square, bright-white house had a silver metal roof and huge porch on the front and sides. Architecturally, it would have been correct in Jamaica. The shutters were green, and front door, an orangish yellow. The family had to drive around back to pull into the garage.

The McDonalds showed no sense of style, or common sense for raising a child. Marilyn considered them a joke. She was overjoyed when her parents said they were retiring and moving to Florida. Marilyn made them an offer to buy the house. They accepted it. She would pay them thirty thousand a year for twenty years, and the money would be used as a portion of their retirement cash flow. Payments started when Marilyn got promoted to vice president at Gibbous Metals.

Elijah Ashby moved to Cincinnati after graduating from Transy. He took a position with a louver manufacturing company in quality assurance on the shop floor. After two years, he expressed an interest in being a salesman, so the company sent him out to sell louvers. No one knew the product line better. He also had the gift of gab. He'd go home often to see his parents and would always try to see Cheryl Welch. A few times, he stopped at Gibbous Metals to check in on both childhood friends. Elijah introduced them to the purchasing department at his company, and before long, Gibbous Metals was its major supplier of aluminum parts.

Beatrice Ashby died of breast cancer on Elijah's twenty-fourth birthday. Marilyn and Cheryl felt bad for him. His mother was considered a saintly woman by everyone who knew her. In less than a year, Isaiah Ashby fell dead while preparing a lesson for Wednesday-night bible study. To Elijah's surprise, his father owned a ten-million-dollar life insurance policy with him as the beneficiary. It paid off in fifteen days. He quit his job and moved back into the house where he had grown up.

Marilyn had an idea how Elijah could use the ten million he'd just come into. He knew louvers, and Gibbous Metals was experienced at making parts. She convinced him to open a louver manufacturing company. The three friends had a difficult time coming up with an interesting name for the business. They almost settled on Saratoga Louvers, but in the end, chose something corny: Real Buy Louvers.

Ashby spent that fall building an enormous manufacturing plant. He had big plans. People who watched what he was doing thought he was spending money like a drunken sailor. Elijah found a location near the Bluegrass Parkway with easy on-and-off access for truck freight. He purchased lots of equipment, hired engineers, and shop workers, and began the arduous task of building a business from scratch. Cheryl Welch urged him to hire Marilyn McDonald to watch over things on the inside while he went out selling. The business did four million in volume the first year and lost a half million dollars.

After Marilyn left Gibbous Metals to join Real Buy Louvers, Cheryl sold her place in Saratoga Estates and moved to downtown Danville, near her business. Marcel Sutherland had been looking for a home close to Harrodsburg that he could redo to suit his needs, and when he saw the Welch house, he made an offer to buy it for cash at the asking price. Marcel had only seen Cheryl Welch one time, when he closed on the home. She said little, professing no emotional ties to the property. He thought that a little odd.

By the third year, sales at Real Buy Louvers topped fifteen million, and the business broke even. Cheryl Welch joined the board and had been active on it since. The next year, Marilyn McDon-ald became a board member. Since louvers were made almost completely out of aluminum parts, Gibbous Metals had the ben-efit of being Real Buy's major supplier. Once again, the three musketeers from Saratoga Estates were in league together. They had known each other all their lives. The odd thing about the relationships among the three was that no romantic interludes had occurred between them since Cheryl's mother had died.

Cheryl had come on to Elijah in junior high school. Some necking and heavy petting between them died out when she took an inter-est in another boy. Marilyn, a consummate flirt, had guys chasing her off and on, throughout high school. On three occasions, she threw herself at Elijah when she was between men. He felt it ap-propriate to fill the void in her love life, knowing full well it was a temporary situation, and he was good with that. When the three of them were at Transy, Elijah had more opportunities with the ladies than he could follow up on. His two girlfriends from the neighborhood were attracting plenty of attention of their own.

Real Buy Louvers had experienced remarkable growth over the last seven years. Ashby got the final numbers for last year from the CPA a week ago. Sales were over one hundred million, and operating earnings were nearly ten million. Net income came in above five and a half million.

~ ~ ~

On Tuesday, at nine thirty in the morning, Marilyn McDonald planted herself in the black-suede chair in front of Ashby's desk. He was looking out the window with an empty expression on his face. She said, "I'm eager to hear what you'll have to say about Sutherland and Skinner after you meet with them."

"Yeah. I'll give you a full report." He smiled at her weakly.

"How much do you want them to know about the company?"

"Enough to do what we're putting them on the board for," he said.

"I hope they're not too inquisitive," she warned.

"Don't worry. I can handle them. Everything will work out. Now, get back at it before they get here." She left his office quietly.

24

CHAPTER 4

The big plant where the louvers were made was a thirty-foot-high, rectangular concrete structure with clerestory windows around the tops of the walls, and single windows in each of the offices. The main entrance doors were on the right-front corner of the building. Marcel Sutherland eased his red Mercedes to where Brock stood, shielding his eyes from the morning sun. Marcel had on a dark blue jacket, blue slacks, brown shoes, and gold-orange-and-blue paisley tie. Brock wore a gray-and-black-thread sport coat, bright-white shirt, and yellow tie with oval gold-and-black emblems. Both men had expensive watches strapped to their wrists. They looked like a million dollars.

The reception area featured a mezzanine with a blue-metal staircase leading to the upper floor. Elijah Ashby stood by the railing at the top. "Up here, gentlemen." He had on a brown tattersall sport coat and tan slacks. He led the visitors toward his office, introducing himself to Skinner on the way. Ashby took a seat at the round-glass table across from his burl-top desk and made a hand gesture for them to sit.

Marcel said, "From what I can see on the Internet, you're the king of louvers."

"And, you're the king of tailored clothing," Ashby commented pleasantly.

Marcel added, "And my partner here is a court jester." He pointed at Brock, and they all laughed the way men do when they're breaking the ice.

Elijah Ashby, broad-shouldered with long arms and legs, had short black hair, combed in one direction, brown eyes, and naturally brown skin that made his white teeth stand out. He fit the mold of a hapless salesman who people would trust and want to buy from.

"Can you tell me a little about your business, Marcel?"

"When I was growing up, I hated shopping for clothes. Nothing ever fit right, and you couldn't find what you wanted. When I got to college, I began noodling on whether there was a way someone could look in a catalog and pick out clothes that fit, and have them delivered within days. I figured out how to do that."

"How?"

"We found a company that had the technology to take a person's measurement in seconds. We put booths in big cities where people could come in, strip down to their underwear, and get digitally measured. That was the easy part. The hard part was finding contract sewing operations willing to put in software that created custom patterns for garments. An even more daunting task was assembling a team to design clothes and refresh the styles continually, but we did it."

"What a great idea. If you don't mind sharing, roughly how big is the business?"

"We franchised it outside the United States, and the royalties are sizable. Here in the US, we sell over three hundred million in clothing. If it hadn't been for Brock, I wouldn't have had the capital to start the business. He put the money up to get us off the ground."

Elijah turned his attention to Skinner. "Don't you just love America? Take a risk, get a nice reward."

Brock said, "Sir, I'm afraid it was nothing but dumb luck on my part. We were friends in college, and I knew he was smart. I trusted him."

Elijah's face turned lugubrious. "Trust. Isn't it interesting how two of the most important words in the English language are similar? Trust and truth. Both somewhat elusive."

Brock sought to lighten the mood, and said, "I can attest to that. I'm married to Marcel's sister, and she'd tell you she doesn't trust me to tell the truth."

Ashby cackled before asking him, "What about your business experience?"

"I've got a degree in accounting from UK, but never took a steady job in the field. I'm pretty good at analyzing financial information, though. I own a majority interest in a lumber company in Hazard, and my wife runs a well-respected winery there. We love Appalachia but spend a fair amount of time in Lexington as well."

Brock and Marcel waited for Elijah to move the conversation along. Finally, he said, "Let me tell you a little about Real Buy. I was selling louvers when my father died and left me ten million in insurance. I decided to start this company with the money."

"I saw on the website where you just had your tenth anniversary. Congratulations. Looks to me like it's been a great success," Sutherland said.

"Yes, we've been blessed. Last year the company topped one hundred million in sales."

"How did you develop that much business in just ten years?" Brock asked.

"I've got a lot of contacts, and the market has been good."

Brock leaned back and reflected seriously, "I'll say. Growth and success like that are usually driven by one of three things: you make something nobody else does, you've figured out how to be the lowest-cost producer, or your service is so good, customers will pay a premium for the product."

Ashby looked at Marcel. "I like the way this guy thinks. I know it's not normal to be all three, but we are. We have better lead times on commodity products, lower-cost designs on the more complex louvers, and a few products that no one else has."

"Interesting," Marcel commented.

Ashby stood suddenly and said, "I'm sorry, men, I didn't offer you anything to drink. Can I get you something? I'm going to have a cup of coffee."

"Black for me," Brock said while Marcel nodded in the affirmative. When Elijah left the room, Brock whispered in a low voice, "He's lying."

"What?" Marcel rubbed the side of his face and frowned.

"That's a load of crap. No company can be all three."

"Well, just don't get us thrown out of here by arguing with him about it."

Elijah returned with the fingers of one hand through the rings of two cups, and the other hand around his logoed mug of coffee with cream. "Here you go." Brock and Marcel each took a cup and set it on the table.

Brock waded in a little deeper. "I take it you're happy with the earnings of the business?"

"They've been good. We're fortunate."

Marcel asked, "So, if I may inquire, what value would you expect us to bring if we became board members?"

Ashby put his arms on the table and picked lint off the right sleeve of his sport coat. "I mentioned truth. You should know I did extensive background checks on you guys because I need to trust you."

Marcel and Brock looked at each other. Brock asked, "Are you in some kind of trouble?"

"No, nothing like that. Do you mind signing confidentiality and nondisclosure agreements?"

"I don't. How about you, Brock?"

"As long as the liability is limited."

"Oh, there's very little liability in the agreements. They're primarily for good faith."

"Okay. Now, do you want to share with us how we can help you?" Skinner asked.

Ashby got up and walked over behind his desk. "I want to sell the company for at least fifty million dollars, maybe more, and need you guys to approach the right group of strategic buyers to create a bidding war."

Marcel said, "You're a young man. Are you planning on retiring at such a young age?"

"No. I want to do some other things."

Brock asked, "Do you have in mind who the potential buyers would be?"

"Yes. Bigger companies: Grayhill Louver, Cadence Enclosure, Orson Pound, or Deimos Fan."

"Why not let a business broker or attorney do the deal for you?"

Elijah sat in his desk chair and looked out the window as he had done when Marilyn McDonald was in his office less than an hour before. "Because I don't want to take a chance of anyone finding out the business is for sale."

Brock said, "The problem wouldn't be on our side. It's usually the buyers who leak information, especially if it helps them in the marketplace. Do any of these potential buyers compete with you directly?"

"No. That's why I targeted them."

Sutherland stated, "Well, that's good. You told me the other day that Marilyn McDonald and Cheryl Welch were on the board. Do they know you're planning to sell?"

"Of course."

Skinner played dumb. "How do you know them?"

"We grew up together in the same neighborhood and have been friends since we were born. Marilyn is second in command here at Real Buy, and Cheryl is the president of our biggest supplier, Gibbous Metals in Danville. They both buy clothes from Sutherland Tailoring. They've met Marcel. He lives in Cheryl's old house between Marilyn and me."

Brock smiled and said, "Looks like I'll have to buy a house on your street to fit in."

"That won't be necessary." Ashby got up from his desk and returned to the round table. He stared at each of them, and asked, "Are you ready to join the board?"

Brock put it out there without checking with Marcel, "First, would you mind telling us how much the business made last year?"

"Operating income was $9.7 million on $108 million in sales. Net income was right at five million, six-hundred thousand."

"That's a nice business," Brock replied, in a complimentary tone. "There'll be plenty of interested buyers."

"I'll send you the agreements I want you to sign, and compensation schedule for being on the board. I'll also include the fee I'll pay you if we sell the company."

"Sounds good," Marcel said. The three of them exchanged contact information.

Brock added, "I'd like to learn more about the company. How do you recommend I do that?"

"Come back and meet with Marilyn McDonald when it's convenient. She can answer your questions."

"Good. One more thing, would it be okay if I visited a customer to learn why they buy the product?"

"No problem." Elijah Ashby concluded the meeting with more pleasantries and escorted the men back to the stairs leading out.

When Marcel and Brock got outside, Brock said, "Don't look at me or stop to talk. He might be watching us. I'll meet you at your office. We'll talk there."

"Whatever you say, boss." After knowing Skinner for nearly twenty years, Marcel could tell the man's head was about to explode. He just prayed his sister wouldn't go off the rails when Brock told her what was going on.

~ ~ ~

Marilyn McDonald came back into Elijah's office ten minutes after Brock and Marcel left. She spoke tersely, "Well?"

"Well, what?"

"You know what. Do you think they can pull it off?"

"Marilyn, I asked Brock Skinner to visit with you. You can judge for yourself. Those guys are smart."

"What's he going to ask me?"

"About the business. I'm sure he wants to understand just exactly how we're making ten million dollars here. He's married to Marcel's sister, so I'd be careful about turning on the charm."

"You should call Cheryl and bring her up to speed," Marilyn advised.

"I think we should give them a while to learn about the company, and then have a board meeting. It should be a light-hearted affair of some sort to show we're one big happy family."

"I agree. Otherwise, they'll smell a rat."

Between Cheryl Welch and Marilyn McDonald, Elijah Ashby was walking a very fine line, much like Kyle Becker, whom he didn't know.

They planned the next board meeting for April 10 at Keeneland. Marilyn said, "I'll get a corporate box where we can have some privacy."

Elijah suggested, "I think we should talk about the process for selling the business. We'll want to make sure Sutherland and Skinner are prepared to approach the potential buyers."

~ ~ ~

Marcel called Brock while driving to his office at Sutherland Tailoring. "I want to congratulate you for staying cool in the meeting. I'm proud of you. I hope Maude doesn't throw you out when she hears about it."

"Remember, you got us into this, not me. If she gets mad, I'm blaming you."

"That's courageous."

"I want to know why Cheryl Welch sold her house. They all seem so cozy. Why did she move away?"

Marcel speculated, "Single woman, big house, bad karma."

"Yeah. It's the bad karma part that has me worried."

When they walked into Marcel's office, Brock closed the door. Marcel asked, "So, what's on your mind?"

Brock leaned on Marcel's desk with straight arms. "We're going to have to hack into Real Buy Louvers and Gibbous Metals." The IT department at Sutherland Tailoring had become so sophisticated that it could break into just about any database out there.

Marcel responded sarcastically, "Let's do it right after we sign nondisclosure and confidentiality agreements. That way, when we get caught, the police can handcuff us and take us straight to jail. Remember, we're not in Hazard where the cops are friendly to you."

"All the more reason not to get caught."

"What are we looking for?"

"The final accounting trial balances of both companies for the last five years, for starters."

"That shouldn't be too hard. What are you hoping to find?"

"I'm not sure. I'll know when I see it," Skinner said.

Brock looked up Real Buy's phone number, dialed it, and asked for the vice president. "Ms. McDonald, this is Brock Skinner. Would you have time to see me this afternoon at three o'clock?"

Chapter 5

Kyle Becker owned a lackluster house on Paris Pike, between Lexington and Paris, north of I-64 and I-75, not far from the OTB he frequented. He bought the place several years ago, doing a poor-man's fixer-up job on it over the last five years. The story-and-a-half, with two gray dormers, had a steep roof with mottled brown shingles. Porch posts had been reclad in tapered, natural rustic cedar, and the brick painted a light gray. The pumpkin-colored front door and shutters didn't look the best, but Kyle didn't care. He planned on buying an expensive condo in downtown Lexington when he got enough money.

Kyle was slouching comfortably in the squishy chair in his house's small upstairs office when he placed a call a little before noon. "Penny, this is your Beau Brummel, Kyle Becker." He sat up and leaned forward.

"Ah, I'm guessing you want something." She sounded mildly annoyed. Becker had a feeling that soon, dinners at nice restaurants wouldn't be enough for Penny. She was trending toward dinner *and* keeping company with him for the rest of the night at his house. He liked the idea but couldn't conjure up a way to extricate himself from a relationship that he was certain would go nowhere. That was always the problem. Kyle had visions of finding a sharp-looking woman, like what he had missed out on in high school. Penny Gaines wasn't that woman.

"I'll admit, it is rude of me to call you only when I want something. Does throwing myself on the mercy of the court count for anything?"

"Kyle, if I didn't like you a lot, I wouldn't let you do this to me. Where are we going to dinner this weekend?"

"I say Blue Heron. I'll reserve the table by the fireplace for six o'clock on Friday night."

"Okay, but I'm expecting a kiss when you drop me off at my place afterward."

Becker was in a bind now. He sincerely didn't want to hurt Penny's feelings. He offered a solution, "Why don't I give you that kiss when I pick you up?"

"I like that even better," she answered enthusiastically. "What are you after?"

"Can you get me the details on the entrants of the tenth race at Keeneland on April 10?"

"That's easy. Of course, it's not strictly ethical."

"I've got an idea. Just print the information out. That way, there won't be any record in your email system. I'll pick up a meat-lover's pizza for us, and swing by your place after you get off work."

"Good plan, as long as it includes that kiss."

"I'm looking forward to it," he said. Kyle figured this would be the night things got more complicated with Penny Gaines. She was a wonderful person, and he intended to treat her right, if at all possible.

A few minutes later, Kyle fixed himself an egg salad sandwich and called Esther Rice. Two of the men he met at the party last weekend had horses running in the Keeneland race he was interested in. "Hi, Esther. You on break?"

"Yes. How are you, Kyle?"

"Ducky."

"What's on your mind?"

"Can you find out who's exercising a couple of horses racing at Keeneland in April?"

"What's their names?"

"Rodesine and Fad Matter. That's R—O—D—E—S—I—N—E, and two words, F—A—D and M—A—T—T—E—R. I heard about them from the men you introduced me to at the party. I want to find out how they're working."

"Okay. I just bought a big-screen TV. Can you come over and help me hook it up on Saturday afternoon?"

"Sure. It'll have to be after five o'clock. I'm betting on a race at four thirty. If I win, I'll pick up supper for us."

"Why don't you do that win or lose?" she asked.

Becker scolded himself for being so cheap. "I'm sorry, Esther. I don't know why I didn't suggest that myself, without any conditions."

"Because you think you have to punish yourself or someone else when you lose a bet. I hope you grow out of that."

"I'm trying."

"So, you never told me what you thought of the guy I introduced you to at church on Sunday. Out with it," she demanded.

Kyle had somewhat prepared for this moment but didn't relish it. "Esther, you know I care about you. I think you'd be disappointed if I didn't tell you how I really felt."

"You didn't like him, I take it?" She sounded a little put out.

"I think he's probably clean cut. What worries me is his talking and listening," Kyle said.

"What do you mean?"

"I've met people like him who focus more on themselves than anyone else. You can tell by how they speak. In conversation, they constantly talk about themselves and have no interest in you or what you have to say."

"Well, I *have* noticed he talks a lot," she agreed.

"I find those people lack self-awareness, or even worse, to be very selfish." He was building up to the worst of it.

She said nothing for a few seconds. "That's disappointing."

"The thing that got me the most, Esther, was the fact that he said nothing about you. If he really liked you, he wouldn't have been able to hold it in." Kyle heard a sniff come through the phone. "Esther, you okay?"

"Not really. I'll find out about your horses and see you Saturday afternoon." She cut the line. He knew she was badly shaken over what he had told her. He began second-guessing his direct approach.

The past performances of Rodesine and Fad Matter were available online. Brock knew how to interpret every number in their charts. He studied the data carefully for the next half hour.

There were many ways to fool the public as to the readiness of a horse to win a race. One way, as in the case of Fad Matter, was to put him in over his head off a layoff. The next race, the connections dropped the horse in a longer race and made the jockey run the Thoroughbred's brains out, extending him. In the last race, the confused horse got put in a shorter sprint and was only asked to rate near the front of the pack. He was eased in the lane to reduce his speed rating. Fad Matter would be ready to fire in less than four weeks at his preferred distance of seven furlongs, provided he was fit and training well. That's what Kyle needed Esther to find out.

Rodesine only had four lifetime starts, all mediocre. The trainer, whom Becker had met, said the horse was spooked by his and other horses' shadows. After the shadow roll was added to Rodesine's face, he purportedly began training like a beast. Once again, it would be up to Esther Rice to assess just how far the horse had come. That evening, Kyle would get the list of other horses in the race from Penny, to craft a strategy for a winning bet.

He heard an urgent knock on the door and went downstairs to see who was there. It was Esther Rice. She had on her riding out-fit, dusty boots, and a grim look on her face. A green, canvas duffle bag was hanging from her shoulder. Kyle asked, "Esther, everything okay?"

"No. I'm done riding for the day. Do you mind if I shower off here?"

"Certainly not. The bathroom is down the hall." He waved her in and shut the door. "I'm sorry if I upset you when we talked earlier." She said nothing, sat in an upholstered chair, and pulled off her boots.

Kyle looked out the front window of his house for a long time. Budding green leaves on the spring trees across the way were flut-tering in the wind. The faint noise of the shower eventually ceased. Esther emerged from the bathroom barefooted with a towel cinched above her breasts. She said, "I need a hug." Kyle put his arms around her, and she exhaled audibly.

At one thirty, Esther dressed in the clean clothes she had brought in her duffle bag. She walked to the front door to leave, and said, "I'll see you on Saturday. Hopefully, I'll have some good infor-mation for you by then." Just as she grabbed the doorknob, the doorbell rang.

Kyle barked, "Open it."

Penny Gaines was standing there. She ran her eyes up and down critically at the woman inside the door, and asked, "Is that you, Esther? I haven't seen you in forever."

"Penny. Nice to see you again."

"Come on in," Kyle urged. "Esther's chasing down some information for me. What are you doing here?"

"I was out running errands, so I thought I'd drop these papers off to you."

He took them and said, "Thanks." He followed by saying, "Between what the two of you are helping me with, I'm trying to figure out how to score on a race in April." He looked at them, back and forth, knowing full well he was in hot water with both.

Penny thought she smelled sweet moisture in the air, leftover from a shower. She considered mentioning the pizza date Kyle had scheduled with her that evening but decided against it. Instead, she said, "I'd better get going. Good to see you again, Esther."

"You too." Esther watched her leave, closed the door, and turned to face Becker. He had no clue what might come out of her mouth. She asked pointedly, "Which of us do you like better?"

"You, by a long shot," he said. It was the first bald-faced lie he'd told in a while. He wondered if this was how his own father started down the wrong road.

"Well, that's good to hear. You've told me on several occasions you're not the marrying type. That's a shame because I'd make you one hell of a wife." She went through the front door, got in her car, and sped away.

Kyle figured he better try to patch things up with Penny Gaines in person. He drove over to the farm office in Bourbon County where she worked and looked in the parking lot for her car. It wasn't there. He waited until two thirty before he tried to reach her by phone. "What do you want, Kyle?"

"Where are you?"

"I'm heading home."

"Aren't you coming back to the office?"

"No. I don't feel like it."

"I just wanted to make sure we're still on for pizza tonight," Becker said, lacking conviction.

"What's the use. I'm not interested in that kiss anymore, especially since you were in the sack kissing Esther Rice only an hour ago."

"I was not!" That was the second whopper he'd told in less than an hour. "She's a friend of mine just like you are."

"I don't think so. She's at another level. Tell me this? If you were forced to marry me or her, which would it be?"

"You," he said without hesitation.

The line went silent for several seconds. She finally spoke, "When you bring that pizza over tonight, I suggest you come prepared to express your appreciation for what I do for you."

Kyle had reached a fork in the road. He took the dangerous one. "I think we better call it off for tonight. It doesn't sound like you're in the mood for company."

"Yeah, that's what I figured. When it gets right down to it, you're not really interested in me as a woman."

"And you're ruining a perfectly good friendship. I like being with you, and respect you. What more do you want?"

"I want to be at the top of the list, not just part of your harem."

Everything had gone sideways in Kyle's world, all in one day. He truly liked Penny Gaines and Esther Rice, cared for both, and wanted the best for them. He was like Captain Ahab, however, in search of his own Moby Dick, that stunning-looking woman who had eluded him in high school. He'd come to realize he couldn't have things both ways. If he was going to hold out for pulchritude, he'd need to fight shy of women with their own designs. He thought if he could just win enough at the track, the money would help him get what he was after. Yet, inexplicably, he said, "Penny, you are at the top of my list. I'm sorry if I hurt your feelings. There's no need for that. I'll come around at six."

She said nothing and hung up.

Becker got back home a little before three. He stomped up to his office and flopped down on the bulbous sofa against the wall. He said loudly, "Alexa, play 'You Shook Me' by John Lee Hooker." As the song came on, he picked up a wooden pencil lying on the side table and threw it in disgust at the window across the room. He shoved the papers of horse performances onto the floor, kicked them angrily, and yelled, "Alexa, stop!" The music ceased abruptly.

CHAPTER 6

At three o'clock, Marilyn McDonald stood behind the mezzanine railing at Real Buy Louvers, staring down at Brock Skinner, who had a marvelous view up her skirt. She had a devilish grin on her face, which Brock interpreted as genuine trouble. He waited for her to speak. "Come on up, Mr. Skinner."

When he got to the top of the stairs, he peered at her guardedly, and said, "Call me Brock."

"Let's go back to my office." She closed the door after they went in. He ambled over to the window to check the weather. Small, high clouds had formed that were moving quickly to the northeast. "Well, Brock, you can sit down over there in front of my desk if you're ready to get down to business." She sounded like a busy hooker urging the john to pick up the pace.

Skinner complied. He watched her stroll around the black granite desktop, remembering a line from a blues song: *She walked like she had oil wells in her backyard.* He said, "Shall I call you Ms. McDonald?" She was a knockout. Her light-brown hair had been precisely parted on the left side. It fell to mid-torso. She had mesmerizing olive-green eyes and was built like a proverbial brick shithouse. Her smooth skin was flawless. She wore light makeup and clear fingernail polish. The chartreuse skirt and jacket she had on seemed too bright for her eyes.

"Call me Marilyn." She'd been around men like Skinner and wasn't the least bit afraid of him. The fact he looked like he could break somebody's neck in two seconds put most women off. "What would you like to know about Real Buy?"

"Everything."

"That'll take more than this afternoon."

"I was being facetious," Brock said to loosen the dialogue. "I guess I'm most interested in how a ten-year-old business like this can get so big, so fast, and make so much money, so quick."

"You sound like you don't believe Elijah and me are smart enough to make that happen."

"It takes more than two smart people."

"Why do I feel like I'm being interrogated by the FBI?" she said to back him off.

He leaned forward and grinned slightly. "Oh, I'm sorry. I had assumed you didn't want me to waste your time on frivolous conversation," he said.

Her attitude toward Skinner turned on a dime. She knew he was smart. "In human relations, Brock, I've found you should build rapport first, and rapport builds trust. Once there's trust, you can talk like that."

"Okay, since there's no trust between us, let's keep it on that level then. Can you give me an overview of how the company got to where it is today?"

Marilyn considered turning on the charm but chose not to. "Let me see if I can put it on your terms. Who makes the best chicken sandwich in the business?"

Brock brushed off the insult, and replied, "Chick-fil-A."

"Right. So, what if we could make a sandwich as good, sell it for less, and get it to the customer faster?"

"I suppose we'd take market share quickly."

"Bingo," she said, winking one eye and using her right hand as a pistol.

"That explains the commodity products. What about the more complicated ones?"

She responded, "Copy and improve. We evaluate competitors' products and make them better."

"I guess I already know what you'll tell me about louvers you make that no one else has. The competition isn't savvy enough to knock off your products and improve on them," he offered with a flourish.

"Something like that," she replied nonchalantly.

Brock said, "I don't think I'll take up any more of your time. I have one last request, though. Can you think of a customer in Appalachia whom I could visit? I'd like them to share with me why they buy from the company."

Marilyn McDonald tapped the keys of her laptop. She studied the screen and said, "Laurel Mechanical, in Harlan, Kentucky."

"Do you have the name of the person I should call on?"

"George Pelham. I've met him. They're a pretty big outfit."

"Could you call and tell him I'd like to come by?"

"Sure. When?"

He checked the calendar on his phone before saying, "Next Tuesday. Ten o'clock."

~ ~ ~

Elijah Ashby was studying sales reports when Marilyn McDonald marched into his office with an ugly look on her face. She stood over him, pounding her forefinger on his desk as she declared, "Skinner is going to be trouble. Why didn't we get some stupid banker?"

"Because a stupid banker couldn't do what we need done. You of all people should know that."

"Yeah, well, this guy is nobody's fool. He'll figure out what's going on."

"Oh, really? Now, how's he going to do that?"

She turned her back on him. "I don't know, but if he does, you understand what that means, don't you?"

"Marilyn, I'm getting tired of this. We're going to sell the company for a lot of money and get this over with."

"You better hope so."

~ ~ ~

Maude heard her husband key open the door and yell her name. She called out, "I'm in the kitchen."

He loosened his tie and gave her a kiss. "Well, I had an interesting day."

"How so?" She was chopping vegetables for a Cobb salad.

"Ashby wants us to help him sell his business for a lot of money."

"Huh. Go ahead, tell me what's wrong with the idea," she goaded.

"The guy built a company in ten years that's making ten million dollars. I'm sorry, but the business he's in just ain't that easy."

Maude laid down the knife and asked, "You think he's cooking the books?"

"I don't know." He went to the refrigerator to get a can of flavored sparkling water.

"How are you planning to find out?"

"I'm going to study the financial statements and look for Waldo. We saw Ashby this morning. I met with Marilyn McDonald this afternoon. She's one good-looking woman. Not as beautiful as you, of course, but right up there."

"Marcel said she was a bit of a flirt. Did she try any feminine wiles on you?"

"No. I think she's saving them for the right moment," Brock said, half seriously.

"What's next?"

"I'm going to try to get a meeting with Cheryl Welch, and then go see a customer over in Harlan next week. I'm hoping he'll tell me the truth about Real Buy."

Maude brought salads to the table, and said, "Well, there's one good thing: no dead bodies yet. That's always a good sign."

"Now, dear, let's not borrow trouble."

She fluttered her lips and sang out, "No, let's not."

~ ~ ~

Elijah spoke to Cheryl and agreed to drive to Danville for a late dinner with her. They met in a downtown bar that offered a simple menu of broiled salmon or filet mignon with a house salad and vegetable of the day. The shoe-box establishment had a high ceiling, 150-year-old brick walls, and distressed oak floor. The orange light gave the place a club feel. Most people came there to drink. Neither Cheryl nor Elijah partook of alcoholic beverages—her because of alcoholic parents, and him due to a legalistic upbringing. Elijah said, "Are you interested in the details of my meeting this morning with Marcel Sutherland and Brock Skinner?"

"Shoot." Cheryl Welch wasn't quite as tall as Marilyn and was fuller figured. Her streaked-blonde hair had been done in a chin-length layered Bob that made her limpid blue eyes look bigger than they were.

"They may be more than we bargained for."

"How so?"

"Sutherland is a brilliant businessman, and things need to make sense to Skinner, or he'll try to figure out why they don't." The tattooed bartender brought the house salads and silverware. "Skinner met with Marilyn later in the day. She came into my office afterward, all steamed up."

"Fine, you've given me the report. Can we not talk about business anymore?"

Elijah raised his eyes and met hers. Cheryl's face looked sad in the dim light. "All right, what shall we talk about?"

"Do you remember when you and I were seeing each other in junior high school?"

"Of course," he said in an offhand way.

"I dumped you for another boy."

"A lot of water under the bridge since then."

"Did you ever consider pursuing me again?" she asked.

"Certainly, but I was afraid to."

"How come?"

"Marilyn."

"I thought so. You and her have been a lot more intimate than we have."

"Yes. That was before Toni died."

"She's better looking than me and has the charm I don't have."

Elijah stared at Cheryl, disappointed. "Don't sell yourself short. You're the most beautiful person I've ever met. I've known you all my life. Your parents were a hard case. So were Marilyn's, but yours were worse. Who knows what'll happen when this thing is over."

"Will it ever be over?" she asked.

"Yes. I'll make sure of that." Neither of them talked much while they ate.

When they left the bar at nine thirty, she said, "I want you to come over to my place."

"I'll follow you." Elijah Ashby was in no position to refuse her invitation.

Cheryl had a modest house near downtown that lacked character. Overgrown bushes immured the tiny porch. Compared to what she grew up in, it was a dump. Elijah followed her through the front door. After some awkward milling around, they went to the bedroom to make love, which they had never done before. Elijah remembered how Marilyn looked without her clothes on. She was a Ferrari. Cheryl was a comfortable model, much to his liking. While they were lying in bed, she put a few thoughts in his head that he would need time to reflect on. He gave her a long hug and rubbed her back before he left.

Elijah pulled in his driveway at eleven fifteen. As the door to the garage was going down, a ring came from his cell phone. "Marilyn, what are you calling for this late at night?"

"Did you speak to Cheryl?"

"Yes. She didn't show much interest in what's going on."

"Have you been in Danville with her all this time?" she asked.

Ashby wanted to keep the upper hand. "What are you getting at, Marilyn?"

"I just don't want any funny business between you two."

"Go ahead. Blow the deal up if you want to," he said stridently.

"I'm not going to do that. You know, we haven't been close since before Toni died."

"Right, and for good reason."

"I'm walking over to your house. I think we need to talk things out," she said.

"Come on, Marilyn, don't do that." He ended the call and checked to make sure all of the doors were locked. Elijah looked out the front window and saw Marilyn marching in his direction with her bathrobe on. When she got to the stoop, he yelled through the window, "Go home, Marilyn. I'm not going to let you in."

"Why not?"

"It's late."

"What's Cheryl got that I don't have." She opened her robe to flash her naked body.

"Nothing. You've got it all. Now act like it. Go home and go to bed. I'll see you at work." He retreated from the window. She cinched her robe again and stomped back to her house.

Elijah entered his home office, turned on the light, and dropped into his desk chair. He was smoldering with anger. He said, "Alexa, play 'I Can't Quit You Baby' by Otis Rush." He sat still and listened to most of the song with his chin cradled in his right hand. Before the song was over, he said, "Alexa, stop." Elijah had only been furious a few times in his life, and when he had, he'd snapped. One of those times got him into the mess he was in. His parents had taught him to have self-control. Elijah had it 99.99 percent of the time. He thought about what Cheryl had shared with him earlier in the evening. It might be worth a try. If he could pull it off, things could go in a different direction.

~ ~ ~

A light fog hung in the air the next morning, visible through the windows in the kitchen of the Skinner condo. Brock called Marcel and asked if he was able to hack into Real Buy Louvers and

Gibbous Metals. Marcel said, "We got the files. I'm going to send them to you encrypted."

"Nice. I'll get started figuring out what's going on over there."

"There's something else. Last night about eleven thirty, I was awakened by Marilyn's loud voice outside. She was standing in Ashby's yard. He wouldn't let her in his house. She marched back home in a huff."

"Well, that confirms what I thought. Things aren't all hunky-dory at the louver works."

~ ~ ~

The Skinners and their dog, Truman, left Lexington for Hazard at ten o'clock in the morning. They pulled into the driveway of the log cabin shortly after noon. Maude fixed ham sandwiches for lunch while Brock downloaded all the files Marcel had sent him. She asked, "You ready to find Waldo now?"

"Yep, after I go work out at the gym and take Truman for a walk."

Maude noticed the lightning in his eyes. She liked it. Sort of.

Chapter 7

Brock was able to draw several conclusions from the Gibbous Metals and Real Buy Louvers accounting information. Both were C corporations, which was unusual in today's world of limited liability and Subchapter S corporate structures. Five years ago, Gibbous Metals did $20 million in sales and made a small profit. Volume had increased to $60 million last year, and the company bled money the larger it got. Last year's losses were six million. A carryback provision in the tax code allowed Gibbous to recover two million in taxes paid in prior years. In all, five and a half million in taxes had been recovered on seventeen million in losses over the last five years. The net worth of the company had dwindled from $15 million five years ago to $3 million at the end of last year, and at that rate of decline, the operation would soon be broke.

Meanwhile, profits at Real Buy Louvers had increased percentagewise with each passing year. Ashby had capitalized the company with $100,000 in common stock and put the rest of the ten million in the business as a loan, which had been fully paid back.

Brock looked up a number on his phone. "Elijah? Skinner here. How's it going?"

"Fine, Brock. What can I do for you?"

"I met with Marilyn, and she's arranged for me to see Laurel Mechanical next week. In the meantime, I was hoping you could call Cheryl Welch and set up a meeting with her for me."

"I can. What are you after?"

"I'd like to see her operation and learn a little about it."

"When you want to do that?"

"Tomorrow at ten o'clock, at her place of business, if she's available. My wife will be opening her winery for the season on St. Patrick's Day, and I'd like to see Ms. Welch before things get hectic around here."

"Smart move. I'll set it up," Elijah said pleasantly.

Brock placed a call to his brother-in-law. "You busy?"

"Yes."

"Can you meet me at your house for lunch tomorrow?"

"Works for me. What time?"

"I'm calling on Cheryl Welch at her office in the morning. I'll ring you when I'm heading your way."

"Sounds good."

~ ~ ~

Driving a Lamborghini across the state from Hazard to Danville was better than competing in the Grand Prix. Bouncing back and forth over the Kentucky River offered a real-life road course that had jaw-dropping scenery of lush deciduous trees, spectacular limestone palisades, and contented cows on intermittent rolling hills and dales.

Brock felt the heat radiating off the engine of his sports car when he climbed out of it after parking in the lot at Gibbous Metals. The concrete-block building had a barrel roof covered in tar. White paint on the block sidewalls featured black grime at the mortar joints, accumulated over the years, making the building look like it would crumble in a mild earthquake. The Gibbous Metals sign, vintage 1960, set the tone for what went on inside the business. A woman came out the office door and started walking toward him. As she got near, he said, "You must be Cheryl Welch."

"And you're Brock Skinner?"

"Don't let that get around. I'm wanted by the police, FBI, and Interpol."

A twinkle came in her otherwise vulnerable eyes as she stifled a laugh. "We better hurry inside then."

She led the way to her office. He noticed the hallway was devoid of decoration, making the operation feel like a utilitarian government building. The place seemed dour, strictly business. The windows in her office had old putty-glazed steel frames painted black and the picture window behind her oversized, antique hickory desk looked out onto the shop floor. There were several noisy machines visible, spitting out shiny aluminum parts. The employees knew what they were doing, expending as little energy as possible.

Brock sensed he would like Cheryl Welch better than Marilyn McDonald for one simple reason—the look in her eyes. Windows to the soul, and a troubled soul it was. He had always been a sucker for wounded birds. His inclination was to stop her from stepping into moving traffic and getting herself killed. "It looks like you guys are cranking out a lot of stuff. Has business been good?"

"Decent. Can't complain. I noticed you pulled up in a half-million-dollar machine out there. Most people form an opinion about a person by the car they drive."

"And what's your opinion of me?"

"You've got to have pretty big britches to whiz around in that thing, especially in this part of Kentucky."

"I suppose so," he replied diffidently.

She moved on. "Elijah told me you're new on his board. What can I tell you about our company?"

"How much business are you doing with Real Buy?"

"Sixty percent of our output goes to them."

He took the conversation down another path. "I'm not sure you know this, but I'm married to the sister of the man who bought your house in Saratoga Estates: Marcel Sutherland."

"Of course, I've met Marcel and was told you were his brother-in-law."

"How come you decided to sell and move away from your friends Marilyn and Elijah?"

"Bad memories. My parents were alcoholics, and it was tough seeing them kill themselves in that house."

Brock was good at reading people. "I'm sorry," he said. "I can understand that. Is there anything I can do for you? A guy like me who drives a car like that can do most anything." He jerked a thumb over his shoulder in the direction of the parking lot.

"What do you mean?"

"Well, sometimes people need a helping hand with something in their lives. I know I've needed one at times."

She raised her shoulders and asked, "Are you coming on to me?"

"Absolutely not. There's nothing in this world that could pry me away from my beautiful wife. I hope you get to meet her."

Her shoulders dropped, and she said contritely, "That was stupid of me. I've never been able to talk to men, other than Elijah. My mom and dad were difficult to be around. I've kind of been on my own since I was little. I'm sure a psychiatrist would say it has affected my relationships."

"You seem like a wonderful person to me. What about Marilyn McDonald? How do you get along with her?"

She wriggled in her seat and said, "We get along fine for the most part. You know, when I inherited this company, I hired her to be second in command. When Elijah got his business up and running, she went over to help him."

"Were you upset she left here?"

"Heavens no. There was plenty of work to be done at Real Buy."

Brock leaned to the right and looked through the window behind Cheryl's head. "I take it you get along well with Elijah Ashby?"

"Everybody does. He's a really nice guy."

Brock stood and asked, "Say, would it be okay if I went out on the shop floor to look around?"

"By all means. Do you need me to accompany you?"

"Not necessary. I'm curious about the manufacturing equipment. It's interesting to me."

"Don't go too near the presses. The aluminum is a thousand degrees as it goes through the dies." Cheryl held out a pair of safety glasses and escorted him to the plant entrance.

Sibilant floor fans were running on high to dissipate the heat coming off several big machines. A chain-link fence along one wall secured racks of dies and logs of aluminum used in the presses. Hundreds of sticks of shiny material were stacked on rolling carts throughout the plant. A man with a crew cut, wearing gray khakis, was sitting at a computer in a corner office. Skinner popped his head in to introduce himself, "Hi there. I'm a friend of Ms. Welch. Can I ask how you sell those parts?" He pointed to the aluminum extrusions on one of the runout tables.

"What do you mean?"

"By the foot or the piece?"

"By the pound," he said. "The die weight is on the extrusion drawing. That part over there, for example, is the blade for a Real Buy louver." He flipped to the drawing, and said, "The shape is one point one seven pounds per foot. You multiply the number of feet times the weight per foot times the pound price."

"That makes sense," Brock commented as he nodded his head. "I notice they cut off the ends. Could I have a short piece? I'd like to drive it in the ground and put a wren house on top of it."

The man walked over to the scrap bin by the saw and retrieved a two-foot piece of drop. "Here you go."

"Thanks." Skinner surreptitiously ran the louver blade out to his car and placed it in the passenger seat floor. He went back to Cheryl's office door, letting her see that he'd returned from the plant. She waved him in as she was finishing up a phone call. He said, "Busy place. Those are some massive machines."

"It's really a boring business. We've added a few new presses, and it's grown a lot, but we've been doing the same thing out there for years—pushing metal."

"Ashby told me you knew he intended to sell his company. If 60 percent of your business goes to them, do you worry that the new buyers might drop you as a supplier?"

The look on her face told Brock what he wanted to know. She said woodenly, "Wouldn't bother me a bit."

~ ~ ~

After he left Gibbous Metals, Skinner pulled into a lumber yard on the main highway leading to Shaker Village. He took the aluminum piece in and asked the man at the service desk to cut a one-foot section out of it for him. A twenty-dollar bill did the trick. For another twenty, the man agreed to weigh the piece on the accurate digital scale the yard used for nails. "One point seven one pounds," the man reported with a smile.

Brock called and told Marcel he'd bring salads to the house for lunch at noon.

When Skinner came in, Marcel asked, "So, how was your visit with Cheryl Welch?"

"Good. I like her, but there's something rotten going on there." Brock handed Marcel the one-foot piece of louver blade. "That's the kind of material she sells to Real Buy Louvers. The problem is, she should be charging him 46 percent more for that part based on the weight of the aluminum. Somebody was smart enough to transpose the die-weight numbers in the records to make it look like an honest mistake. It would also be hard to find in an audit."

Marcel said, "Let me guess . . . the deal Real Buy is getting on the metal is why their profits are so high."

"And the losses at Gibbous Metals are mounting. She has gotten some big tax refunds, which may be why they're pulling this stunt, but that business will run out of cash by next year."

"So, what's going on?"

"My brain has been mulling that over the whole way here. The most likely scenario is the three amigos got together and decided to push all the profits into Real Buy Louvers so they could sell it for fifty million dollars with the idea of carving a big melon."

"Are there holes in that theory?" Marcel asked.

"Unfortunately, yes. Elijah Ashby might simply be blackmailing Cheryl Welch to get low metal prices, but the bigger head-scratcher is Marilyn McDonald. How is it she gets a free ride off both of them? I'd like to know if she has any ownership in either Gibbous or Real Buy. If not, what's going on between the three of them?"

Marcel got up from the breakfast counter and went over to look out the dining-room window at Marilyn's garish plantation-style house. He said, "Maude was right. They're setting us up for a fall. If we go out and get a bidding war going among the buyers, we'll have to keep quiet about the phony profits."

Brock replied sharply, "We ain't doing that. We're going to find out what's happening before we get that far."

"*You're* going to find out. I've got a business to run."

"I knew you were going to say that. After meeting Elijah and Cheryl, I could swear they're on the level. Maybe Marilyn is blackmailing them. That would fit her profile. She's a hellcat."

"One good-looking hellcat."

"Got that right."

Marcel came back into the kitchen and said, "So, it looked like Elijah refused to let Marilyn in his house the other night. Begs the question . . . is there some kind of love triangle going on?"

Brock said, "I don't know about that, but based on the fact that Elijah lets Marilyn work at the company and serve on the board, he either loves her or she's part of whatever big-time grift they're running."

"I'm warming up to the blackmail idea. What could she have on them? If there is anything, I think I know where she'd have it parked," Marcel said, grinning.

"Where?"

"Follow me." They went into the closet of the master bedroom in Marcel's house. He showed Brock the safe with the dial. "I'll bet all three houses back here have the same setup."

Brock fingered the dial, and asked, "Is it a left-right-left pattern?"

"Yes, and I happened to notice the combination is the first two digits of the house address, followed by the second two digits, and then the third two digits. And the code for the alarm is one number added to each number of the street address entered backward."

"I wonder if your two neighbors are smart enough to figure that out?"

"Hard to tell," Marcel said pensively.

~ ~ ~

Brock made his way back to Hazard, arriving late in the afternoon. Maude was over at the winery getting ready to open on Monday, and he was sure she'd say *I told you so* upon hearing about his meeting with Cheryl Welch.

He was right.

CHAPTER 8

Kyle sat on a green, dew-glazed bench along the guardrail near the finish line of Keeneland Racecourse on Saturday morning at seven o'clock. His coffee had gone tepid, so he tossed what was left of it through the fence onto the track. He stood when a couple of horses he'd come to see began chugging down the homestretch. One of them would likely be the favorite in the tenth race on April 10. Before he committed to bet against the eleven-hundred-pound animal, he wanted to make sure it looked beatable.

Penny Gaines had acted like she'd enjoyed the dinner Kyle treated her to at Blue Heron the night before. Thankfully, she hadn't brought up Esther Rice but did tell him it would take 10 percent of his winnings on the race she'd gotten him information for to keep her happy. The *quid pro quo,* Kyle told her, was for her to come to the track with him the day of the race. Penny turned down the invitation because she had to work, so she said, but squeezed Kyle to agree to give her the 10 percent, anyway. He acquiesced.

After watching a few more horses train, Becker walked down the hill between the barns to the track kitchen. He saw Esther Rice through the window, sitting at a table, eating eggs, bacon, and fruit. She had on riding gear, which meant she was taking a food break between mounts. Esther saw Kyle come in and waved him over. "I didn't know you were going to be around here this morning."

"Nice to see you, Esther. I wanted to watch a couple of horses work out. Can I join you?"

"Please do." He got a burrito, another cup of hot coffee, and sat down across from her. She said, "You know, I've been thinking on what you said about the man I had my eyes on. I'm thirty-six years old now, and I'm running out of options."

"Does that mean you're going to pursue him then?"

She looked away, threw her fork on the half-eaten plate, and stuck her hands in the pockets of her jeans. "I don't know. Is there something wrong with me? I mean, are men not attracted to me?"

"There's nothing wrong with you. The right guy will come along when you least expect it." What Kyle didn't say was that if she were a little stronger in the beauty department, he'd throw a net over her. Esther had frizzy brown hair, a round face, shallow gray eyes, and calloused earth hands she'd gotten from riding hundreds of miles on Thoroughbreds.

After a nearly full-body shrug, she said, "I'm putting you in charge of finding me a man. One that *you* approve of, that is. Until then, you're my backup plan." She reached over the table and grabbed his hands.

Kyle got the inference. If he wanted her to stop pestering him, he'd have to do some recruiting. "Have you found out anything about Fad Matter and Rodesine?"

"Boy, you can pick 'em. One thing I'll give you, you're smart as hell. Both horses are burning up the track. And their trainers are trying to keep it quiet. They're hunting a big payday just like you are."

"Esther, I want you on my arm upstairs that day if I hit it big." He figured since Penny Gaines had turned him down, he was in the clear.

"That's three weeks off. I'm more interested in tonight. You're still going to stop by and help me hang the new TV I got, right? If not, I'll be wondering if you're out shagging that frump, Penny Gaines."

"Yes. I'll bring linguini and clams, and a big salad to go with, whether my ticket pays off this afternoon or not." He gave her a warm smile.

"See? Everybody says you can't change men. I've already gotten you to quit pouting when you lose. No telling what other magic I can work." Esther picked up her tray, took it to the drop-off bin, and waved goodbye as she blasted through the double doors and back up the hill to the concrete-block barn where her next ride was being saddled.

~ ~ ~

Becker entered the OTB a half hour before the race he was going to bet on that afternoon. The manager saw him come in, made a sour face, and turned his back. Kyle surveyed the crowd, reflecting on his own station in life. Most of the male patrons sitting around didn't have a pot to piss in or a woman to call their own. The few women in attendance were skanks, hoping someone would buy them a drink and take them home. He thought, *What the hell am I doing in this godforsaken place? I'm smarter than everybody in here. Is this the best I can do with my life?*

He went to the betting machine and purchased a superfecta ticket that read: 2,7-with-2,7-with-3,4-with-3,4,5,8. It cost him $240. The order of finish was 7-2-4-5. He had it twenty times. It paid $642 on one dollar, which meant his ticket was worth $12,840. After the tax withholding, the window handed him $10,272. He left a $32 tip on the bar, put his original bet of $240 in his wallet, and shoved an even $10,000 in his pants pocket. The money took the sting out of his self-perception of being a lowlife. All he needed to move up in the world, he reminded himself, was more money, and a beautiful woman on his arm. Becker couldn't wait to get a cushy condo downtown and take up residence with a classy female who everyone would ooh and aah at. For the time being, he hadn't turned out much better than his old man. That would never do.

~ ~ ~

Kyle picked up two orders of linguini and clams from Joe Bologna's. He carried the sack full of food into Esther's apartment at six o'clock. She asked, "How'd you do?" Becker put down the sack, reached in his pocket to extract the stack of bills, and handed it to her.

"Hot damn! There's ten thousand here."

"Need a loan?" he asked smugly.

"No, but if I do, I'll know where to come. Let's eat." She gave him his money back.

Esther's face glowed, signaling her very good mood. She talked incessantly during dinner, and afterward, the two of them tackled hanging and hooking up her new TV. She turned to the blues channel that had a picture of Duke Ellington accompanying his version of "Mood Indigo."

Becker figured he'd better do some talking while he had the chance. "So, what kind of man is it you'd like me to find?"

"One just like you," she said.

"Now think about that. I'm not right for you. First off, I have a crappy personality."

"Horse manure," she muttered.

"I don't have a steady job, don't want any children, and can't be depended upon."

"You care about me. I know that. So, what exactly is the problem?"

Kyle wished he'd kept his mouth shut. He decided to be honest with her. "You're going to laugh when I tell you."

"Try me."

"I'm looking for a bimbo," he said shamefully.

She did laugh, but it was an evil one. "A bimbo? You were salutatorian of our high school class, and you're stupid enough to chase after a bimbo?"

"I told you I had a crappy personality," he shot back.

"No, it's something more like derangement. Well, one thing's for sure, I ain't one. I'm glad we cleared that up. You need to leave now," she demanded with fire in her eyes. The very good mood she'd been in had turned dark. He got up from the couch and walked out without looking back at her.

Becker climbed in his car in the parking lot at Esther's apartment and reached for his phone. "Penny, do you have anything going on tonight?"

"Kyle, I didn't expect you to call. Uh, no, not really. What do you have in mind?"

"You didn't bring up Esther Rice last night when we were at dinner. I just wanted to set things straight."

"Okay. Why don't you come over? You can tell me some more lies about that trollop."

"Come on, Penny. Give me a chance," Kyle pleaded.

"Pick up some cheesecake somewhere. We'll play a couple of hands of gin."

"That sounds good," he said. She hung up. He looked at Esther's apartment door for what he thought might be the last time. He'd lost an important conduit to information that had made him a lot of money. It couldn't be helped. Eventually, he concluded, every woman wants to go forward or backward. They never want to tread water. He didn't much want to do that anymore himself.

Penny Gaines wasn't unattractive. If you were to see her face closeup on television, with lots of makeup on, she'd almost pass for a hot babe. In person, five feet away, it was hard to get past the short legs and round shoulders. Kyle was trying to downplay those attributes in his mind as he stepped through the front door of her house. She took the cheesecake he'd brought in a plastic container into the kitchen.

"Do I get another kiss like the one I got last night?" She didn't wait for him to answer.

She put the cheesecake on plates, and they set up the card table. Kyle marked columns on a piece of paper to keep score. He dealt her eleven to start the game. She arranged her hand, and said, "So, what is it you wanted to tell me about Esther Rice?"

He closed his fanned cards and laid them on the gray table, face down. "It seems to me that maintaining a friendship with two eligible women is somewhat treacherous."

"You just now figuring that out?"

"Well, frankly, yes."

She discarded a king of spades to start the game. They played on a few draws without talking. Penny finally ginned and caught him with a pair of twos. She took the cards and started shuffling them for the next hand. She slapped the deck down, waiting for him to cut. "Are you ready to dump Esther and stick with me?"

He took half the deck and placed it toward her. "Yes," he said.

"You're going to have to prove it. Why don't we forget about this card game?" she suggested with a twinkle in her eye. He looked at her and smiled.

An hour later, they got around to eating the cheesecake. She said, "Maybe I can get off work on April 10 and go to the track with you after all."

"I would recommend it. If I win, you'll want to collect on the spot. Otherwise, how will you know whether I actually won or not?"

"You *are* a big-time liar. I see your point."

"So, it's all set. I'll pick you up at two o'clock at your office on Thursday, April 10. I'll get a box for us on the fourth floor. The tenth race will go off at about five o'clock. We should be out of there by five thirty. I'll get a dinner reservation at Coles for six o'clock."

"I'm looking forward to it." She reached up to give him another kiss, and before their lips met, a fender-bender-like crunching sound came from the driveway. Kyle moved to the window, pulling the curtain aside to see what was going on. A pickup truck with its lights off had just backed out onto the main road. The driver stepped on the gas, and the pickup lurched down the road.

Penny ran ahead of Kyle after they scurried outside. She blurted, "Look, whoever that was rammed the backend of your car." The rear of the silver Toyota was crumpled with the bumper displaced, hanging down.

"Yeah." He knew that pickup truck.

"What are you going to do?"

"Get it fixed."

"Why don't you chase after who did it?"

"I don't have to."

"You mean, you know who it was?"

"Don't worry about it," he said.

Penny walked back into her house. Kyle followed, expecting a lecture from her. She had a dangerous look on her face. "Now I'm getting the picture. It was Esther Rice, wasn't it? She just finished second in a two-horse race and isn't too happy about it.

You tell her if she comes around here again, she can deal with the business end of my shotgun."

"Drop it, Penny. Let's not ruin a good thing we've got going." Becker pulled her in close and peered down at her with a reassuring expression.

Becker checked to see that the taillights were still working on his car before backing out of Penny's driveway. His relationship with Esther Rice had ended with a bang. Literally. If he ever found the bimbo he was looking for, his relationship with Penny Gaines would end with a shotgun blast right between the eyes. He was beginning to understand why his father went to bars for companionship, where the women were harmless.

CHAPTER 9

The weather rarely cooperated for a pleasant St. Patrick's Day. The cold, windy drizzle curtailed the number of visitors at Vigneron on opening day. Maude stood behind the tasting bar, trying not to let her disappointment show. Brock came up behind her and asked, "Want me to go downtown with a sign and stand next to the guy selling tax preparation services?"

"I have a better idea. Why don't you buy the place?"

"Sounds like I might get a good deal," he said.

"For you, it would be free."

"Does that include the inventory?"

"Certainly not," she answered, walking out from behind the bar in high dudgeon. "I want a thousand dollars a bottle."

"How many do you have back there?"

"Oh, about five thousand."

Brock put a hand to his lips, looked down, and frowned. "Let me see, that would be five million smackeroos."

"You're pretty quick." She could always count on her husband to raise her spirits when she was down.

"I think I'll pass. There'll be better days ahead. You can take that to the bank," he told her. Brock was liveliest when he had something to work out in his mind. He was counting on George Pelham at Laurel Mechanical to fill in some of the gaps on Real Buy Louvers.

~ ~ ~

Harlan, Kentucky, one of the oldest towns in the state, was once known as Mount Pleasant. In recent years, the population had been declining, now under two thousand people, signaling it was not that pleasant a place to live during these modern times. The biggest business around, Laurel Mechanical, had a terrible time finding and keeping good employees. Motivated kids went off to college and never returned. Other young people, who didn't pursue higher education, were plentiful, but a lot of them had been raised with crazy ideas, such as being intelligent was somehow an embarrassment. George Pelham was born and raised there and had bucked the trend. He was in his late forties. He'd made a lot of money as a mechanical subcontractor, taking work up to eighty miles from the office. In that part of the world, good subs were hard to find, so in the land of the blind, the one-eyed man was king.

Skinner pulled into Laurel's lot promptly at ten o'clock on Tuesday. The establishment wasn't exactly what he'd been expecting. An attractive split-face concrete block building had a band of hunter-green windows running around the front half of the structure. The side yards and landscaping were impeccably manicured. A big flagpole in the sidewalk, bifurcating the asphalt parking lot, flew the American flag. The green letters identifying the business had been mounted on a steel frame perched on the roof. Around back, fleet trucks not in use that day, were parked inside the chain-link fence.

"I'm here to see George Pelham. Brock Skinner. He's expecting me."

The gaunt fellow at the front desk picked up the phone to announce Brock's arrival. Within thirty seconds, a man who could pass for a Baptist-church deacon, presumably Pelham, appeared with his hand out to shake. "Welcome, Mr. Skinner. I hear you live over in Hazard. How do you like it there?"

"Love it. My wife owns Vigneron Winery near downtown. That keeps us busy."

"Is that right? Constance and I have been there a few times. Great place. We're not big wine drinkers, but we enjoy the Appalachian scenery. Come on back." He windmilled his arm and led the way down the hall.

Pelham's office was peppered with pictures of his wife and children. By all indications, he was a clean-cut man who assiduously managed a good-sized, professional business. Brock said, "Thanks for seeing me."

"Marilyn mentioned you wanted to ask me why we do business with Real Buy."

"That's right."

"What's your interest in the company?"

Skinner had to think fast. "Elijah Ashby asked me to gather some unfiltered information from a few customers for planning purposes. I told him if he wanted the truth, I'd have to promise anonymity to get honest answers. Do you know Mr. Ashby?"

"I should say. I'm on the company's customer council, and some other members are, shall we say, bigger partyers than Elijah and me. He was raised in the church and doesn't do much carousing."

"How is it you started buying from him?"

"Well, we were having quality problems with our regular supplier several years ago, so we got other prices on a big job we had. Real Buy's price was very competitive. We gave them a chance to prove themselves."

"I take it they did."

"Yes. We buy over five million a year from them these days, and other companies can't understand how their prices are so low."

"You buy on price then?"

George Pelham put his arms out to the side and leaned forward on his desk. He said, "It's more complicated than that. We do get volume discounts, but I also like the people at the company."

"How well do you know Marilyn McDonald?" Brock could tell by his expression that he knew plenty about her.

"Funny thing, when I first attended a council meeting, and she was introduced, I thought she was the owner of the place. It seemed like Ashby was trying to please her."

Brock saw fit to finesse the point. "Well, she is the vice president *and* a very attractive woman. I'd say most men try to make her happy, including myself."

"You should see the other council members when they get liquored up. They do more than try to please her."

"I can imagine," Brock replied.

"I'm going to share an opinion of mine not based on any evidence. I don't like to gossip about people," George whispered.

"So noted."

"I think she's smarter than Elijah, and frankly, I can't figure out why she hasn't left the company to be the president of a competitor. There's something else holding her there."

Brock offered, "Maybe they are romantically involved."

"I think it's more than that," he rebutted. "I believe she's got something on him."

"Like what?"

"I don't know."

Brock spoke to George Pelham for another forty-five minutes, talking about the details of the business, trying to water down the comments made in the earlier part of the visit. He didn't want Pelham to call Ashby and ask what the hell the guy who called on him was doing. The two men walked out front together after Skinner confirmed he'd gotten the information he needed. George said, "Best of luck to your wife and her winery. I hope to see you when we visit there again."

"Her name is Maude. Just introduce yourself and tell her I said to find me."

"We'll do that."

As Brock was driving back to Hazard, he rang Marcel. "Hey, I just left one of Real Buy's biggest customers."

"Please tell me your visit was uneventful."

"On the contrary. He confirmed what we were thinking. Marilyn's got some sort of hold on Elijah, and we know he's got something on Cheryl Welch, ergo Marilyn has something on both."

"Like what?"

"As you said, it's probably in her safe."

"Yeah, but what is it?"

"There's one way to find out," Brock said.

"I'm not breaking into her house."

"I figured as much. I'll do it. We have to plan it out."

"When?" Marcel asked.

"In a few days," Brock suggested.

"I can't wait." He didn't mean it. "What are you going to do in the meantime?"

Brock fleetingly considered keeping his brother-in-law in the dark. "I think I heard the parents of Elijah and Cheryl were both dead. What about Marilyn's folks?"

"She told me a few years back they had retired to Florida."

"Find them."

"Come again?"

"Find out where they are."

"I can do that. I don't want to know anymore, though."

"Good. The less you know, the better," Brock added. Twenty minutes later, Marcel called with the address of Mindy and Peter McDonald.

~ ~ ~

When George Pelham got back from lunch, his phone rang. The woman on the line identified herself as Marilyn McDonald. "Oh, hi," George said pleasantly.

"I wanted to call to see if Mr. Skinner paid you a visit this morning," she said.

"He certainly did. Nice fellow."

"He is. Elijah asked him to visit a few of our most important customers to make sure we're on top of our game at the company."

"He was here for an hour. I told him what I thought of Real Buy, which was all good. You guys run a tight ship."

"We're trying. It's important to get feedback on our performance, and always strive to be better," Marilyn preached.

"Right. We feel the same way about our customers."

"Did Mr. Skinner ask you anything that was out of bounds?"

"Not in the least. He seemed to be an astute businessman himself. He had our operation figured out in no time. I'd like to have someone like him on the board of my company."

"Did he tell you he was on the board of Real Buy?"

"No, he didn't, but if he is, I can see why."

"Thanks, George. Call me if you ever need anything."

"Will do. Enjoy the rest of your day." Pelham didn't get where he was by missing many tricks. Somebody had sent Brock Skinner to find out what he himself had wondered about: *Why didn't Marilyn McDonald leave Real Buy Louvers in favor of a bigger job with another company?*

Pelham Googled Vigneron Winery's website for the phone number and dialed it. "Is Maude Skinner there?"

"This is she."

"Hello. This is George Pelham over in Harlan. Your husband came to see me this morning."

"Oh, yes. He told me he was driving over for a visit."

"Would you do me a favor? When you see him, ask him to call me?" He gave her his number.

"I sure will. And, by the way, please come over and visit us when you can."

"That's very gracious of you. My wife and I will do that."

Maude went back to the maintenance shed at the winery, where Brock was cleaning the spraying equipment. She said, "Your buddy over in Harlan just called. He wants you to call him at this number." Brock looked up at her to make sure she wasn't on edge. Maude had turned and walked away before he could get a read on her.

"George, Brock here. You wanted me to call?"

"Yes. Thanks. I left something out of our conversation this morning that I thought you ought to know."

"What's that?"

"Well, when my wife and I were out to dinner with Ms. McDonald one time, my wife asked her if she had ever considered pursuing other employment opportunities."

"What did she say to that?"

"She'd had a fair amount of wine, and I'm sure she wouldn't have said anything if she were more in control." George hesitated and Brock waited him out. "She said she was in love with Elijah Ashby and could own his company herself if she wanted to."

Brock replied, "Sounds like she was drunk. I don't think I'd read too much into what she said."

"Maybe not, but I've got a hunch you're trying to figure out where Marilyn McDonald fits in the picture."

"I think we understand each other, George. Thanks for calling me with that information."

~ ~ ~

Marilyn McDonald sat in an unmarked company vehicle alongside a tractor in the farm implement dealer's lot next to Real Buy Louvers. When Elijah Ashby drove past her, she fell in behind him at a distance. He passed by the turnoff to go home, and she had a good idea where he was headed. When he stopped in front of Cheryl's house in Danville, Marilyn cruised on by and parked across the street. She sat there, waiting for the two of them to come out. Elijah and Cheryl got in his car and pulled away forty-five minutes later.

Marilyn went around to the back door of the house and twisted the knob. It was unlocked. She entered and worked her way back to the master bedroom. Gaudy floral wallpaper made the room look smaller than it was. The drawn raspberry-colored drapes kept most of the light out. The sheets and bedspread were rumpled at the foot of the bed. Cheryl's lingerie was in a pile on the floor. Two wet towels hung on towel racks in the bathroom.

When Elijah Ashby pulled into his garage later that evening, he saw Marilyn in the rearview mirror, standing behind his car with arms crossed. She came around to the driver's side and waited for him to get out. "What do you want?" he asked.

"You," she said in an ominous tone.

"It's a little late for that, don't you think?"

"I'm smarter, a better lover, and better looking than Cheryl. Why are you messing around with her?"

Elijah shut the car door and moved past her. "Because she's got something you don't have."

"What's that?" She followed him to the door leading into his house.

"A soul." He spun to see what her reaction would be to that insult.

Marilyn McDonald's face had desire written all over it. "That's not true," she said as she grabbed him around the neck. "I've worked hard to make you successful in business. That should count for something."

Elijah put his arms around her waist, smiled, and said, "You did that for your own benefit. I can't say that I blame you. Before we talk romance, let's finish what we've started."

"Why wait?" she asked.

"To keep our eye on the ball, stay focused," he responded.

"Okay. Just know what you're missing." She kissed him and then smacked his face gently.

"My memory is good, Marilyn. You are what most men would call the perfect woman." She grinned at him.

Chapter 10

Penny Gaines had cleared the way to get her hooks in Kyle Becker, and knew if she rushed things, he might get spooked. She asked, "Can you tell me how the Keeneland race you're working on will set up?"

Becker was sitting at one end of the couch upstairs in his house. Penny was lying next to him with her sock feet in his lap. They had just finished eating the Chinese food Penny picked up on her lunch break. "I'll play three tickets, one heavy for a big payoff, and two more for insurance."

"How so?"

"I'll put Rodesine and Fad Matter first and second, and the favorite third. For insurance, I'll move the favorite up to second on one ticket, and up to first on the other."

"What about the fourth-place finisher?"

"That's what I'm working on now. Since nine horses will be in the race, there are six back there to consider. I want to throw two of them out if possible. In a superfecta, that's where mistakes are often made."

"So, how much are you going to wager?"

"Five hundred and sixty dollars. Eight bets on each ticket. Forty dollars on the best play, twenty on my second preference, and ten on the third."

"Why don't you go all out and bet twice that amount on the heavy one?"

"Law of diminishing returns. The pool only has so much money in it. A bet twice as big does not get twice the payout. If I hold forty of the fifty winners, let's say, of a net one-hundred-thousand-dollar pool, I'll get 80 percent, or eighty thousand. If I have eighty of ninety winners, I'll get 88 percent of the pool, or eighty-eight thousand. And if there are no other winners, I'd get the whole hundred grand, whether I have it forty or eighty times."

Penny thought about it and said, "In the first scenario, you'd get eight thousand more on another three hundred and twenty dollars wagered."

"Yeah, but many times I have the only winning ticket, or I lose the bet. Pigs get fat—hogs get slaughtered."

"Well, you know what you're doing. What're you going to do with the money if you win?"

"Give 10 percent of the winnings to you and buy a condo downtown," he announced emphatically.

Penny sat up and bellowed, "Go, Kyle!" She slipped on her shoes and said, "I've got to get back to work."

Becker asked, "Can you take a vacation day tomorrow?"

"Probably. What do you have in mind?"

"Visiting a couple of horse owners and trainers. We can get lunch at Shaker Village."

"Let's do it." Penny Gaines tried to look pretty when she sashayed out of the room.

~ ~ ~

Kyle picked up Penny at her house and drug her to two separate farms the next morning, where two of the other six horses in the tenth race on the tenth were boarded. One of the owners told him the track secretary had called and pleaded with him to enter his horse even though it hadn't been doing any speed work since being laid off. The owner said, "I'm going to run him, but I've already told the jockey to take him to the back for a breeze. There's no way he'll finish in the top six."

The horse at the other farm was a different story. He had been training well and could possibly run the race of his life to finish fourth. Any higher would mean every other horse upfront had collapsed, which was unlikely.

It was a short trip from the second farm in Versailles to Shaker Village. The bright sun had warmed the air sufficiently, making the ride on the winding roads a pleasant one. Penny, in a happy mood, said, "Kyle, I'm getting kind of used to you being around."

"Don't run me off now, Penny. I've been playing the field since I first met you in the ninth grade."

"All that means is you know me pretty well."

An image of Penny's shotgun trained on his forehead flashed through his mind. "And you know me pretty well by now too."

"Probably too well," she commented.

"What does that mean?"

"You really don't understand women, do you Kyle?"

"Apparently not," he replied as they pulled into the parking lot at Shaker Village.

The two-hundred-year-old Shaker compound had been smartly preserved and was a major Kentucky tourist attraction. The maroon-brick restaurant had a double row of gunmetal-gray arched windows and outdoor seating in between. Kyle and Penny were led to a nice table against the inner brick wall, away from the traffic pattern. She said, "You know, if it weren't for our friendship, I don't think I would have eaten at half the places you've drug me to."

"Nice to know I'm good for something."

"You're good for more than that."

He changed the subject. "What are you going to have for lunch?"

"Whatever they recommend," she said.

As Becker looked over the menu, the hostess seated two women across the way from where he and Penny were sitting. One was the most beautiful woman he'd ever seen. It was all he could do to not get caught gawking at her.

~ ~ ~

The server brought menus to Cheryl and Marilyn. Each of them ordered a glass of unsweetened tea. Marilyn asked, "What do you think of Brock Skinner and Marcel Sutherland being on the board?"

"Fine by me. Brock Skinner came to see me the other day. I like him."

"Seems the rugged type."

"He's married to Marcel's sister. I'd like to know what she's like."

"I'm curious myself," Marilyn said. "I'm going to encourage Elijah to invite her to Keeneland on the tenth. That way, we'll have three women and three men. She can step out for a few minutes while we discuss business."

"Does Marcel have a girlfriend?"

"I think so. I've seen a girl go in and out of your old house a few times."

"What are you going to do with your share of the money once we sell Real Buy?"

Marilyn decided to reveal her intentions. "I'm going to move to Lisbon."

"Oh, really?"

"Yes. I hear it's the place to go with a wad of money. They like Americans."

"You planning on finding a man and getting married?"

"Let's not put the cart before the horse."

Cheryl would mark that spot off the list if she and Elijah consummated their romance. "What do you think Elijah has in mind?"

"Let's stop beating around the bush, Cheryl. You're trying to snag him, and so am I. We'll see how it plays out." They ordered lunch and talked about frivolous things during the meal.

Marilyn saw the girl sitting with the man against the wall in the dining area get up and head for the powder room. The girl had short legs and droopy shoulders, and as soon as she was out of sight, the man looked in Marilyn's direction. She was used to that. Every red-blooded male who saw her eyeballed her. *He can do better than that,* she thought. The man was good looking. He had light-brown hair, plain features, and attractive proportions. Cheryl interrupted her train of thought, saying, "I'd better get going."

Marilyn gave her a parting shot, "I know you're sleeping with Elijah."

"It's nothing you haven't done before," Cheryl remarked. She found the cash to pay her half of the lunch tab, dropped it on the table, and strolled out. The girl had returned across the way. The man gave Marilyn one last glance before turning his attention back to his companion. Marilyn sat and waited for them to leave. She went out in the parking lot after they left to get the license plate number off his car.

As Becker's vehicle crossed the Kentucky River bridge, Penny asked, "Did you notice the beautiful women across from us in the restaurant?"

"No, why?" he lied.

"I just wanted to know if you have a wandering eye."

"Next time, please alert me so I can enjoy the scenery."

"You're such a liar, Kyle. Are you a sociopath?"

"That's for me to know, and you to find out."

"Where are we going now?"

"I want to catch a couple more farms before I drop you off at home."

"Lead on," she said.

They pulled into a big spread east of Harrodsburg Road, past Wilmore. The trainer was there loading up the horse Kyle wanted to learn about. It was a small animal, more along the lines of a router than sprinter. Kyle, as if he didn't know, asked, "When's he racing again?"

"Tenth of April. He's off his feed and has lost seventy pounds. I don't think he'll be sharp until he gains weight."

"What's the distance of the race?"

"Seven furlongs. A little short for him. I took the race because the secretary said he needed to fill the card. He promised to drop another horse I'm training in a good spot."

"Well, I hope he gets his appetite back soon," Kyle said encouragingly, with a broad smile on his face.

Becker saved the farm closest to Penny's house for last. The trainer told him the condition of the horse was none of his damn business and to get the hell off the property. He got a glimpse of the roan with the white patch on his face. He was a big, mean-looking animal. Kyle concluded he couldn't throw him out.

"Have you decided who to eliminate?" Penny asked.

"I have."

"Good. Take me home, James."

"No. I think you should walk from here. You need the exercise."

"Ha-ha. You can walk. I'm taking your car," she boasted.

"If you think you're big enough, try it." Penny jumped across the console in the middle and started tickling him in the ribs. "Okay, I give," he said.

"Are you going to come in?"

"No. I've got a date with Esther Rice."

"You can say the darndest things. If I ever catch you with her, you're dead. I'm not kidding."

"Luckily for me, I was kidding." When they pulled into Penny's driveway, Kyle hit the brakes. Red paint had been thrown on the front door of the house. It had splattered in all directions.

Penny sat up in her seat and hollered, "What the hell! I'm going to kill Esther Rice. You wait here while I get my shotgun."

"How do you know she did this?"

"Come on, Kyle, who else would have done it?"

"You can't accuse somebody without any evidence," he scolded.

"All right, fine. I'll drive over there myself." She got out of the car and chugged toward the house. Becker hadn't intended to stay with her, but knew if he didn't, she'd do something foolish.

He parked and chased after her. "I'll call somebody to come clean it off and repaint the front of the house."

~ ~ ~

Marilyn McDonald had gone to the CFO's office at Real Buy Louvers after she returned from lunch and asked him to find out who the plate on a car she had seen was registered to. "Why do you need to know? Did the driver sideswipe you or something?"

She had to make up a quick story. "No, I saw the person who got in the car steal something from the gift shop over at Shaker Village. I wanted to give them the information."

"Okay, I'll have the dispatcher run it down. You could just give them the plate number, you know."

"Just do it," she ordered.

Late in the day, the CFO called Marilyn to give her the name the car was in: Kyle Becker. The registered address was on Paris Pike in Lexington. The location piqued her interest in that it might be a prime piece of real estate in horse country. She left the office and fought rush-hour traffic until she worked her way over to the location of Becker's house. It was a modest story-and-a-half with mundane landscaping, devoid of a woman's touch. The vehicle was not in the driveway. Her curiosity had been satisfied. She was hoping the property belonged to a well-healed horseman. She should have known better since the car had been hit in the rear, and the driver hadn't seen fit to get the damage fixed.

Marilyn drove to the local address in Lexington that Brock Skinner had given Elijah when he signed onto the board. It was a three-story, modern, red-brick fourplex with each unit having a roof-top patio. The Skinner unit was on the back left of the building, with the patio facing south and west. There were single garage doors on the first floors of each unit. After looking the place over, she decided to get an early dinner at Tony's on Main Street, before the crowd became obnoxious. Every man at the bar saw her come in.

CHAPTER 11

As the weather improved, business at Vigneron Winery turned brisk the last two weeks of March. Maude's mood brightened with each compliment she received on her delicious wines. Her husband bellied up to the tasting bar just before the doors of the winery were to open at ten o'clock, and said, "Now that things are going better, I'm planning to take a road trip."

"What kind of road trip?" she asked with a furrowed brow.

"To Jacksonville, Florida."

"What for, a beach vacation without your wife?"

"Tempting, but no. I want to see if I can find Mindy and Peter McDonald."

"Marilyn McDonald's parents? Are your expenses being reimbursed?"

"No."

Maude backed away from the bar, and said in jest, "Here I am slaving away as the breadwinner of the family, and you're flitting around chasing unicorns."

"That's right," he confirmed.

"Have a nice trip. Please come back alive."

"What fun would that be?" Brock kissed his wife and walked through the vineyard to the driveway in front of their log cabin, where the Lamborghini was parked with his overnight bag already loaded in the trunk. He hurried to Knoxville, exceeding the speed limit, to catch the next direct flight to the sunshine state.

The plane landed in Jacksonville a few minutes before three. Brock had a rental car and was heading south by three thirty. His hotel was the closest one to the retirement community where the McDonalds had been living for several years—inventoried for death. The snowbirds had pulled out the day before, April 1, as the leases expired on their wintertime accommodations.

Jacksonville was a bit of a mystery: too hot in the summer, too cold in the winter, yet a popular place for Easterners and Mid-westerners to hole up or escape to. Brock checked into the hotel and made his way by five o'clock to where the McDonald's lived. The ornate sign in front of the retirement community had grif-fins on each end in gold-tone bas-relief and the green words Bamboo Dunes carved in whitewashed wood. Brock thought the name was odd, given there weren't any bamboo trees in sight. Tri-fold brochures with the usual blandishments were in a clear plastic pouch hanging from a shepherd's hook. He took one.

Florida housing was notoriously stratified by wealth. Bamboo Dunes was geared toward people with a net worth of five hun-dred thousand to a million. The McDonalds were at the top of the spectrum because they had twenty-five hundred a month coming in from their daughter, and Peter was getting a handy pension from the Harrodsburg police department. Throw in a couple of serviceable social security checks, and things had been, and continued to be, pretty cushy for them.

The two wings of the three-story structure were bright-tangerine stucco with white trim. The McDonald's lived in Unit 247, near the end of the second level of the wing on the left. Skinner in-tended to catch them walking to the dining hall, engage them in conversation along the way, and invite himself to join them. He would pose as a prospective buyer and open the McDonalds up with a phony story about how hard it was raising a teenage daughter. He located their place and waited down the hall for them to come out, and when they never did, he decided to change his story and say someone recommended them as a reliable reference on whether Bamboo Dunes was worth a plug nickel or not.

He knocked on their unit, expecting a response. Instead, the door across the hall creaked open. A woman with a dowager's hump, in her eighties, came out to report, "They're not home. They went to St. Augustine for a couple of days." She had on brown slacks and a black-and-white blouse that made her white hair look yellowish.

"That's a shame. Someone suggested I ask them whether this would be a good retirement community for my parents. They're in their sixties."

"Well, you can ask me. I've been here since the development opened. Come on in."

"That's kind of you ma'am," Brock said as he stepped into the narrow, tiled hallway of her unit. He could see the place was sparsely decorated, and it smelled faintly of floral perfume. Paperbacks were packed in a white-painted bookshelf that had gimcrack in front of the books on every shelf. "I'm not keeping you from going to dinner, am I?"

"Heavens, no. Please sit down." He decided on the brown chair that had a pleated skirt. She sat on the small, powder-blue sofa. A white ceramic pot with a variegated mother-in-law's tongue in it was perched on an iron stand next to her. "What's your name?"

"Duncan Whitehead. And yours?"

"Bonnie Pratt. Where do your parents live?"

"Kenosha, Wisconsin."

"Well, I've been here fourteen years. I have nothing bad to say about the facility. It's clean, and they use butter and salt in the kitchen, so the food's got some taste."

"That's good. Do you live alone?"

"Yes. I moved in here when my husband died," she reported, as though she'd long gotten over his death.

"I guess you know just about everybody here."

She got up and tottered to the hall closet. "Let me show you something." She retrieved three poster boards that were loosely rolled up, reverse rolled them, and laid the flattened-out charts on the coffee table. "I keep all the names of the people currently on these floor plans. That way, I know what's going on."

Brock leaned forward to inspect the top sheet. Names were penciled in each unit. "Marvelous," Brock said. "How many of these people do you know?"

"Oh, about a third."

"Any nefarious characters?"

"I can only judge by the families that come to visit. Some kids and grandkids look a little shifty, but I guess you can't really control the way your kids turn out," she said dismissively.

"Do you have any kids, Mrs. Pratt?"

"No, I married late in life. It's just as well. I wasn't cut out for motherhood. How about you?" She pinched off a weak smile.

"None for me either. How about your neighbors across the hall? How long have they been here?"

"Almost as long as I have. They moved in when they were in their fifties."

"That seems a little strange. I would have thought people that young would have preferred a place with a bigger kitchen and area for entertaining."

"Not them. They don't make friends. I don't even think they like each other."

"I wonder why?"

Bonnie Pratt stood and went to the window to look out at the pool. The diehard sun worshippers were still there, and the rest of the crowd had headed in for cocktails and dinner. She said, "I suppose because of their daughter."

"What about her?"

"Mindy came over one day a couple of years ago and told me that Peter was not the father of her child."

Brock replied, "I'm surprised they're still married. Does the daughter ever come to visit?"

"As far as I know, she's never been here."

"That's sad. Say, how about I escort you down to the dining hall for dinner, and you can tell me everything you know about this place? That way I can give a complete report to my parents."

"That's a capital idea, Mr. Whitehead. If I had a son, I'd want him to be just like you."

"Flattery will get you everywhere, Mrs. Pratt. Lead the way." He pulled the door shut after they stepped out into the hall.

They both had beef daube and carrot clafoutis. She was right. There was plenty of butter and salt on the food. Two hours later, Brock was able to gracefully take leave. He felt a little guilty giving her a false name. Not guilty enough to fess up to what he was really doing. He had gotten more than he bargained for from her.

Skinner kicked back on the king bed in his hotel room and called his brother-in-law. "Where are you?" Marcel asked.

"Jacksonville."

"Any luck chasing down Marilyn McDonald's parents?"

"No. I found something better. A chatty neighbor."

"What did she allow?"

"Peter McDonald is not Marilyn's father."

"Uh-oh. Who is?"

Brock sat up in bed. "There's two good candidates—Carson Welch and Isaiah Ashby. I'm betting on Welch."

"If that's the case, it would explain why Cheryl hired Marilyn at Gibbous Metals."

"There's still more to it than that. I want to crack her safe and try to find out the rest of it."

Brock finished his conversation with Marcel and called Maude. They talked for forty-five minutes about what went on at the winery, and the pleasant visit he'd had with Bonnie Pratt. She asked, "You think Marilyn knows Peter isn't her father?"

"I assume she does."

"If so, I wonder when she found out?"

"What difference does that make?"

"Blackmail," she said.

"You've got a point. I'm going to drive straight to Marcel's tomorrow when I get to Knoxville. I should make it back to Hazard by suppertime."

"Be careful."

~ ~ ~

Skinner was sitting in the bustling Jacksonville terminal the next morning, waiting for his plane to board, when Elijah Ashby was keying in the code to disarm the alarm at Marilyn McDonald's house. She had left for work two minutes earlier. Elijah retrieved the door key from under the flowerpot and let himself in. He knew where the safe was since he'd been in the house dozens of times, for as long as he could remember. When the safe popped open, Elijah surveyed the contents without touching anything. There were papers stacked on the right, and a memory stick next to them. He grabbed the stick and slinked back over to his house to see what was on it. He downloaded the file that came up on his computer. It was the video that brought back terrible memories.

Elijah found an identical memory stick in his desk that had no files on it. He went back across the street and put it in Marilyn's safe, closed the house, and reset the alarm. When he got back home, he put the stick he'd stolen in his safe. He called Cheryl with excitement. "I got it! It was on a memory stick. I put an empty one back in her safe."

"That's wonderful. When do you want to get together to talk about what's next?"

"I don't know yet. I'll call you as soon as I can," he said.

~ ~ ~

Brock parked in a vacant garage bay at his brother-in-law's house and waited for him to arrive. When Marcel pulled in a few minutes after two, they quickly reviewed the plan for breaking into Marilyn's. Brock said, "I'll get the tools out of my car to pick the lock."

Once he successfully cracked the safe, Skinner carefully reviewed the stack of loose papers. It was the usual stuff: birth certificate, passport, insurance, titles, list of passwords, and other trivial documents. He turned his attention to the memory stick and made a call to Marcel. "There's nothing here except a jump drive. What should we do with it?"

"Leave the house open, bring it over here, and I'll download what's on it. Then you can take it back and lock up."

Marcel put the stick in his computer, only to find it blank. "Why would she have an empty drive in her safe?"

"She wouldn't. What's happened?"

"Occam's razor. The law of economy."

"What the hell are you talking about?" Brock asked.

"It's too hard to explain. The upshot is that Elijah Ashby must have beaten us to it."

"Unless Marilyn occasionally checked to make sure the files were on there, she wouldn't know they'd been pilfered."

Marcel said, "I bet she checked the stick regularly for a while but became lax after nothing ever happened."

"That would mean the information was in there for quite some time. I doubt she knows it's gone."

"Let's assume she doesn't know. The bigger question is whether she has another copy of the files. If not, the tables may have turned on her, and she doesn't know it yet."

"You think we should break into Elijah's house to see if we can find anything?"

Marcel replied, "I think we wait until after the Keeneland board meeting."

"What Keeneland board meeting?"

"Look at your email. Ashby sent out an invitation for the tenth of April. He invited you, and Maude, so we'd have three men and three women. Take the jump drive back and lock up the house." He pulled the stick out of his computer and handed it over.

After Brock returned, he said, "I bet the missing file has information about who Marilyn's father is, and if it's Carson Welch, that might be the leverage she has."

"But what about Ashby? Why's he caught up in this? I mean, he must be involved in the phony profit scheme at Real Buy. Why?"

"There's still something missing. Maybe we'll be able to pick up on it at the board meeting."

Marcel said, "Having Maude there will be a plus. She's pretty good at reading women. Maybe she'll catch something we don't see."

Brock commented, "I find it hard to believe that Marilyn could be one step behind instead of one step ahead. If she has another copy of those files, she may have been baiting Ashby with the jump drive in her safe."

"Well, there's no way we can determine that now."

On the ride back to Hazard, Brock had a long conversation with his wife, explaining everything he and Marcel talked about. She said, "Did you ever consider that if Carson Welch is Marilyn's father, she may have some claim of ownership in Cheryl's company?"

"That could be, but what about Ashby? Marilyn certainly has no claim on his company."

"Then she must have something else on him," she conjectured.

"That makes the most sense. I need to find out what that is."

Chapter 12

Kyle Becker parked in front of Esther Rice's apartment on the first Sunday night in April. After his three loud bangs, she opened the door. "What the hell do you want?" she asked.

"To talk."

"No." She tried to kick the door shut, but Kyle's foot got in the way.

"Ramming my car is one thing, Esther, but throwing red paint on Penny's door is something else."

"What are you talking about?"

"You know damn well what I'm talking about."

Esther retreated into her apartment, leaving the door open so Becker could follow her in. "I was mad when I hit your car, but I didn't throw paint on anything," she said in one long huff, then turned to face him.

"I know you're unhappy with me because of her, but I'm worried you've gone off the deep end."

Esther said, "When I smashed the back of your car, all the anger I had went out of me. I figured when you tired of Penny, you'd come around to see me again, anyway."

"Who else could have done it?"

"There's only one answer to that."

"What?"

"*She* did it or paid somebody to do it."

"Why?"

"Because she's circling in for the kill. She wants to make extra sure I'm out of the picture before she gets you in a headlock."

"Are you implying she thinks I'll marry her?" Kyle asked naively.

"She and I are the same age. We're in the back half of our thirties. Both of us want to find husbands. You, apparently, don't want either one of us. But as women like us are wont to do, we stupidly continue to chase after what we can't get. Kind of like you, and your dream of finding a bimbo."

Becker thought out loud, "How in the world did I get myself in this position?"

"You led us on. If the situation was reversed, we'd know how to handle it."

"What do you mean?"

"Good-looking women don't give oafish men the time of day, and for good reason. If the men get visions of sugarplums, things can get rough."

"This whole thing is ridiculous," he said.

"I'll make it clear for you. You've been using both Penny and me, and neither one of us likes it anymore. Here's some advice: break it off with her, and never call either one of us again. Otherwise, I promise you, things *will* get rough."

Kyle slinked back out to his car, and for the first time in his desultory life, he worried about his safety. If Penny Gaines hired somebody to throw red paint on her own house, she'd have no compunction using that shotgun. In four days, he'd be escorting her to Keeneland. Esther was right. He should break it off, but he didn't have the courage.

~ ~ ~

The Monday lunch crowd at Vigneron Winery was surprisingly robust due to the lovely weather that had moved in over the weekend. Maude went through the door behind the tasting bar to find her husband carrying a case of wine out of the cellar. She said, "Can you go in the kitchen and help Joan? We've got an army of hungry people out there."

"Sure. What's on the menu?"

"Chicken with bacon-mustard sauce, and Croque-Monsieur."

"What's that last thing?"

"Ham and cheese with a bechamel sauce."

"Dang, woman, if you keep putting stuff like that on the menu, we'll have to add on."

She didn't respond to his raillery. "Afterward, I want to talk about what we're going to wear to Keeneland on Thursday."

"I thought I'd wear cutoff jeans and a wife-beater," he said, to elicit a guffaw from her, which it did.

"I bought two new outfits and need to know which one you like the best."

"Is this going to be one of those 'Does this dress make me look fat?' affairs?"

"Maybe, and you'd better give me an honest answer."

"Oh, boy." Brock set the wine case down and marched toward the kitchen with a stoic look on his face.

Maude had gone back to the house to try on her new clothes by late afternoon. Brock was sitting in the family room, waiting for her to model them. The first dress was honey-yellow, covered with small white flowers. It had stylish ruffled sleeves that flared out at the shoulders. Brock said, "Wow. You're a goddess. Helen of Troy."

"One big difference," she said. "I'm not planning on leaving my husband for another man."

"That's a relief. The dress is beautiful. It'll be hard to beat." The second one was white and platinum paisley, and there were two light lavender ribbons at the waist and one at the hem for embellishment. Brock asked, "What's the weather forecast for Thursday?"

"Sunny and seventy-three degrees."

"That dress is also spectacular. The two are equal, in my humble opinion."

"Okay. What are you going to wear?"

"Blue jacket and yellow tie."

"Then I'll go with the yellow dress. It's springier. That way, we'll match."

"Marilyn McDonald will be jealous when she sees you."

"Good for her," Maude replied. She put her work-a-day clothes back on and returned to the winery.

Brock picked up his phone to call Marcel. "Hey, do you think you can get thirty-five-year-old pictures of the Ashbys, McDonalds, and Welches off their drivers' licenses?"

"I might be able to."

"Something is bothering me. Cheryl's parents were alcoholics. I want to know why."

"How you going to find out?"

"Ask somebody who knows."

"Like whom?"

"Elijah Ashby."

"Call him," Marcel urged. "I'll send the pictures if I can find them."

Marilyn McDonald sat with her legs crossed in Elijah Ashby's office at Real Buy Louvers when his cell phone rang. "Yes, Brock. What can I do for you this time?"

"When I met with Cheryl Welch recently, she told me her parents were alcoholics. Do you have any idea what drove them to that?"

"Why are you interested in knowing?"

"Just curious. She seemed despondent when I met her. I was wondering if the trauma of her early home life has affected her personality."

"I think it's fair to say, Brock, that each of us has been shaped by our upbringing. Marilyn McDonald and I were with Cheryl when her mother died. Pretty tough stuff for all of us."

"What I'm really trying to figure out is whether her business is going well or not. If not, has that been weighing on her?"

Elijah knew right then that Brock Skinner was going to be a problem. "Frankly, that's none of your concern, but you're certainly free to speak with her about it directly. I don't think you should share anything you learn with anyone else. That would be unprofessional."

"Yes, it would be. Maude and I will see you at Keeneland."

After Elijah finished the call, Marilyn asked, "What was he talking about?"

"He wants to know why Cheryl's parents were alcoholics."

"That son of a bitch is going to unravel everything. He'll sink our ship, and when he does, I'm going public."

Elijah stood and said, "Where's that going to get you? I thought you wanted to strike up a romance again."

She got up and fired back, "I want seventeen million dollars, one-third of the fifty-million-dollar sale price for Real Buy."

Elijah had a serious look on his face. "I've got an idea. Why don't I just borrow the money you want against the company and give it to you? Then I can keep the business, and you can fly away."

"We're doing things my way."

"So, you say."

"What does that mean?" she asked.

"Oh, nothing. You know something, Marilyn? You are the most beautiful woman I have ever seen. What are you doing running around without a man?"

"I'm waiting for you to tell me you love me and put a ring on my finger."

"I love you, Marilyn. I'm sure we'll have an interesting time at Keeneland on Thursday."

"Yeah, maybe you'll *win* that seventeen million." She gave him an unpleasant stare and walked out of his office.

~ ~ ~

Cheryl Welch waited patiently for Ashby to come through the door of the bar they frequented in Danville. He saw her sitting in a leather chair in the dimly lit alcove in the back. As he approached, he could tell she was more relaxed than he'd seen her in a long time. "How are you?"

"Better than usual, now that you have the video. Thanks for coming over. Anything been going on?"

"Brock Skinner rang me today and wanted to know why your parents became alcoholics."

"What did you tell him?"

"To talk to you about it. Marilyn was in my office when he called."

"I suppose she's all geared up. Sounds to me like Mr. Skinner is sticking his nose where it doesn't belong."

Elijah sat down on the leather couch next to her chair. "If I throw him off the board, he'll become even more suspicious that something isn't right."

"I think it comes down to one thing . . . if Marilyn doesn't have another copy of the video, it'll be her word against ours."

"She'll claim she has a copy whether she does or not."

"Which means we'll have to call her bluff," Cheryl said.

"She keeps saying she wants seventeen million."

"You know, you could borrow against Real Buy to get the money."

"I told her that," Elijah said. "I've also got a lot of money in my personal account."

"It might be better to pay her off the books."

"There's one problem . . . she seems to be insisting that I put a ring on her finger."

"She kind of inferred that when I had lunch with her at Shaker Village. What will she do if you refuse?"

"Take the money, and then go public with the video."

"So, it comes back to that."

"Yes, but I have a plan to force the issue," Elijah allowed.

"What's that?"

"We should tell the board that we need audited statements to sell the company. Then, I'll anonymously tip off the auditors where to look for the short payments to Gibbous."

Cheryl sat up and said, "That'll unwind everything and put a lot of money back into my company."

"If she has another copy of the video, and uses it, we'll just have to weather the storm."

"I agree. I don't see any way around it. We have to roll the dice."

"Are you ready to order some food?" Elijah asked.

"Why don't we get it to go and take it back to my house."

"Sounds good."

When they had finished eating the carryout meal laid out on Cheryl's kitchen table, she said, "There's another way to smoke Marilyn out. We could get married."

Elijah Ashby chose his words carefully. "There's no sense poking the bear. Let's follow the plan and let the auditors flush her out. We'll see where she stands then."

"Are you avoiding the topic of marriage?"

"We shouldn't get married until this mess is behind us."

"Well, that's encouraging. At least there's a chance you'll put a ring on *my* finger instead of Marilyn's."

Ashby didn't say anything.

~ ~ ~

Marilyn McDonald kept watching for Ashby's car to pull into the driveway across the street from her house. By midnight, she had decided to go find him. The ride to Danville took twenty minutes, and as she approached Cheryl's house, Ashby's car passed her, going the other way. She didn't see him, but he saw her, which caused him to U-turn as soon as he could.

Marilyn parked and got out of her car, and went to the windows to look in. There were no lights on, or any noise coming from inside, so she gave up the quest and returned to her vehicle. Elijah was standing there on the sidewalk with his arms crossed. "What are you doing? Stalking me, or her?" He pointed at Cheryl's house.

"I'm just trying to figure out what's going on between you two."

"Why?"

"Because if I can't have you, she can't either."

"Is that a threat?"

Marilyn stepped in close to his face, and said, "You know, you should be in jail right now. It's only because of my generosity that you're walking around free."

"There's nothing going on between Cheryl and me. I'd dial it down a little if I were you."

She grabbed him around the neck and kissed him passionately. "You know, you can end all of this. I don't even care about the money anymore. I just want you. How's that for a bargain?"

"I'll consider it. Now, let's go home and get some sleep."

When they got back to Saratoga Estates in separate cars, she pulled into his driveway, where she followed him into his house. As Elijah was lowering the garage door, he failed to notice that Cheryl Welch was driving with her lights off and turning around in the cul-de-sac.

~ ~ ~

At seven the next morning, Marilyn walked from Elijah's house over to hers, got cleaned up, and put on work clothes. They both arrived at Real Buy Louvers at eight fifteen. When Elijah entered his office, Cheryl Welch was sitting in a chair at the glass table. "I wasn't expecting to see you here this morning," he said.

She replied, "You're planning on taking up with Marilyn now, aren't you?"

"She's dropped her demand for the seventeen million dollars if I'll marry her." Elijah sat at the table and leaned back in his chair.

Cheryl said, "Well then, I guess I'll be the one to tip off the auditors. If I can't have you, the twenty million short pay to Gibbous will have to come back to me."

"You better hope she doesn't try to get the company away from you then."

"How could she do that?"

"Prove who her parents are."

"It's a little late for that kind of maneuver, don't you think?"

"Don't give up yet on us getting together, Cheryl. Remember, we've got the video, and she doesn't."

"We hope."

Chapter 13

Brock pulled up to the valet stand under the dark green awning at Keeneland a little before noon on Thursday. He presented the tickets Ashby had sent over to gain entrance to the fourth-floor club area. The elevator, to the left of the big sycamore tree inside the grounds, on the other side of the paddock, carried the couple up to the elderly hostess standing in the hall. She directed them to the glass-fronted box that overlooked the homestretch. Elijah Ashby, Marilyn McDonald, and Cheryl Welch were seated around the six-top covered with a starched, white tablecloth. They stood when the Skinners came in, and polite introductions were made with firm handshakes all around.

Marilyn had on a champagne-colored skirt and short jacket that looked like Matisse had painted pale melon squiggles on it. She said to Maude, "I love your dress."

"Thank you. What a lovely place this is." She stepped near the glass to take a long look at the groomed, tawny track.

Cheryl asked, "Have you been to the races here before?"

"Yes, but never in a spot with this kind of view."

Brock said, "We'll be spoiled after this."

"All it takes is connections," Elijah remarked. "Come on, I'll show you the place where we'll step outside to watch the races." The five of them took the short walk to the heavy doors leading out onto the big semi-circle veranda equipped with a tall glass railing. The calm sunny weather was indescribably good, and the breathtaking view over the rolling hills to the west made it obvious why people flocked there to experience what some called the center of the universe.

The elite gathering stopped to give their respects as the national anthem played, and when it ended, Marcel, who had just arrived, came out to join them. He quipped, "I wonder how the other half lives?" Before returning to the private box, the group peered down at the rows of benches along the rail, commenting on the sartorial splendor of certain people in the crowd.

Once everyone had taken a seat, adjusted their clothing, and settled in, Elijah said, "So, there are ten races today, and I want to bet on eight of them. We'll skip the second race for first-time starters and have a quick business meeting during that time. I think we should also leave out the fourth race for maiden claimers."

"I know what you've got in mind," Cheryl said. She had on a blue, multi-shade pantsuit that matched her eyes. "You're planning on selling shares in a betting corporation."

Brock said, "Uh-oh. Here comes a capital call."

Marilyn laughed and asked, "Where can you get a 100 percent return on your investment in four hours?"

"Nowhere. Who's going to be president of this corporation?"

"Elijah, naturally," Cheryl chimed in.

"After a couple of races, we'll evaluate the first-quarter results. If they're bad, we might fire him and look for a new CEO," Marilyn warned.

Elijah boasted, "I'm highly qualified for the position. What usually happens is a dividend is declared and paid after the first quarter, or there's a stock buyback at a substantial premium."

Maude finally spoke, "Remember, pride goes before a fall."

"My sister has been called a naysayer by some. Not by me, of course," Marcel said with a silly expression on his face.

"How much is the buy-in, Elijah?" Brock asked.

"How about fifty thousand each?" No one dared to comment on that shocker. "I'm kidding. Let's put in a hundred dollars a person."

"That's more like it," Marcel responded with relief.

"Yeah, but if we double our money, you'll wish we'd have ponied up a lot more."

"I'm just hoping we don't go bankrupt and have to fund another venture." Everybody laughed heartily as the server entered the room to take lunch orders.

The food wasn't gourmet, and certainly not in the same league as Maude's fare at the winery, but it hit the spot. Fifteen minutes before the first race, everybody was studying the program to find a horse they liked. "Let's go outside and watch them come through the tunnel," Cheryl suggested.

The majesty of horse racing at Keeneland was bolstered by the purity of colors—the rainbow seen on the tote board and silks of the horses and jockeys. Maude said, "Look, there's my pick."

Brock asked, "Number seven? Why'd you pick him?"

"The little rider on him is so cute."

"Oh, boy. That's scientific."

"And the fact that all of the touts like him."

"What kind of a bet are you going to make?"

"Twenty dollars to show."

"He'll only pay two twenty on a two-dollar bet."

Maude feigned indignance. "So, where can you get a 10 percent return in two minutes?"

Elijah interjected, "She's got a point there, Brock."

At post time, there were approximately forty elegantly dressed people standing out on the veranda watching the race. Horse seven cruised to victory, and Maude made her 10 percent. Elijah bet one hundred to win on seven, and the corporation netted a seventy-dollar profit. When the group came back inside, Maude said, "I'm going to visit the gift shop while you folks have your meeting."

When Maude departed, Elijah said, "We don't have much to cover today. I've gathered the names of the people inside the four companies we want to approach to determine their interest in acquiring Real Buy Louvers. I'm going to send them anonymous certified letters through an attorney in Chicago. If they express interest, we'll have them sign a nondisclosure agreement. After that, I would like either Brock or Marcel to confidentially meet with them."

Marcel said, "I recommend Brock do it since he has a more flexible schedule than I do."

"That good by you, Brock?"

"Yes."

"Okay. We'll get the ball rolling. Hopefully, in a month or so, there'll be some action."

Cheryl took the floor. "Shouldn't we have audited financial statements available for a prospective buyer?"

"Why? They'll tell us what they want," Marilyn remarked defensively. Brock took note of her demeanor.

"What do our new board members think about that?"

Marcel said, "If a buyer is planning on borrowing any money to do the deal, a bank will absolutely insist on audited statements."

Brock added, "Any buyer of an operation this big will probably insist that an audit be done before closing."

Marilyn looked out the window aloofly and said nothing. In her mind, she figured where this whole affair was headed. Auditors would ask Gibbous to confirm the pricing Real Buy paid for parts. If Cheryl authenticated the pricing, then an audit would certify Real Buy's profits, as now shown. If she pointed out the short payment for parts, then the auditors would go back and determine the magnitude of what Real Buy owed Gibbous over the years. By her estimation, it was at least twenty million dollars. The bottom line was, if Elijah took up with her, Cheryl would make them pay what was owed to Gibbous. Marilyn knew she was in a bad position and would have to figure a way out of it. What puzzled her was why Ashby acted like he was in the clear. She wondered why he might think so.

Elijah said, "Well, we might as well get an audit done to speed things up. You have anything to add, Marilyn?"

She looked at him with a hollow expression, and then over at Cheryl. "No."

"I say we adjourn the meeting and start searching for a horse in the third race."

Maude returned to the box twelve minutes before post time, carrying a small green bag. Brock asked, "What did you get?" She showed him the "horsey" jewelry and asked him to pin it on her dress. He said, "You better go place your bet on the third race."

"I already have."

"Let me guess. You bet twenty dollars on the favorite to show."

"You're a fast learner. At this rate, I'll win enough money to pay for our gas home."

"I'm glad one of us is a responsible citizen." Brock grinned at his wife and took her by the arm as they headed outside. The favorite finished third, and Maude got a 20 percent return on her ticket. Elijah bet fifty dollars across the board on the same horse. He lost ninety dollars of syndicate money, which hung him with a net twenty-dollar loss after two races. "I think we'll take a walk around since the corporation isn't going to bet the fourth race," Brock said to Elijah, who was licking his wounds.

"I wouldn't be gone too long. The board might fire me as CEO."

Marcel walked up. He said, "I think I speak for Brock. We're backing you, so tell the ladies they can't remove you, unless of course, you decide to fire yourself."

"Thanks for the vote of confidence. I won't let you down," Ashby assured him.

"I'm going to take a stroll with the Skinners," Marcel said. "We'll be back in a bit." They took the elevator down to the ground floor and weaved through the crowd over to the paddock area where the horses for race four were being paraded. Marcel got Brock's attention. "I found the pictures of the parents and have them here in my coat." He patted the right side of his sport coat with his left hand.

"Don't give them to me yet. Let's walk down to the end of the grandstand." He pointed to the north and led the way. Once there, Brock took the enlarged photos and studied them intently. A troubled look came over his face. "I thought I had everything figured out, but these faces don't support my hypothesis."

"Which is?" Maude asked.

"I'll tell you at dinner." He tucked the papers in his jacket.

~ ~ ~

Marilyn had gone out on the veranda to watch the fourth race, and when it was over, she hustled back to the hallway leading to the company box just as the stainless-steel elevator doors were sliding open. The man and woman she had seen at Shaker Village were first to debouch. The woman was wearing a burnt-orange dress with shoulder pads. It was cinched under the bosom and fell near the floor to deemphasize her short legs. The man had on a hard-blue jacket, light gray slacks, white shirt, and solid-silver tie. Marilyn got a better look at him this time. She liked what she saw.

Kyle Becker escorted Penny Gaines down the hall, past Real Buy's box, to an exclusive dining room packed with two-and-four-tops against the window. Becker's table, the lone empty, had a tall, slender vase with a raceme of orange orchids in it that were the color of Penny's dress. She saw the flowers, and before she could say anything, he said, "I had those delivered because they match the stunning outfit you're wearing."

"Oh, how beautiful. Thank you for being so thoughtful, Kyle." He meagerly tipped the hostess, and they settled into their seats. "Did you happen to notice the girl in the hall we saw at Shaker Village the other day?"

"No. Are you sure it's the same woman?" He did see her and knew it was.

"A woman who looks like that, one doesn't forget."

"What would you like to drink?"

The horses for the fifth race were warming up on the homestretch. Penny watched them turn around and head back up the track. "A Mimosa."

"Waiter, bring the lady a Mimosa, and Mark and water on ice for me. We'll just be having dessert. Bring a bread pudding we can split in a few minutes." The young waiter backed away without speaking.

"Are you going to bet on this race?" Penny asked.

"Might as well, to keep my interest level up. I think I'll play five two-dollar exactas. The second through sixth best horses to beat the favorite."

"Then I'll buy the insurance. I'll take the favorite over the next five choices."

"Good strategy."

"Do you know anything about any of these horses?"

"Not a thing," he said blithely.

They went out to watch the race. Kyle worked his way over to the right edge of the glass handrail, closest to the finish line, and tucked Penny in front of him so she could see. The favorite won with a hand ride. Penny collected thirty-two dollars on her ten-dollar bet. She said, "I'm hot, baby."

"Yes, you are," he replied enthusiastically.

Marilyn McDonald followed Kyle and Penny back to the entrance of their dining room and watched to see where they were sitting. She rejoined her group. "How did we do, Mr. President?"

Ashby, rather despondently, said, "We lost. We're down one seventy now."

"I say we fire the CEO." Marilyn appealed to the others to weigh in.

"By the time we do a search for another more competent replacement, the year will be over. I say we put a warning in his file and give him one more chance," Brock suggested, facetiously.

"Thank you, Mr. Skinner. I appreciate your willingness to give me another opportunity to prove myself." Everybody in the room laughed except Marilyn.

Before the sixth race, Kyle walked up to the electronic betting machine and carefully placed his bets for the tenth race. He went back to the table to review the wagers, to make sure they were correct, and then put the three tickets in the front pocket of his sport coat, pushing them down in, so they wouldn't fall out.

The featured ninth race attracted the largest group on the veranda. By that time, most people who had come to Keeneland for the day had gotten sufficiently liquored up on Kentucky bourbon. A few people were happy with the results of the race, but many groaned and threw down their losing tickets.

About two-thirds of the crowd left before the last race. Kyle and Penny relaxed at their table as most people in the room settled their bills. Elijah Ashby, in the Real Buy box, studied the racing form with a sense of urgency. He needed to win the last race to save face.

Chapter 14

Elijah had heard the final race of the day was frequently won by long shots. He took the last one hundred and twenty dollars of corporation money and bet forty on the nose, and twenty to place on the two longest-odds horses: Rodesine and Fad Matter. Marilyn said, "I hope you can pull your chestnuts out of the fire."

"If not, I might as well go down in flames," he replied.

The Real Buy contingency trotted out to the rail of the veranda at post time for the last race of the day. The horses were already loaded in the starting gate, set up in the short chute past the first turn. Marilyn took the spot on the veranda rail next to Kyle Becker. Penny Gaines was on his other side. Marilyn dialed up the charm. "Didn't I see you at Shaker Village not too long ago?"

Kyle looked at her askance, and said, "That's the rumor."

"Good luck. I hope you picked a winner."

"And the same to you." Becker looked away, hoping Penny wasn't about to claw his eyes out.

When the horses hit the top of the stretch, it appeared Rodesine had a big enough lead to hold on, and Fad Matter was second along the rail. The favorite was charging in tight, and at the finish, Rodesine came across first. Fad Matter had to settle for third. Becker took the three tickets out of his pocket and made sure he had the fourth-place horse before he smiled at Penny. "We hit it. Not the big payday, but it'll be pretty good."

Suddenly, Elijah hollered, "We've got forty dollars on the winner!"

"What were his odds?" Maude asked.

Ashby turned around to see the tote board and jostled Becker in the process. "Oh, excuse me, sir. He went off at sixty-two to one!" Becker tucked his tickets in his pocket before escorting Penny back inside.

Brock said calmly, "It'll pay twenty-five hundred dollars."

"Hot diggity!" Cheryl chirped. "That means each of us will get over four hundred dollars back."

Elijah raised his arms victoriously, and the two tickets he was holding fell out of his hand. The group pivoted to head back inside. Ashby bent over to pick up the tickets he'd dropped and scooped up two or three more lying nearby. Marilyn saw him put them in his shirt pocket.

Kyle and Penny returned to their table. He said, "I'll pay the bill, and we'll go to the window down on the first floor where they write checks."

"Mighty good handicapping, Kyle," she said. He reached in his pocket to retrieve the tickets and panicked. He looked at them quickly and let out a sigh of relief. The winning ticket was there, but he had lost the most expensive one, which wasn't a winner.

In the next room, Elijah reported, "I also had a place bet on the third horse. It would've been nice if he'd have come in second." Elijah looked out the window and saw "OBJECTION" in big red letters on the tote board. "Hey, something's going on. It'd be my luck they take the winning horse down."

"They're looking at the second-place finisher. Right there, he jammed the third horse into the rail," Marcel said as he pointed at the replay on the TV overhead.

"That's a relief."

Next door, Kyle Becker saw the inquiry and panicked again. He got up, ran out to the veranda, and began checking all the tickets on the floor for the one he'd lost. It wasn't there. When he came back in, Penny asked, "What's wrong? You're sweating."

Becker said nothing, keeping his eyes on the tote board. Within a few minutes, Fad Matter got placed second, and the favorite was moved down to third. The results were made official. "Oh, no," he said, putting his face in his hands.

"What's the matter with you?"

Kyle stared at Penny in bewilderment. "They've changed the results, and I can't find the winning ticket."

"What do you mean, you can't find the ticket?"

"Just what I said. It was in my pocket, and now it's gone."

"That's bullshit. You're conning me." Penny had flown into a full-blown rage. "I'll tell you what. Why don't you invite that hot babe to dinner who snuggled up to you out on the porch, because I'm not going with you." She checked the payoff on a one-dollar bet—$3,691.40. "You have it forty times, which means the ticket is worth nearly one-hundred and fifty thousand dollars. My cut is close to fifteen thousand."

"You don't seem to understand, Penny, I've lost the ticket."

"Frankly, I don't care if you have or haven't. Don't ever come near me again unless you're delivering what you owe me, in cash." Penny Gaines marched angrily toward the elevator. In the scheme of things, her being mad was the least of Becker's worries. He gazed out over the track, and up at the TV, trying to figure out what to do next.

Ashby cried out, "Look! Now we've got a place ticket on the second horse. That's another three hundred." He pulled the tickets out of his shirt pocket to review them. The first one was the win ticket. The second, a loser he'd scooped off the veranda floor; the third, another dead soldier. The fourth was the place ticket, and the fifth was a superfecta—another ticket he'd scooped up. It read 5,6-with-5,6-with-2-with-1,3,7,8. He looked at the tote board to see the superfecta results: 6,5,2,3. Elijah took his pen and did the math longhand on a page in the program: $147,656. He damn near fainted. He regained his composure, and asked, "Marilyn, would you be kind enough to cash these tickets?" He handed her what the corporation was due.

"Sure," she said, stone faced.

After she'd collected the nearly twenty-nine hundred dollars, Marilyn walked into the room, where she saw Kyle Becker sitting listlessly at his table. She approached and said, "Hi, I'm Marilyn McDonald. And you are?"

Becker, still in stupor, said, "Huh? Oh, I'm sorry. My name's Kyle Becker." He stood to be courteous. She was the most beautiful woman he'd ever been close to.

"I think I saw you drop a ticket out on the porch."

"I did," he replied.

"Well, I've got some encouraging news for you. I believe I know who picked it up, and there might be a way you can get it back."

"Ma'am, if I may say so, telling me that is too good to be true. First, you're gorgeous, and second, why would you want to help me?"

Marilyn was in her element now. "And you're a nice-looking man. You deserve to get back what you dropped by mistake. What happened to your lady friend? Is she one of your fair-weather fans?"

"She left me sitting here when I told her I'd lost the winning ticket." He swung for the fences. "May I escort you to dinner this evening as a thank you?"

"What did you have in mind?"

"I have a reservation at Coles for six o'clock."

"Would it be okay if I met you there?"

Is it okay? It's better than okay . . . "Fine, Ms. McDonald. I'll be waiting for you to arrive."

"Call me Marilyn." She stuck her hand out to shake. He took it, and she kept ahold of his hand for several seconds.

Marilyn returned to the Real Buy box with the fanned bills in her hand. "Here, Elijah, you do the honors."

He divided the money six ways. "Okay, shareholders, I'm happy to report that your return on investment has exceeded 350 percent. We'll be liquidating the corporation now, but if another lucrative business opportunity presents itself, I'll be sure to send you the prospectus."

"Thanks for a wonderful afternoon," Maude said.

"Would anyone like to join me for dinner?" Elijah asked.

"I have an engagement," Marilyn reported.

Brock said, "Thanks for the offer, but Marcel, Maude, and I have other plans this evening as well."

Not wanting to, Elijah said anyway, "And you, Cheryl?"

"I'd love to join you," she replied, intending to needle Marilyn.

~ ~ ~

Cheryl Welch arrived at Holly Hill Inn in Midway a little before six, a couple of minutes before Elijah. She ordered two glasses of club soda that arrived just as he entered the bar. "That was a fun day," she said in an upbeat voice.

"Did you catch Marilyn's expression when you suggested an audit?"

"Yes."

"She's wondering now why we're not sticking to the script."

"Which means she'll look in her safe when she gets home to make sure the video is still there." Cheryl put her arm around Elijah. "Have you figured out what kind of pickle you're in now?"

"You mean if Marilyn has another copy of the video?"

"No."

"What do you mean then?"

"If you take up with me, she's going to burn you. If you take up with her, I'm going to tell the auditors that Real Buy has under-paid Gibbous by more than twenty million dollars."

"The only way she can burn me is if she has another copy of the video."

"That's true."

"You've left out one minor detail, Cheryl."

"What's that?"

"If twenty million goes back to Gibbous, and Marilyn has lost her leverage on me, she'll look for another way to get at your money."

"And what would that be?"

"She'll try to get a copy of your parents' wills. And then she'll run into court asking for DNA testing."

"How is she going to DNA test my dead parents? They were cre-mated."

Elijah leaned on the bar and looked into Cheryl's eyes. "It's not your parents' DNA she'll want. It's yours."

~ ~ ~

Becker came across North Ashland to Main Street and pulled his car into the cramped parking lot alongside Coles. Once inside the restaurant, he asked the hostess to seat him. Marilyn came through the door within minutes. Kyle discreetly raised his hand. She saw the signal and joined him at his table. She said, "What a nice surprise: dinner with a handsome man at a great place."

"You don't know the half of it."

"What do you mean?"

"This day has been an emotional roller coaster." He put his cloth napkin in his lap.

She said, "You know, when I saw you at Shaker Village, I wondered why I had never seen you before."

Becker was too smart for his own good. He deduced immediately that she must have known or found out he lived in the area and was not a tourist from out of town. That implied she was working a plan or setting a trap. "Probably because I don't work. I'm a professional gambler."

"That's funny. You look too smart for such a profession. I think that came out wrong. What I meant to say was, most professional gamblers I've seen or met appear more sinister than you."

"I was salutatorian of my high-school class. I'll take any compliment I can get," he said pleasantly. "Would you care to share a bottle of wine?"

"Cakebread Chardonnay," she replied without hesitation.

"I can see you're the strong female type."

"To use your phrase, you don't know the half of it," she blurted. He chuckled and waved at the waiter.

After they had a relaxing meal together, she broached the subject he was most interested in. "The guy who scooped up your ticket lives across the street from me. I saw him pick it up and put it in his pocket."

"And you know a way I can reclaim it?"

"I do."

"How?"

"The man's name is Elijah Ashby. He'll take the ticket and put it in his safe when he gets home tonight."

"That doesn't sound promising."

"I know how you can disarm the alarm at his house, and best of all, I have the combination to his safe."

There it is, he thought. *The trap.* "This might be a naive question, but are you setting me up?"

"No. I'm hoping after you get your ticket back, we can strike up a relationship. After all, what woman would pass up the chance to be seen with a good-looking man with a fat wallet?"

Kyle Becker saw how it was. What lengths would an otherwise honest man go to for a chance to reel in a woman of her caliber? "I just hope he doesn't take the ticket out of his safe and drive to Keeneland to cash it right away."

"He won't. He's got plenty of money. Meet me in the parking lot at Shaker Village in the morning at seven o'clock. I'll pick you up. We'll go to my house and wait for him to leave for work. You can get in and out of there in less than three minutes. I'll take you back to your car, and you can go on your merry way."

On the drive home, Becker thought there must be a catch.

CHAPTER 15

Brock, Maude, and Marcel left the Skinner condominium at fifteen till eight, after Marcel had completed a video conference call with a group of Sutherland Tailoring managers from the west coast. They entered Columbia Steakhouse and claimed the roomy, poorly lit booth near the kitchen. The smell of cooking beef billowed through the service window. The sound of a fan and muffled radio could be heard in the background. When the insouciant waitress stopped at their table, all three of them ordered Diego salads and filets done medium.

Marcel implored Brock to share his thoughts by bouncing his hands up and down. "Okay, tell us what you thought you knew."

"I had a plausible story all put together until those pictures you showed me today at the track knocked it into a cocked hat," Brock confessed.

"Give us what you were thinking, anyway," Maude urged.

"I tied two threads of information together to construct a scenario that doesn't contradict any of the facts."

"What threads?"

"When I asked Ashby why Cheryl's parents became alcoholics, I think his reply was a slip of the tongue. He said he and Marilyn were with Cheryl when her mother died. I looked up the details of Toni Welch's death. She hit her head on the fireplace and died the Wednesday before Thanksgiving, during the kids' senior year of college. She was dead drunk and must've revealed why her and her husband turned to the juice."

"What do you think she said?" Marcel prodded. The waitress brought the salads and threw them on the table. Maude gave her a dirty look.

"Cheryl inherited Gibbous Metals from her mother, and after she went to work there, she put Marilyn on the payroll. That implies Marilyn had something on her."

Marcel jumped in, "You told me Mindy McDonald, Marilyn's mother, confessed to a neighbor that her husband was not her daughter's father."

Brock added, "I mistakenly thought that Carson Welch was Marilyn's father, and that an unforgivable dalliance drove him and his wife to alcoholism. The neighbor of Marilyn's parents in Florida told me Peter and Mindy McDonald don't like each other very much. Infidelity will do that."

Maude surmised, "So, Marilyn told Cheryl she deserved a job at Gibbous based on something she heard from Toni Welch."

"That would make sense, but how did Elijah Ashby get hooked into the deal?" Marcel asked.

"Something happened or was said that Elijah wanted kept secret. Marilyn used the information to concoct some sort of blackmail scheme and install herself as the vice president of Real Buy. A customer in Harlan told me Marilyn, after a little too much to drink, said she could own Ashby's company if she wanted to. She also said she was in love with him."

Marcel rehashed what had been hypothesized previously. "The scheme Marilyn must've come up with was to suck Gibbous dry and push all of the profits over to Real Buy, so it could be sold for a lot of money." The waitress comported herself more professionally when she brought the steaks. Marcel cut into his to make sure it was cooked to his liking. He wiped his lips after devouring the tender piece of meat, and remarked, "To get the other two to play along, Marilyn would have to promise a big payday for each of them when the company got sold." Maude, after eating half of her steak, asked the waitress to box up the rest. Marcel went on, "Something has changed. Brock, did you see the look on Marilyn's face when Cheryl suggested an audit?"

"Yes. What's happened is either Cheryl or Ashby, or both, broke into Marilyn's house and removed what was being used to blackmail them."

"What do you think it was?"

"A smartphone video of events leading up to Toni Welch's death. Marilyn put it on a memory stick and kept it in her safe. It got pilfered."

Maude said, "Therefore, Elijah and Cheryl are acting like they have the whip hand. You mentioned Marilyn told the customer she loved Ashby. Is it possible that both Cheryl and Marilyn are vying for Elijah's affection?"

"When I met with Cheryl Welch, whom I like the best of these shady characters, she all but said he was the man for her."

Marcel concluded, "It would seem Cheryl's in the driver's seat now. She can alert the auditors that Gibbous has been underpaid by millions of dollars or leave the money in Real Buy if Ashby puts a ring on her finger."

Maude asked, "What if Marilyn claims she has another copy of the video?"

"The whole thing turns into a high-stakes poker game. Ashby will have to call Marilyn's bluff to see what she's holding."

"What's with the pictures you were talking about?"

"I asked Marcel to find shots of the Ashbys, McDonalds, and Welches from their drivers' licenses thirty-five years ago. Marilyn has a striking resemblance to Peter McDonald."

"If Peter McDonald is, in fact, Marilyn's father, then something's not right."

"We need to get our hands on that video," Brock said as he leaned back and put his arms on the edge of the table. "Ma'am, please bring me the check. Thank you."

~ ~ ~

Elijah Ashby wheeled into his driveway at half-past eight. Rain clouds had formed, the wind was gusting, so he hurriedly closed the garage door. He went to his safe to lock up the superfecta ticket before changing into more comfortable clothes. Raindrops splattered on the windowpanes at the back of the house. He flipped on the patio light to see how bad it was out there.

Marilyn McDonald pulled into her garage to get out of the swirling wind and rain a few minutes after Ashby. She headed straight for her safe to retrieve the jump drive that had the video on it. Clicking the drive into her computer, she saw it was blank. She concluded the only people who could have stolen the video were Elijah, Cheryl, Marcel, or that troublemaker—Brock Skinner. Everyone on the Real Buy board was a suspect.

At seven o'clock the next morning, the ground was still soggy from the heavy rain that had fallen overnight. Marilyn pulled up behind Kyle Becker's car at Shaker Village, which she knew on sight, and waited for him to get out and into her car. "It's a little early in the morning for a professional gambler to be up," he said.

"Early bird gets the worm." Marilyn had on her work clothes.

"Early bird needs a cup of coffee." Becker was wearing black jeans and a seafoam-green chambray shirt.

"I've got a pot on at the house."

"Any croissants to go along with it?"

"I don't eat croissants. I'd be happy to fix you a vegetable smoothie."

Kyle stared at her salaciously, and said, "Ah, so that's how you keep that dynamite figure of yours."

"You're undressing me with your eyes, aren't you?"

"Gentlemen don't do things like that."

"Right." She drove into her garage and put down the door. Once in the kitchen, she poured a cup of coffee for him, and asked, "Cream or sugar?"

"Black is fine. Thank you."

"I was just kidding about that vegetable smoothie. Can I fix you some bacon and eggs?"

"No. I'm good. Thanks for the offer, though. What's the plan?"

Marilyn gave Kyle a door key, the alarm code, and location of the keypad at Elijah's house. She also told him where the safe was, and how to open it. "Your superfecta ticket will be in there. There will also be a memory stick that looks like this." She held up the blank one she had in her hand. "I want you to retrieve it. It belongs to me."

"I'll take your word for it."

They watched for Ashby to leave for work, and after he'd pulled out of the neighborhood, Becker scampered across the street and entered the house. Sure enough, the superfecta ticket was atop the papers in the safe, and the memory stick was there too. He locked up and rearmed the alarm, and then came back through the front door of Marilyn's house. "I got it." He said, as he raised the superfecta ticket.

"What about the memory stick?"

"Not in there." Kyle figured he better see what was on the stick before letting loose of it. If there was nothing important, he could mail it to her anonymously.

"That's disappointing," she said. *Cheryl most likely has it*, she thought. "Come on, I'll take you back to your car."

On the way to Shaker Village, Kyle said, "Let me know if you would like to get together again. After all, without your help, I'd be out a lot of money."

"You would at that. I can't be seen with a man driving a car that's been hit in the rear. Get the bumper fixed or trade the car in on something nicer. What happened to your car, anyway?"

"A disgruntled girlfriend rammed it with her truck."

"The one who walked out on you at Keeneland?"

"No. Another one."

"Man, you've got 'em coming and going. Doesn't look like you make 'em very happy though."

"No need to worry about that. I can make you happy," Kyle said as he opened the door of her car to get out.

She said, "That's a bold statement. After I get off work, I'll go home and change clothes, and then drive over to your place. We can go into Paris for dinner."

"You know where I live?"

"I do."

"What should I wear?"

"Oh, something corny. I'll have on an ornate Spanish dress and short jacket."

"I've got just the outfit. How about a white shirt, black vest, hat, and bolo tie, with blue jeans and fancy boots?"

"Perfect. Until this evening," she said as she flipped her hand in his direction.

It was nine o'clock when Kyle walked back in his house. He knew when things were too good to be true. He'd learned that gambling on horses.

~ ~ ~

Marilyn McDonald stepped into Elijah Ashby's office unannounced. He saw her out of the corner of his eye, and said, "What can I do for you?"

"Nothing. I just wanted you to know I have another copy of the video in case you and Cheryl thought by stealing the one in my safe, you'd be in the clear."

Ashby leaned back in his chair, and asked, "But what about us? Have you lost interest in me?"

"Sadly, I have. I don't need to beg any man, and besides, I have a boyfriend who's smarter and better looking than you."

"Ouch. That hurts," he squealed.

"You better tell Cheryl not to screw things up."

"What makes you think she listens to me?"

"Come on, Elijah, who you trying to fool?"

Ashby stood and threw down the pen he had in his hand. "I'd be more worried about Brock Skinner than Cheryl or me. He's likely already figured out what's going on and might anonymously tip off the auditors himself."

"I doubt it. Oh, by the way, I saw you scooping tickets off the veranda floor yesterday. Any of them winners?"

"All of them. I'm rolling in dough."

"I think a case could be made that any winnings belong to the betting corporation."

"I scooped up those tickets on my own time."

"Yeah, sort of like you and Cheryl did when you broke into my house and stole a copy of the video. On your own time."

"And I'm pretty sure it was the only copy," he said.

"You'll find out differently if the two of you try to double-cross me."

Elijah sat back down. He leaned forward and wove his hands. "You know, I've got half a mind to fire you and make you clean out your desk."

"You'll be sorry," she sang out as she left his office.

~ ~ ~

Kyle walked into Keeneland at twelve thirty and headed for the "big money" window. The track cashiers knew there was one un-cashed ticket out there that would claim the entire pool for yesterday's tenth race superfecta, so they weren't surprised when Becker presented it for payment. After the IRS got their piece, the check was made out for $118,124.

The money got deposited at Chase Bank by one fifteen. Becker wrote a first check made out to cash for seventy-five hundred, then waited fifteen minutes, and wrote another for the same amount, to stay under the ten-thousand-dollar limit the govern-ment used to catch drug dealers and money launderers. He pocketed the fifteen thousand and drove to the farm in Paris where Penny Gaines worked. Through her office window, she saw his car pull in. She figured it would be better to bust his chops in the parking lot than have a screaming match inside the building.

Kyle peremptorily remarked, "You should have stuck around yes-terday. I found the winning ticket in another pocket." The money was dangling in his left hand.

Penny looked at the cash and stopped dead in her tracks. Finally, she said, "I take it that's for me?"

"All of it. Fifteen thousand." She snatched it out of his hand and said nothing. Kyle quipped, "I believe a thank-you is in order." She went back to her desk and left him standing in the parking lot.

Chapter 16

After lunch, Maude took the recently waxed Lamborghini to Louisville to do some business with the company that printed labels for her wine bottles. She told Brock to expect her back by five o'clock. He spent two hours in the gym sparring with a good young fighter, and took a long, cool shower at the condo afterward. He didn't recognize the number that came up on his ringing phone. "Hello."

"Brock, this is Cheryl Welch."

"And how are you?"

"Okay."

"What can I do for you, on this fine day?"

"When you came to see me, you said if I ever needed a helping hand, you could lend it."

"Yes?"

"Are you still in Lexington?"

"We are."

"I'm over at the Financial Center visiting my lawyer. I was wondering if you could run over here and meet with me for a few minutes, in their conference room?"

"Sure. What floor?"

"Twenty-third. The offices of Scales and Drumright."

"I'll be there in ten minutes."

The reception area was a throwback to the solicitors of the nineteenth century. Damned good copies of Victorian-aged mahogany furniture looked authentic. The walls were covered with coarse, wheat-colored grass cloth. Cheryl poked her head out of the conference room on the back wall and waved Brock in her direction. She closed the door after he'd taken a seat at the oblong table that had smudges and drink-rings on the glass top. There were four large original paintings of flower arrangements in the room, one on each of the windowless walls. The dress Cheryl had on was dark purple and baggy, making her look frumpy and older. She sat across from him. Her eyes were locked on his.

"Is everything all right?" he asked.

"Well, I'm not destitute, if that's what you mean."

"How can I help you?"

Since her first encounter with Skinner, Cheryl had a feeling she could trust his discretion. "I want to know what you know." She looked away.

"You want the long or short version?"

"Short."

"The day your mother died, something happened that put Marilyn McDonald in a position to blackmail you and Elijah. She forced you to put her on the payroll at Gibbous after you inherited the company. At that time, there was nothing to squeeze out of Elijah, but when he got the ten million in insurance, Marilyn cooked up a plan where all of you could get rich. She went over to Real Buy to keep an eye on Elijah and make sure you sold aluminum to his company at a loss. Marcel and I have been brought in to legitimize a sale of Real Buy for a high price based on inflated profits we're not supposed to know about. If the company were to be sold for fifty million, how would you and Marilyn get any money out of the deal?"

"Each of us has an option to purchase one-third of Real Buy at par value when there is a contract to sell."

"So, you buy a third for thirty-three thousand, and sell it for nearly seventeen million, and pay the capital gains tax."

"Yes. How do you know what the option price is?"

"Because Elijah capitalized the company with a hundred thousand in stock, and then put the other nine-point-nine million in as a loan. He paid the loan back to himself with profits created from losses you incurred at Gibbous. Seems to me, the joke's on you so far."

Cheryl looked confused. "Have you seen the company's financial statements?"

"Yes, and those of your company too."

"You heard me call for an audit during the meeting yesterday?"

"I did. My guess is that you and Elijah got your hands on the video Marilyn has been using for blackmail and decided to try to cut her out. I'd like to know what's on it."

"I'll tell you if you can keep quiet about it."

"I will."

"My mother was drunk. She told Elijah that his mother had had an affair with someone, calling her a religious hypocrite. Elijah jumped up in anger when my mom said that, and he shoved her into the fireplace. She hit her head and died. Marilyn said she wouldn't go to the police with the video if things went her way."

"Your mother said more than that. Care to tell me the rest of it?"

"Let me know what you think she said. I'll confirm or deny." Cheryl got up and went to the corner of the room to get a bottle of water.

"At first, I thought she revealed her husband, your father, was Marilyn's father, not Peter McDonald. I figured if she was a blood relative of the Welch family, she might have some sort of claim on Gibbous Metals."

"What derailed your theory?"

"Marilyn McDonald looks like her father, not Carson Welch."

Cheryl sat back down. "I can confirm that fact. Peter McDonald is Marilyn's father, and Carson Welch was mine."

"So, what does Marilyn have on you?"

"I've got a feeling you'll be able to figure that out without me telling you. The point is moot now. I'm in a spot and need your advice."

Brock wandered over to the corner of the room to tap a cup of coffee from the silver samovar. "I've got a theory on that, too," he offered.

"Let's hear it."

"You and Marilyn are after Elijah Ashby but aren't sure whom he'll pick. Both of you have enticements to offer, but the woman scorned can also drop the hammer on him. It appears to me he's the one in the bind."

"Marilyn only can if she has a copy of the video. I'm willing to accept whichever one of us he chooses. I've dealt with disappointment my whole life."

Brock smiled at her, and said, "Cheryl, I can tell you without fear of contradiction, the man who falls in love with you will have a happy life. If Elijah takes up with that harpy, he'll rue the day."

"I wish all the men I met were as nice to me as you are," she said sincerely.

"I take it I'm missing something else?"

"Yes. If Elijah picks Marilyn, I'll expose the fact that Gibbous is owed over twenty million for aluminum parts that were underpriced. If I do that, and lose Elijah, Marilyn might find a way to get at the money pulled back into my company."

"You already have an idea if she can get at it or not, but I can see you're not going to tell me how. I'm okay with that. Consider this, however, you must tell the auditors about the invoicing irregularities, regardless."

"And why is that?"

"Because if you don't, someday it will be found out, and you could face jail time for fraud. Somehow, I don't see you as the type of person who would give up integrity for money or love," he stated in an avuncular tone.

"I suppose you're right."

"I've got a feeling if he chooses Marilyn, you'll have to sue Real Buy to get the twenty million owed to Gibbous. Who has the video now, you or Elijah?"

"He says it's in his safe."

"Based on the fact that you lived in the neighborhood, I'm sure you know how to break into his place."

"I do," she said with certainty.

"I recommend you go in there and get the video so that you have some leverage against him if you need it in future."

"I can do that."

"Then, you'll want to get on his computer. He would have downloaded the files off the memory stick to confirm what was on it. Take your own jump drive and copy the video just in case the one in the safe is blank, or not there. After that, permanently delete the file on the computer. You'll need to know his password."

"I know it." She stood and frowned wanly. "I'm not sure I love him anymore."

"Why is that?"

"Because I don't think he loves me. Women can tell, you know." She seemed resigned to her plight.

Brock got to his feet, sensing the meeting was about to end. "Would you be kind enough to confirm one more thing for me?"

"Probably. What is it?" She put one hand on the table.

"Did you come here today to look at copies of your mother and father's wills?"

"I did."

"I'm sure you'll tell me the last piece of this puzzle when the time is right," he said.

"I will. I promise. Thanks for helping me." The formalness of the conversation shifted when she gave him a hug.

~ ~ ~

Becker parked his silver Toyota in the "pre-owned" section of the luxury-car dealership, anticipating that an anxious salesman would accost him within seconds. He wasn't disappointed. "How can I help you, sir?"

"I want to trade this in on a used Mercedes," Kyle said.

The salesman walked around the car, noticing the damage to the rear bumper. "How many miles does it have?"

"I don't know. Forty thousand or so, I think."

The salesman opened the door and stuck his head in to read the odometer. "Forty-one one fifty-seven." He backed out, shut the door, and reported, "The damage to the rear is about three thousand dollars' worth, but these cars hold their value pretty good. I'll give you ten thousand on trade, as is."

"Okay."

"Now, what can we put you in?"

Kyle scanned the lot, and said, "A roadster. One that smells good inside."

"Are you just kicking tires, or do you want to drive out of here in a new car?"

"Here's the title to my vehicle." He took the paper out of his shirt pocket, unfolded it, and put it in the salesman's hand. "It's signed over. Once we make a deal, I need to be out of here in twenty minutes. I'll want you to transfer my plates while I call my insurance company."

"I'm not sure we can get you out of here that fast," he replied.

"Okay, then I'll run over to Lexus, and see what they've got for sale." Kyle started to get back in his car.

"Not necessary. Let's find you the right car. You mentioned it had to smell good inside?"

"Yes. All in, I'll give you no more than twenty thousand dollars, plus my car."

"Well, let's get sniffing then. Why don't you sit in a few of them and take a whiff?"

"What about that roadster over there?" Becker pointed to a midnight blue SL 550 at the end of the row.

"I'm not sure I can put you in that for what you want to pay."

"Go see, if you don't mind." Becker started walking toward the car when the salesman went inside to talk to the boss.

He returned and said, "We can make that work. Here are the keys. You want to drive it?"

"I don't have time." Becker got in the driver's seat and closed the door. He started the vehicle and turned on the heat, and then the air conditioning. The vehicle had the new-car smell even though the odometer read seventy-nine thousand miles. He got out, and said, "I'll take it."

"You don't want to drive it?"

"Yeah, when I pull out of here."

The salesman scratched his head and had a scared look on his face. "Come on inside."

Becker reached for his wallet. "Here's my driver's license and the credit card I want to purchase the car with."

"We can't put twenty thousand on a credit card."

"Yes, you can, if you want to make the sale. I didn't haggle on the price, so you needn't haggle on the terms." Twenty minutes later, Becker was on New Circle Road, heading toward Paris Pike. The car he'd bought was faster and quieter than his old Toyota. He turned north and into his driveway a little before five o'clock.

Once inside, Kyle dug in his pocket to fish out the memory stick he'd taken from Ashby's safe. He downloaded the video and hit play. Marilyn McDonald's voice came on, saying, "That's your choice, a bad one." A drunken woman fired back, "Why, you little whore." The woman kept on talking for a couple of minutes until a man came across the frame. He yelled, "Stop it!" before shoving the drunken woman into a limestone fireplace. Becker recognized him as the man who owned the house he'd broken into that morning. He looked much younger.

Now that Becker had been ensnared by the Valkyrie, Marilyn McDonald, he thought for sure he was halfway to Valhalla. The rest of the journey was a condominium in town. Kyle wondered how much Ashby would pay to get the video back. He put the jump drive in a baggie and buried it in the blue sugar tin on the cabinet shelf in the kitchen. Just in case someone broke into his house and stole his computer, he permanently deleted the down-loaded file.

Kyle showered off and put on the outfit Esther Price compelled him to purchase for a party weeks ago. He looked in the mirror and laughed at himself before shutting off the fan in the bathroom, just as the doorbell rang. When he swung open the door, there stood Marilyn McDonald. Becker wasn't particularly religious, but at that moment, he knew there was a god. A Venus de Milo such as her was indescribably beautiful, a work of art by the master of the universe.

"I see you got some new wheels," she commented. Her Spanish dress had been cut tight. The whites of her green eyes were bright and clear.

"Have to keep up with the Joneses," he quipped.

"Between those clothes and your upgraded fly hoopdy, I see you're moving up in class," she said.

"Be careful, that's a horse racing term," he explained. "I hope I'm not in over my head."

"What's next? Are you getting a fancy place downtown?"

"As a matter of fact, I am."

"Where are we going to eat?" she asked.

"Trackside. Not as good as Coles, but you'll like it." They climbed in his car and sped north to downtown Paris.

Chapter 17

When Maude came in from the garage of the condo, Brock was on the phone with Marcel. "Do you think you can find the wills of Carson and Toni Welch?"

"How am I going to do that?"

"I don't know. Hack the government files from fifteen or twenty years ago?"

"Oh, sure."

"I've got a better idea. Hack into the database of the law firm of Scales and Drumright. They'll have copies."

"That might be a possibility," Marcel said.

"That's the spirit. Call me if you find anything." Brock went into the kitchen and asked Maude, "Did your label business go okay?"

"It went well."

"Good. Do you think we should run back to Hazard tonight?"

"I'd like to. I want to be at the winery when we open tomorrow."

"Let's lock up and head out."

~ ~ ~

Cheryl Welch immediately acted on Brock's advice. She parked in Elijah's driveway and knocked on the side door, hoping he wasn't home. When there was no answer, she shut off the alarm and entered the house with the key she'd had for over twenty years. She opened the safe to see if a memory stick was in there. Nothing.

Cheryl put in the password BOOKOFELIJAH as one word, all caps. The computer screen welcomed her, so she clicked on the downloads and inserted the jump drive to copy the video file. After it transferred to the stick, she deleted it from the computer, and then went into the trash bin to permanently delete it. She shut down his machine, closed the house, rearmed the alarm, and got back in her car. On the main road, she turned toward Danville. In her rearview mirror, she saw Ashby's car approaching at a distance from the road to Harrodsburg. Cheryl couldn't be sure if he saw her or not.

Elijah shut off the alarm at his house and went into the kitchen to fix a club soda with lemon juice. Out of curiosity, he opened his safe to inspect the superfecta ticket, to double-check the date and race number for accuracy. It was gone, and so was the jump drive that had the video on it. In a fit of panic, he logged on to his computer to make sure the downloaded copy of the file was still there. It was gone too. He grabbed his phone. "Cheryl, where are you?"

"On my way home from work. What's going on?"

"Someone has stolen the memory stick that was in my safe. The copy on my computer is gone too." He didn't tell her about the superfecta ticket.

"What?"

"Someone has taken it."

"Marilyn is the only person who could have figured out how to crack your safe. She must have stolen the video back."

"Maybe so, but she wouldn't know how to get into my computer to delete the downloaded file."

"Do you use the same password on your computer at work?"

"Yes."

"Well, she probably knows that one, and got lucky when she tried it on your home computer."

"Damn it!" he barked.

"I guess we're right back where we started. You can bet she won't put the video in her safe again. Why don't you drive over here to my house or meet me in Danville at our favorite bar?"

"No. I want to wait around here until she gets home. I'm going to have it out with her."

"Suit yourself. Let me know if anything happens." When Cheryl got home, she took the jump drive and put it under the mattress in the guest bedroom. She placed a call to Brock. "It's me. I wanted you to know I got the video and wiped it off his computer."

"Did you get the one out of his safe?"

"There wasn't one in there."

"That's interesting. I suggest you lay low. Let your friends make the next move."

"Please tell your wife hello for me. Thanks."

Maude asked, "Who was that?"

"Cheryl Welch. She said to say hi. She got ahold of the video and for the moment has Elijah and Marilyn in check, unless Marilyn is the one who stole back the purported copy in his safe."

"If Cheryl comes clean, Marilyn and Elijah might have you arrested," Maude commented ominously.

"I'm willing to take that chance."

~ ~ ~

Trackside Restaurant, a hip refurbished train depot in downtown Paris, Kentucky, fit its name well. The outdoor seating was only a few feet from the greasy tracks running north and south, and unless you were a hobo, the view wasn't what you were accustomed to at mealtime. Washed-out, vertical green siding and a chalky-red metal roof set an arrogantly shabby tone. The inside of the eatery looked like something out of Monticello: cream walls and flat-board colonial window trim painted gray. Kyle Becker followed Marilyn McDonald through the entrance, and every country boy and city slicker in the place noticed them. The consensus, not officially tallied, was that the man in the cowboy hat was her sugar daddy. He had to be because she was so darned good looking.

The wind outside convinced them to take a corner table inside. Kyle took off his hat and set it in the vacant seat to his right. Marilyn said, "You're the first person I've been out with in years, or maybe ever, who wasn't a businessman."

"Those guys are fast talkers. You might find me a little slower on the uptake."

"I doubt that. I'm curious, why'd you become a professional gambler."

"The money, quality of life."

"Sounds lonely. I mean, you're completely on your own."

"Fits my personality, I guess. What about you? How'd you end up where you are?" he asked.

"The money, quality of life."

"Touché. I really don't know what you do for a living."

She said, "I went to Transy, got a degree in business, and now work as an executive for a louver manufacturing company in Lawrenceburg. I've been there for a few years. You broke into the house of the guy who owns the business."

"Ah. So, I guess you know him pretty well." Becker was beginning to put it all together. By some stroke of luck, Marilyn saw her neighbor pick up the winning superfecta ticket and must have figured he would put it in his safe. She needed to have somebody break into his house and steal the video that had been stolen from her. She must have been afraid to go in herself in case he'd set a trap for her.

"Yes. Since birth."

"Did the two of you ever have a relationship?" Kyle now felt that Marilyn McDonald must have been blackmailing Ashby with the video where he's seen shoving a woman to her death.

"Yes. Until yesterday at five o'clock, when I met you," she said, right on the barrelhead.

"You must see something in me I don't see in myself," Kyle responded, in a self-deprecating way.

"Brains, looks, and most of all, courage."

Becker decided to throw her a couple of curve balls. "I must admit, I get along better with women than men. That's how I've gotten myself in trouble before."

"How so?"

"Leading them on. You wouldn't be doing that to me, would you?"

"It's kind of hard to lead a man on in one day, don't you think?"

"You've got a point there. Shall we order?" He had the country ham salad, and she picked the yellowfin tuna. The waiter brought port wine after he'd cleared the table. When Kyle looked up while sipping his drink, he saw Esther Rice walk in. By the look on her face, she'd already seen him. Here she came, like a cat sneaking up on a mouse. "Hello, Esther. Nice to see you again."

"Kyle."

"This is Ms. Marilyn McDonald." He laid open a hand in her direction.

"Hi," Marilyn said.

"Pleased to meet you. It's good to see you're getting some use out of those clothes I made you get. Where's the hat?"

"Right here," he said.

Marilyn swung open the chair she was sitting in and hooked her left arm on the chair post. "You, by chance, wouldn't be the woman who rammed into the back of Mr. Becker's car?"

"As a matter of fact, I am."

"Well, I'm a personal injury lawyer, and will be representing him. He was sitting in the car when you hit it. His neck is injured. Whiplash. I hope you've got enough insurance to cover the claim."

"Nice try, lady. You're the bimbo he's been searching for since we graduated from high school. Looks like he's struck it rich."

"I'll take that as a compliment." Marilyn kept calm.

"Did he tell you he was a dog player?"

"No, he hasn't shared that with me yet."

Becker tried to change the subject. "What are you doing here, Esther?"

"Waiting for Penny Gaines to show up." Esther looked at Marilyn, and said, "She's the other girlfriend he jilted."

"Oh, I think I saw her with Mr. Becker at Keeneland yesterday. She walked out on him. What a shame. He cashed a six-figure ticket."

Esther looked at Kyle, and asked, "What's my cut?"

He said, "Oh, I'd say about three thousand dollars, the amount it will take to fix the Toyota. I hope we can still remain friends."

"Why, of course." Esther turned and headed for the bar.

Marilyn asked him, "Do you think Ms. Gaines is coming to meet her?"

"Not a chance in the world. The only way they'd meet would be for a pistol dual."

"From what I can tell, you know how to mesmerize women," she added comically. "By the way, what is a dog player?"

"A gambler who bets on horses with long odds. I say we finish our wine and pay the bill."

They drove back to Kyle's place. She suggested going to her house in Saratoga Estates, which they did. Elijah Ashby had been waiting for Marilyn to return and decided not to disturb her after he saw the Mercedes roadster pull in her driveway. He swore under his breath and turned away from the window in disgust.

~ ~ ~

Brock wanted to get some exercise on Saturday morning, so he enticed Truman to run along with him while he jogged about a mile, until reaching a fork in the road. They walked a few hundred yards on the one that had little or no traffic. On the way back, Brock sprinted for a hundred yards, and then walked another two hundred, and repeated the pattern until the big log cabin came into view. Truman had no trouble keeping up with his master. In fact, he probably could have kept pace running backward. The dog could catch humans and various other critters in short order.

Maude was already at the winery when Brock and Truman cut through the vineyard to find her, right before the place opened for the day. Once Truman saw her, he went back out on his own to scout for varmints intent on eating the grapevines. Brock asked his wife, "Do you need me to do anything?"

"Bring some more water bottles in and put them in the refrigerator."

"Will do." After he'd finished the task, he went into Maude's office to call Marcel.

"Were you able to find the Welch wills?" Brock repeatedly tapped his pencil on the top of the desk.

"No luck."

"Anything else been going on?"

"As a matter of fact, yes. A little while after Ashby got home last night, I saw him sitting in the front window of his house, like he was waiting for someone to arrive."

"Probably Marilyn."

"That could be."

"Did she ever come home?"

"Yeah, shortly after nine. But that's not all. A dark blue Mercedes roadster pulled in behind her, and the guy driving it went in the house. The car left about eight fifteen this morning."

"Did you get a look at him?"

"No, but I got his license plate number."

Brock asked, "Did you run it?"

"Yes. His name's Kyle Becker. I went ahead and pulled his driver's license picture."

"Do you recognize him?"

"I think so."

"What do you mean, you think so?"

"I'll send the picture to you in a text, and you tell me if you've seen him before."

Brock looked at the picture when his phone dinged. "We saw him at the races on Thursday. I wonder if Marilyn knew him before that?"

"Good question. I did some poking around. The guy is a professional horseplayer."

"How'd you find that out?"

"Looked at his IRS tax return. Why in the world would Marilyn be involved with him?"

"Where does he live?" Brock asked.

"On Paris Pike."

"I seem to remember he was with some girl. I don't suppose there's any way to find out who she was?"

"Dear Brock, you underestimate me. I hacked into Keeneland's database and found Becker's table reservation. There was also an invoice for orchids for his guest, Penny Gaines."

"Isn't that sweet of him. What's the problem with getting the wills?"

"It looks to me like Scales and Drumright don't store things on a computer. I can't find where they have a database."

Skinner said, "That figures. Their offices would fit right in 150 years ago. See if you can turn anything up on Penny Gaines."

"That should be pretty easy to do."

CHAPTER 18

Kyle Becker returned home from placing bets on two races at the OTB and was sitting in the front room eating a peanut butter and jelly sandwich, waiting for the horse racing channel to broadcast the first race at Keeneland. The Kentucky Derby was only three weeks off. The ninth race on Keeneland's card was one of several derby qualifying events around the country that day. Becker didn't care about the big race. He'd gotten a tip on two dogs running; one in the first race, the other in the fifth, but he didn't have time to craft an exotic wager. Instead, he purchased five-hundred-dollar win tickets on the two animals and hoped for the best. His horse in the first race went off at 16 to 1. It paid $34.60 on two dollars. Kyle had it 250 times, which meant he won $8,150 after getting his bait back. He had already made good money for the day, even if the dog in the fifth race didn't come in.

Kyle was in an optimistic mood, so he shut off the TV, ran upstairs to his office, and opened his computer. Alarmingly, the number of condos advertised for sale in downtown Lexington was limited. He liked the looks of the 1,340 square-foot three-story listed for $334,900. *For $250 a square foot, it better be nice*, he thought. The pictures showed a patio off the third floor, which, along with the garage, would be extra footage not figured in the published size of the unit. The write-up had something that caught his eye: RENT TO BUY. He called the number of the listing agent and set up an appointment for one thirty.

The good-looking female real estate agent saw Becker pull his Mercedes up to the curb in front of the condo. She hailed him when he got out of his car. She had already raised the garage door and told him to go right in. The ground floor had storage closets, a small workbench, and an enclosed utility room. He liked the layout. The single bay for parking the car was spacious enough. Stainless-steel elevator doors were next to the fire stairs. The agent pushed the button and said, "Do you have a house to sell?"

"I own a home, but if I make an offer on something, the purchase would not be contingent upon the sale of the house."

"I wasn't thinking in those terms. I'm always looking for listings," she said.

Kyle liked the women a lot. He felt he'd been a little boorish with her, causing him to say contritely, "I'm sorry if I sounded brusque. I didn't mean to be rude."

"Sir, you don't know what rude is. People generally treat real estate agents like garbage, bottom feeders. I'm touched that you're worried about my feelings. Let's take the elevator up so you can see the rest of the place."

The second floor featured a family room, small dining area, kitchen, pantry, coat closet, and half bath. The appliances in the "one-butt" kitchen would satisfy the best of cooks. The multi-colored granite countertop looked expensive. Kyle said, "I noticed your ad had rent to buy in it. Can you explain that?"

"Sure. The man who owned the unit passed away. His heirs don't want to sell it this calendar year. Something to do with taxes. They would like to rent to the buyer for a year, and then reduce the price by the amount of the rent paid."

"Sounds reasonable."

"The snag for a buyer is that the rental amount is high. The sellers want to protect themselves in case the purchase deal falls through in a year for some reason."

"What's the rent?"

"Three thousand a month."

Kyle suggested, "That's not too bad. Shall we go up another level?" They stepped back into the elevator.

Third floor amenities included a luxurious master bath, bank of closets, washer and dryer, and small master bedroom. The sliding glass door across the back wall led out to the patio facing west and north. Kyle went outside to check the view. The patio of the unit to the south was visible through the vegetation growing on a wire-mesh divider. "Do you know who lives next door?"

"A rich couple from Hazard. They're here about 10 percent of the time. I offered the unit to them first, but they didn't express any interest in it."

Kyle went back inside and said, "Let's go down to my car. My checkbook is there."

"Okay," she said. Most real estate agents would have started running their mouths. Becker appreciated the fact that she kept quiet.

Kyle made out two checks and handed them to her. He said, "One check is for thirty-six thousand, which is a year's rent. The seller can cash it now. The other one is for three-hundred thousand, to buy the unit. It's postdated by a year. I'm paying the asking price, so make the paperwork easy for me." He had a year to come up with the purchase amount and thought the video he possessed was worth at least that much to Elijah Ashby.

"Will do." She fidgeted for a minute, and then asked, "Are you married?"

"No, I'm not."

"Don't hesitate to invite me over for a glass of wine after you move in."

Kyle snickered inside. W*hen it rains, it pours?* "I look forward to it."

~ ~ ~

"Marilyn?"

"Yes, Elijah?"

"Can I pop over and have a chat with you?"

"Come through the front door," she said, and hung up.

The low cloud cover on late Saturday afternoon offered nothing more than depressing, muted light. The house was dark inside. Elijah found Marilyn standing by the back window of the family room, gazing out at the nervous birds pecking away at a dangling cage of suet. A trumpet vase of orange and red roses sitting on the low coffee table seemed dreary in the shadows. He said, "It wasn't long ago that you said you wanted me and not the money. Now you don't want me, but you want the money again. Am I reading the situation correctly?"

"Yes. My new boyfriend treats me better than you ever did." She tilted her head back, rubbed her neck, and continued peering out the window.

"That's disappointing. You just got me started liking you again, and *wham*, out I go. Feels like high school all over."

"You know what did it for me? Jumping in the sack with Cheryl. At first, I wanted to win you back to prove I could, but the more I thought about the two of you together, the more I began to despise you."

"And I suppose your relationships with other men over the years should mean nothing to me?"

"I guess you've got a point there," she admitted.

Elijah stepped closer to her. "Okay. I understand. So, let's talk about the money. You want seventeen million. Taxes will take

25 percent of that. I don't know whether you've got a copy of the video or not, but I'd like to end this thing now if we can."

"What are you offering?"

"You know, we paid back the loans I made to the company from the ten million in insurance money I got. It amounted to 9.9 million dollars. All that cash is in my personal bank account."

She said, "Yes. That's the way I planned it based on the idea we'd get married."

Ashby talked past her. "Here's the deal. I'll give you ten million dollars, tax free, in exchange for all copies of the video you have, and settlement for all future claims against Cheryl and me. You will also agree not to divulge anything said or done the day Toni died."

"Deal. Have the agreement drawn up and bring me a check. I'll give you all the copies of the video that I have. After that, I'll try to sell this house and move somewhere exciting."

Elijah began walking toward the front door through her immaculate living room. He stopped, pivoted, and said, "Oh, one more thing. Please don't tell Cheryl we've made this deal. I'm going to have to work something out with her too."

Marilyn laughed loudly. "When she finds out you don't love her, she'll tell the auditors about the twenty million due Gibbous. That's going to leave Elijah a dull boy, with no money."

"I've got a plan. Maybe things will work out, and we can all be friends again. You know, I should have been smart enough to make this deal with you when I got the ten million to begin with."

"Building a nice business has given us purpose in life. It's been worth it. That means something, doesn't it?"

"I guess so," he said. "By the way, when you broke into my house, why'd you take the superfecta ticket?"

"You mean the one you scooped off the floor at the races?"

"Yes, that one."

"I haven't the foggiest idea what you're talking about." She turned to face him, looked up at the ceiling, and stuck her nose in the air.

"Then tell me this . . . why did you go on my computer and permanently delete your video that I downloaded? I mean, what difference does it make to you if I have a copy?"

"I didn't touch your computer," she replied indignantly.

"Well, who did?"

"Maybe, the same person who took the superfecta ticket?" she said to keep him confused.

Marilyn wasn't sure who had taken the video out of his safe. She figured it must have been Cheryl. But why did she go on his computer and delete the downloaded copy? There was only one good explanation. When she opened the safe, the video had already been removed. To get a copy, she had to go onto his computer. That meant Kyle Becker had the video even though he claimed he didn't. She'd have to clean that up somehow.

"No, I've got a hunch Cheryl did it. You must have beaten her to the copy in my safe, so she figured there was one on my computer."

Marilyn added, "And she'll use it to make sure you pay her back the twenty million."

"Do you think Cheryl is smart enough to look on my computer for a copy?" he asked.

"Frankly, no. She told me one day that she liked Brock Skinner. I'll bet she's opened up to him, and he's helping her. If he hasn't figured this whole thing out, he's getting close."

"Likely."

Marilyn said, "Look, why don't you go make a similar deal with her like you just made with me?"

"Whatever arrangement we come to will include relinquishing copies of the video. The first thing I'll ask her, though, is whether she also got the copy that was in my safe. If she did, that means you don't have it. If she didn't, that would indicate it was removed the same time the superfecta ticket was taken."

"Are you looking to welch on our deal?" Marilyn asked.

"No, I'm just wondering if you enticed someone to remove the ticket from my safe and grab the video at the same time. If that's how it went down, I hope the person didn't make a copy. Then, I'll have to buy that one too. Before you get ten million from me, I'll need assurances that the person who broke into my house doesn't have a copy of the video. That person wouldn't be your new boyfriend, would it? He must be the guy who lost the superfecta ticket, to begin with. I'm sure he's mesmerized by your beauty."

"You bet."

"What's his name, by the way?"

"Kyle Becker. I kind of wish things would have worked out between us, Elijah. You're smart and handsome."

"Do I detect a softening of your position?"

"You get me the ten million dollars, and you'll find out how much I like you then."

"I do want you back, you know." Ashby, as the day was darkening, shuffled through the uncut grass in her yard, around the empty garbage cans at the edge of the street, back to his house.

~ ~ ~

Brock answered his ringing phone while he was cleaning up the dinner dishes. Marcel came on, "Penny Gaines works at a horse farm in Bourbon County. I looked up Kyle Becker's high-school graduating class, and she's part of it. I'm guessing she feeds him tips on horses to bet on from time to time, and he gives her a cut of the winnings."

"What's the name of the farm where she works, and can you give me his address?" Marcel read them off before they ended the call.

Within minutes, Skinner's phone jingled again. "This is Brock."

"Mr. Skinner, this is the real estate agent handling the sale of the condo next to yours in Lexington. You remember me?"

"Certainly, what can I do for you?"

"Well, I wanted to let you know the unit sold this afternoon."

"That's great. Can you tell me who bought it?"

She said, "A gentleman by the name of Kyle Becker."

"Come again?"

"Kyle Becker," she repeated.

Brock looked at the phone as though someone was playing a trick on him. "Thanks for letting me know. If you need help with anything, hunt me down."

"Thanks, Mr. Skinner. Enjoy your evening."

Brock called Marcel back. "You're not going to believe it. This Kyle Becker character just bought the condo next to ours. What are the chances of that?"

"When you tell Maude about it, she won't be happy."

"Boy, that's breaking news. I would have never guessed," he said, tongue in cheek.

"Brock, don't call me again this weekend . . . I've had enough drama."

"Yeah."

Chapter 19

Maude stepped out of her comfort zone on Sunday by offering fried catfish on the lunch menu at the winery. Every hillbilly in Eastern Kentucky heard the news. The place was overrun with customers. By eleven forty-five, she told Brock to go over to the house and quickly thaw another two hundred catfish. The line for seats finally subsided at two thirty. Brock asked his wife, "How's the wine holding up?"

"We'll have to dump more next week, or I'll run out."

"You can always raise your prices," he remarked.

"Bad for our reputation," she said.

"Want to hear the latest news?"

"Fire away."

"A guy who stayed at Marilyn McDonald's house on Friday night has just bought the condo next to ours in Lexington."

"What?"

"His name is Kyle Becker. He's a professional horseplayer. Him and a date were at Keeneland on Thursday. We saw them on the veranda."

"How do you know?"

"Your brother ran the plates on his car yesterday morning and pulled a picture from his driver's license. It's the same guy, all right. Marcel was also able to track down the name of his date."

"How did he end up at Marilyn's house on Friday night?"

"I don't know. You've met the Real Buy board members. What's your take on them?"

Maude gathered her thoughts. "Cheryl is a little slippery. Elijah more so. Marilyn a lot."

"I agree with you. That's how Becker got pulled in by Marilyn. I'm going to drive over to Bourbon County in the morning and pay a visit to his date."

"What's her name?"

"Penny Gaines."

"I don't like where this is going. It could get dangerous." Her facial expression was somewhere between confusion and dismay.

~ ~ ~

A white clapboard house just over the Bourbon County line had been converted into the office for what appeared to be a prosperous horse farm. The slat shutters were chalk blue, and the front door, light purple. When Brock stepped inside, he saw the racing silks on the wall, which explained the color scheme on the outside of the building. "I'm looking for Penny Gaines."

"That would be me. Are you here to pick up horses?"

"No, I'm here to see you."

She sized Brock up quickly, and asked, "What about? Didn't I see you at Keeneland last Thursday?"

"Yes. Is there somewhere we can talk privately?"

"Not until you tell me what this is about."

"Kyle Becker."

"That rat dog? Is he in some kind of trouble?"

"Not yet."

Penny exhaled in exasperation. "Let's go in the conference room." She pointed to the open door in the back corner.

They sat next to each other in rickety folding chairs that were on a tile floor covered with ground-in dirt from muddy boots. The story Brock had thought up was at least half true. "Mr. Becker has purchased a condominium in downtown Lexington. An owner of one of the units in the building heard that he was a professional gambler. I'm trying to find out something about the man. You see, if he's of low character, the owner will want to sell his unit. What can you tell me about him?"

"Everything, but why should I?"

"As a courtesy. My friend has a way of lavishly returning favors. All you need to do is ask."

"What's your name?"

"Brock Skinner." He opened his wallet and showed her the picture on his license.

"I first met Kyle in the ninth grade, twenty years ago. We took the same subjects in high school. He was salutatorian of our class. We were pretty good friends, but he was friendly with all the dogs."

"I don't get your meaning," Brock said.

"It's a joke. He's a dog player, a person who bets on long-odds horses. I heard someone say once that he did the same with his women too."

"Ah, I get the inference. Were you on a date with him at Keeneland?"

"Yes. We've been dating off and on until recently when it got hot and heavy. He was also dating another girl. He broke it off with her, and I thought for sure he'd ask me to marry him."

"I take it he didn't?"

"No. What's worse, his other jilted girlfriend, Esther Rice, called me on Saturday to let me know she'd seen him with a knockout on Friday night at a restaurant in Paris. I think she said the woman's name was Marilyn McDonald. I saw her with your group at Keeneland. Esther did that to rub it in I'm sure, just to let me know I'd taken it on the chin too." She shifted in her seat and looked put out.

A guy with a ruddy complexion, red-gray Van Dyke beard, and yellow pencil behind his ear popped his head in the conference room, and said, "Excuse me. The driver out front needs the paperwork for the horses he's picking up from barn 3."

"It's in a clear pouch on my desk," Penny stated. The man disappeared.

"You planning to do anything about Mr. Becker?"

"Yes. Esther and I are going to kill the man. He used us both for information for ten years, led us on, and dumped us on the trash heap. Look at us now. No husband and no desirable prospects at our advanced age. That's justification for murder, don't you think?"

"Seems a little extreme. How exactly did he go from you to Ms. McDonald so quickly?"

"He hit on a wager in the tenth race on Thursday worth nearly one hundred fifty thousand. He claimed he'd lost the ticket. I was in for 10 percent of the winnings and thought for sure he was lying, so he wouldn't have to pay me. I walked out on him. Ms. McDonald must have slid right in behind me. Funny thing is, he came by here on Friday and told me he'd found the ticket in another pocket and handed me fifteen thousand dollars."

"And you still want to kill him?"

"Yeah."

"How are you planning to do it?"

"Esther and I will work something out. Poison, car wreck, shotgun, push him off a cliff, who knows?"

"I certainly hope you're not serious. Do you know where I can find Esther Rice?"

"I think she exercises horses at Keeneland from seven in the morning until about three in the afternoon. You should be able to find her there."

"Just so you know, it's me who owns the condo next to the one Mr. Becker bought downtown. You should call *me* if you need that favor." He gave her his cell number.

"I kind of figured that. You can do a favor for me right now. Kill that SOB."

~ ~ ~

Skinner got to his condo at noon and took an Italian soup out of the freezer to nuke for lunch. He stood at the window, taking in how the cloud cover had cleared, leaving sunshine to warm and wash the low-rise skyline of Lexington. The flora between the condo and Transylvania University, of lime green and deeper tones, had thickened the view and increased the shade. He cleaned the dishes, set out the trash, locked up, and got back in the Lamborghini at twelve thirty, headed for Keeneland.

To avoid being too conspicuous, Brock parked behind the trees down the hill from the Keeneland Sales ring. He walked to the first row of barn stalls where horses were going in and out. No races were held on Monday, so animals were all over the place. Finding Esther Rice took a little doing. He had to wait for her to return on the horse she was riding.

Brock waved and said, "Are you Esther Rice?"

She guided the spent horse over by him. He took her hand as she dismounted. "Yes. What can I do for you?"

"My name's Brock Skinner. Do you have a minute to chat? I'm trying to get some information on Kyle Becker. I've been told you know him."

"By whom?"

"Penny Gaines."

"If she hadn't lost him, too, I'd be mad as hell at the mention of her name." Esther unconsciously redid her ponytail to corral the wad of unruly hair blowing in all directions.

"Penny shared that with me. She also told me he got information from both of you about racehorses."

"He did. If he won, he'd give us a cut sometimes. Other times, he would take us to nice restaurants. Only recently did we both learn he was two-timing us." The groom led the horse away to be sprayed down.

"I take it you interpreted the nice dinners as more than a professional interest?"

"No, it was the conjugal consummation. He probably bedded Penny as well. I suppose that's not very ladylike." She crossed her arms.

"How did he end it?"

"He didn't. I threw his sorry ass out of my apartment."

Brock felt she might turn into a Tasmanian Devil if he said the wrong thing. "I'm sure he deserved it. What did he do?"

"When I pressed him on the subject of marriage, he told me he was holding out for a bimbo."

"Bimbo?"

"His words."

"Seems like a dangerous way to end a relationship."

"You'd have to know his history to understand him," she said.

"Do you mind telling me about it?"

Esther moved closer. "Are you married?"

"Yes. To a lovely lady. I'm lucky."

"Figures. In our high school grade, there were the same four boys and seventeen girls in our classes. Three of the girls were thoroughbreds, and the rest of us were plow horses. Kyle Becker ended up as forth choice among the three good-looking girls, which meant he had to make do."

"Were the other three guys cleverer, better looking, smarter?"

Esther grunted. "Hell no. Kyle Becker was the smartest, best-looking boy in the class."

"So, why did he get passed over?"

"Because women love security. The other three guys had futures as lawyers, doctors, businessmen. The girls knew Kyle came from a troubled home, and thought he'd probably waste his potential. He's proven them right."

"Did he not make the connection?"

"You mean does he understand why he got passed over?"

"Yes."

She scratched her neck. "You know, I don't think he understands how you make the money is as important as how much you make."

"Would he see having money as the way to get a thoroughbred, so to speak?"

"Indubitably."

"You think he'd cut corners?"

"You mean cheat?" she asked.

"I mean blackmail."

"For the right woman, he'd do anything. I don't think he has to worry about that now."

"How come?"

"Because Penny Gaines and I are going to kill him."

"What good's that going to do?"

"It'll make us feel better," she said with a smirk.

Driving back to Hazard, lost in thought, Brock reflected on the ways of the world. Men chase after beautiful women, while the most interesting females go unnoticed. Women chase after driven men who, in the end, don't have time for them. He knew that was a gross generalization. What he didn't know was how Marilyn McDonald enticed Kyle Becker to steal back the video in Elijah Ashby's safe. It must have had something to do with the winning ticket he cashed for nearly a hundred and fifty thousand. Problem was he didn't give the video to her after he cadged it, and was now in position to blackmail Ashby. Dollars to donuts, that's how he planned to pay for the condo he bought downtown, Brock surmised. Marilyn would learn about it soon enough. Enemies of Kyle Becker were beginning to form a line.

Brock waited to call Cheryl Welch until after he turned off I-75 toward Hazard. He didn't like to chat while in heavy traffic. "I've got some information for you that might be useful. Before I tell you what it is, let's make a deal that we keep everything we talk about between us."

"You're my port in the storm. Mum's the word."

"Marilyn has taken up with a professional horseplayer by the name of Kyle Becker. She talked him into stealing the video out of Elijah's safe, which means that was her only copy. Becker hasn't given it to her, probably claiming it wasn't in there. He is likely going to blackmail Elijah with it."

"Or he could sell it to Marilyn."

"I don't think so. He's smitten with her and fashions himself as her soulmate." Brock went in a different direction. "I've got a suggestion for you. Skip the audit on Real Buy for now. Tell Elijah you'll sell your stock in Gibbous Metals to the company for seventeen million dollars. Real Buy has the cash and borrowing power to do the deal. That way, the historical financial statements can be combined, and there won't be any misrepresentation of the profits. That protects you from being charged with fraud. He can then sell the combined businesses for a decent price."

"There are two snags in that thinking. I can only tell you about one of them," she said.

"What?"

"If Marilyn gets the video back from this Becker character, she can gum up the works."

Brock suggested, "Why don't you tell Elijah to take the personal money he has and buy her off before she has a chance to get the video back. She'd be in the mood to negotiate right now."

"You might be onto something there."

"If Elijah pays her off, buys your company, and sells his, everybody will have plenty of money."

"Then there would only be one loose end."

"Are you ready to tell me about it yet?"

"I'm getting close. There might be a way Elijah can bake solving that problem into a deal he makes with Marilyn."

"So, the unresolved issue is Marilyn having some way to get at your money."

She chose not to comment on that point, and said instead, "Brock, I really appreciate you helping me through this. I'll let you know what happens."

CHAPTER 20

"Are you still at the office?" Elijah asked.

"Just getting ready to leave," Cheryl replied.

"It's warm outside. Why don't you meet me at High Bridge? We can watch the sunset like we used to in high school."

"I'll be there in forty-five minutes," she replied excitedly.

Ashby, already sitting at an octagonal picnic table, saw Cheryl's car make the turn under the sui generis bridge and head in his direction. She backed into a gravel parking spot next to his car before bouncing out to join him. Cheryl was wearing a billowy turquoise blouse and black skirt that hit her above the knees. She pulled the skirt up before throwing a leg over the brown bench seat. "You've got something on your mind?" Both went silent for a minute to drink in the view, reading the shadows on the limestone palisades. The greenery near the waterline had darkened, and orange-gray streaky clouds in the sky were starting to tone down the sun rolling toward the western horizon across the Kentucky River.

"Yes. I want to see if we can end this madness."

"I know how. Get the video back from Marilyn's boyfriend and pay me off."

"How do you know he has it?"

"Simple logic. She took up with him so he'd get it out of your safe."

"And he's probably given it back to her," Elijah added.

"I don't think so. He's a professional gambler. If he did, or plans to give it back, he's already made a copy to blackmail you with. No, I'm guessing he told her he didn't find it."

Elijah rose and walked over to the edge of the cliff. He said, "I've come to the same conclusion myself. I also think you're the one who deleted the copy off my computer, and in the process, made a copy for yourself."

"Wouldn't that be something," she said in a sing-song voice. "Let me ask you a question. Do you love me?"

"I do," he said.

"Enough to marry me? Now?"

"I told you, I don't want to think about marriage until this mess is over with."

"Uh-huh. You know what I think? Marilyn has enchanted you once again. Some things never change." She got up from the picnic table and padded toward the bridge. The labyrinth of rusting, dull-brown steel supports holding up the train tracks under-pinned the man-made railroad that led to mystery and freedom on the other side. Cheryl thought seriously about walking across it and hitchhiking home. Instead, she moved over to where Elijah was standing.

He frowned at her and said, "Think what you will. You mentioned paying you off. What do you have in mind?"

"The original plan was for each of us to end up with at least seventeen million dollars before taxes. I'm willing to sell Gibbous Metals to Real Buy for that amount, to get my share now."

"You want Real Buy to purchase your stock?"

"That's what I'm offering," she said. "You can combine the financial statements of the two companies and sell the whole mess to somebody. You won't get fifty million for it but might get twenty. That should keep you off the street."

"I'll give you fifteen million, and you'll have to relinquish any copies of the video you have."

"I'll consider it if you can guarantee that all other copies have been destroyed."

"I can't do that until I smoke out Marilyn's boyfriend," he whined.

"Well, get to it."

The sun had dropped down, nearly out of sight. When it finally disappeared, the orange clouds ran to purple, and then to a smoky gray. Elijah put his arm around Cheryl. He didn't notice the tears running down her cheeks. He said, "I'm hoping after this is over, we can all be friends again."

Cheryl wiped the tears from her face, pushed him away, and hurried over to her car. She turned and said, "I've already come to grips with the fact that you don't love me. Don't ever touch me again." She got in her car, slammed the door, and drove away.

The scooper and dog player were both experiencing life's vicissitudes. Each was hotly pursued by two women only weeks ago. Those women are gone now, all of them mad as hell. Elijah Ashby was contemplating his second encounter with Kyle Becker, whom he didn't realize he'd already bumped into at Keeneland, in the hopes of emerging safely from the long, dark tunnel he'd been in for fifteen years. Becker had two things Ashby wanted: one was a video that could spell his doom. Ashby only had one thing Becker wanted: $300,000 to buy his dream condo in downtown Lexington. Becker also, for the moment, had the most valuable thing of all: the girl both wanted. They would come to learn what it felt like when the shoe was on the other foot.

~ ~ ~

Marilyn McDonald showed up unexpectedly at Kyle Becker's house the next day at noon. He swung open the door, and she said, "I brought barbecue for lunch." She thrust the box of food in his direction.

"That's timely. I'm hungry."

When they'd finished eating, she said, "Kyle, if we're going to go much further, I need to trust you implicitly."

"Okay."

"I'm not completely convinced you didn't find a jump drive in Elijah Ashby's safe."

"What do you want to do, search the place?"

"Nothing as primitive as that," she retorted. "What I'd like to do is look at what's on your computer."

"Okay, let's go upstairs." Kyle led the way to his home office and sat down behind the keyboard. "I need to trust you too. Don't look at my password when I key it in," he uttered playfully. She did anyway.

"Do you mind if I drive?"

"Be my guest," he said as he hoisted himself out of the chair.

She sat, scooted closer to the keyboard, and went to work. A copy of the video was not in the downloads or trash bin. Marilyn looked in the other folders on the machine and found nothing. She sighed and said, "I guess you were telling the truth."

"What's on there that's so valuable?" he asked.

"Something important to me."

"What do you think happened to it?"

"Well, most likely Cheryl Welch broke into Elijah's house and took it."

"Who is she?"

"She owns a company by the name of Gibbous Metals in Danville."

"Never heard of it."

Marilyn took a piece of paper from her skirt pocket and unfolded it. "Never mind that. I want you to sign this document. Since I'm a notary, I can notarize your signature."

"What does it say?" Becker asked.

"That you do not have any videos with Elijah Ashby in it and do not know where any are."

"Easy enough." He reached for a pen and signed on the line, not concerned it was a false statement. "Now, do you want to do anything this weekend?"

"Yes. Let's go hiking at Red River Gorge."

"You're full of good ideas," he said.

"I'll be here at nine o'clock on Saturday morning. It's about an hour's drive there." She began descending the stairs.

He stopped at the top of the staircase. Pleased with himself, he said, "Oh, there's something I forgot to tell you."

"What?" She turned to face him when she got to the first floor.

"I bought a condo in downtown Lexington this weekend."

"You don't say? Where?"

"Market Street."

Marilyn remembered the Skinner condo address. "Is it a three-story affair in a fourplex?"

"Yes. How did you know that?"

"I'm familiar with the building."

"Small world," he said. She moved out of sight, across the room. He hollered out, "Meet me downtown on Saturday." All he heard was the front door closing after she left.

Becker went back and sat at the computer. He looked up Gibbous Metals to see if there was a picture of Cheryl Welch. She was the woman he'd seen at Keeneland last Thursday with Marilyn, and at lunch before that at Shaker Village. It only took him ten minutes to locate her home address. He changed clothes and went down to the garage to head to Danville in his new ride.

Low clouds were moving fast across the sky. The air had never warmed for the day, and due to a raw, pulsating wind, it felt cold outside. Kyle cruised by Gibbous Metals first. The unsettling weather made the place look foreboding. Next, he drove to downtown Danville and saw that Cheryl's house wasn't much to look at either. The overgrown bushes along the front porch shrouded the front door. He decided to go back to Gibbous Metals to see if he recognized Cheryl Welch if and when she came out.

At a little after three, she exited the building through the office entrance, carrying a small satchel. Kyle let her drive away before following at a comfortable distance. She pulled out onto the main highway to Harrodsburg, Lawrenceburg, and Frankfort. He decided to let her go, turning off to the right, back in the direction of her house. He parked his car a block past in an alley.

Becker knocked on Cheryl's door and rang the bell. Nobody answered. He looked around the porch area and tried to figure out where a door key would be hidden. The casework framing the entrance had a pronounced shelf above the door. He reached up and slid his hand along it until a key was dislodged, falling to the ground. He let himself in the house and stood quietly for a few seconds to make sure the coast was clear. The first place he looked for a memory stick was in the sugar and flour tins. It wasn't there.

Kyle had just about given up hope of finding another jump drive with a video on it until he lifted the mattress in the guest bedroom. He stuck what was there in his pocket, locked up, replaced the key, and walked briskly back to his car.

~ ~ ~

Cheryl Welch marched into Real Buy Louvers to find Elijah Ashby, satchel in hand. He was behind his desk when she entered his office. She offered no greeting. He asked, "What have you got there?"

"The minutes' book and stock certificate for Gibbous Metals. I've also included an affidavit that says I will not divulge to anyone what happened the day my mother died."

"Okay."

"When can I get the fifteen million?"

"The company attorney will have to confirm there are no lawsuits or liens against the assets of your business before I can write you a check."

"How long will that take?"

"Ten days or so. Things don't have to be unpleasant between us, you know."

"They're not. I'm just disappointed in myself for not taking action when I heard what my mother had to say the day she died."

"What were you going to do? Tell the police?"

"No. I should have settled things in court instead of succumbing to blackmail."

"I'll second that," Elijah said. "Can't do anything about it now."

"Are you going to go see Marilyn's new boyfriend?"

"I suppose I'll have to. That'll be a fun meeting. Uh, Mr. Becker, please give me back the video you stole out of my safe. I'm sure he'll play along."

"You'll have to work through Marilyn. She'll need to squeeze him," Cheryl said.

"That won't work. If he signs a statement saying he doesn't have the video, or relinquishes it if he does, and then a copy surfaces somewhere else, there's no way to tie it back to him. No, I'm in a box here, or I should say, we're in a box." He looked at her, eyes wide open.

"Have you considered telling Brock Skinner about the problem? He seems like the kind of guy who can fix things."

"I'd be afraid he'd feel obligated to go to the police."

"I don't get that sense. He seems like a free agent to me."

"What is it he could do?"

"Scare the crap out of him. Threaten to kill him if the video surfaces."

Elijah rubbed the back of his head and stuck out his chin. "I hadn't thought of it that way. No, I think I should at least talk to the guy and see what he has to say."

Cheryl decided to take the country roads back to Danville. She stopped at her favorite bar for a carryout dinner before parking in front of her house. After eating, she went to the guest bedroom to make sure the jump drive was still under the mattress. It was gone. She hurriedly dialed Brock Skinner. "Now somebody has stolen *my* copy of the video!"

"Oh, Cheryl, I should have told you to put it in a lockbox or something."

"Who do you think took it?" she asked.

"My guess is Kyle Becker. If he did, he now has both copies, the only two in existence."

"I shared with Elijah that he should tell you about the problem."

"What would you have me do?"

"Ask him to give the videos back or threaten to kill him."

"Well, that wouldn't be hard. He just bought the condo right next to mine in downtown Lexington."

"How convenient," she said ebulliently.

CHAPTER 21

Esther Rice took a hot shower after finishing another rigorous day of exercising Thoroughbreds. She called Penny Gaines and told her she was coming by for a visit at seven o'clock that evening. Penny watched out the window of her house for Esther to arrive, which she did, right on the dot. "Come on in."

"Thanks." Esther looked around to see if the place had any discernable decorating style. Nothing came to mind. The cheap furniture, though, was in better shape than her own, and at least the pictures in the main room were colorful pastiches of original modern art. The light-mauve carpet didn't go with the sage paint on the walls or whitish-gray baseboard and trim.

"So, give me your assessment of this *bimbo*, Kyle's snagged," Penny demanded, guessing she was the subject of interest.

"I'm not sure she's in the *bimbo* class," Esther corrected.

"How so?"

"Not only is she really good looking . . . she's high-class, smart, and probably loaded."

"And you left one thing out. She's an accomplished flirt. I saw her at Keeneland."

"She made a point of telling me she'd seen you there when I saw her with Kyle at Trackside."

"Right up to the time he claimed he'd lost the winning ticket for the tenth race, I thought I was in prime position A."

"What happened exactly?" Esther asked.

"I walked out and left him sitting there."

"Might have been a poor tactical move."

"No worse than you ramming his car."

"Or you having paint thrown on the front of this house, and blaming it on me."

"Looks like we've both made a couple of unforced errors," Penny admitted.

"The least we can do is blacken his reputation with Ms. Wonderful," Esther suggested.

"Or we could just kill him."

"I wouldn't be against that either. We should make sure she dumps him before we go that route."

Penny said, "I'm not sure where she lives, but I know where she works; a place called Real Buy Louvers in Lawrenceburg. I say we run down there after we get off work tomorrow and catch her at the office before quitting time."

~ ~ ~

At four fifteen the following day, Esther and Penny stood in the lobby of the louver plant, waiting for Ms. McDonald to retrieve them. They both had on gray jeans and different styles of tri-colored paneled blouses. Marilyn skittered down the stairs and asked condescendingly, "What is it I can do for you ladies?" She had on navy pumps and a business suit that accentuated her figure.

"We came to talk to you about Kyle Becker."

"I barely know the man. What could I possibly tell you that you don't already know?" Marilyn said coyly.

Penny said, "It's more what we want to tell you about him."

"Along the lines of something I ought to know?"

"Like that, yes," Esther replied in a benign way.

"I've got an idea . . . why don't we go to my house, and I'll trot out some hors d'oeuvres and an expensive bottle of wine?"

"You may not be so bad after all," Penny said as she shrugged her shoulders and put her hands in her pockets.

"Let me shut down my computer and then you gals can follow me over to the house."

The three women stood in the kitchen of Marilyn's gawdy plantation-style home in Saratoga Estates thirty minutes later. Marilyn hung her car keys on a hook, plugged her smartphone in to be charged, and set it on a stand next to the refrigerator. "Do you like chardonnay? I'm partial to Cakebread." She showcased the cold bottle for them to see.

"Uncork it," Esther urged.

"Here, you do it, Penny. The wine glasses are over there." She handed her a corkscrew and pointed to the glass-front cabinet next to the stove. Marilyn put together a plate of spreadable cheese, crackers, salami, nuts, celery, and grapes. "So, you have some information about Mr. Becker you want to share?"

"Before we get into that, can you tell us why in the world you came on to him? I mean, you can have any man you want. Why him?" Esther asked. She loaded a piece of celery with cheese and chomped a bite.

"You'd be surprised. A lot of men run from pretty women. I saw him, thought he was handsome, and he looked smart. He seemed measured and mannerly when I met him."

"But he's a dog player. They're not even respected in the horse gambling community," Penny argued. She put cheese and salami on a cracker.

"That's of no concern of mine."

"Why not?"

"Because I've got plenty of money. I'd rather date a man like him than one who was married to his work." Marilyn stuck to the grapes.

Penny said, "Ah, now I get it. He's your gigolo."

"Do you think he's good-looking?"

"Well, yes."

"Intelligent? Respectful?"

"Uh-huh. And before you ask, he's a good lover," Penny added.

"I think we can all attest to that," Marilyn averred.

Esther rolled her eyes, and Penny sighed.

"There's one thing you overlooked. He's a user. Not drugs, people. He's used Penny and me to get information on racehorses for years."

Marilyn replied, "And for that, you expected him to marry you?"

"Damn it, he shouldn't have led us on," Penny blustered.

"Do you want him back?"

"Not really."

Talking to Penny, Marilyn asked, "Then what's the problem?"

Esther went to the kitchen window and looked to see if there were any birds at the feeders. A rose-breasted grossbeak was perched on a peg, pecking at the seed. She said softly, "He'll use you too. I don't know how he'll do it, but count on it. He'll find a way to make money off his relationship with you."

Marilyn was now sure that Kyle Becker had the video and was lying to her about it. "I'm glad you warned me. If I get a hint of anything of the sort, he's out on his ear. I can promise you that."

Penny grinned and said to Esther, "It won't be long before Ms. McDonald here gives him the heave-ho."

"And if I do, what are you planning?"

"To kill him," Esther avowed.

"You mean literally?" Marilyn asked.

"That's what we mean," Penny confirmed.

"Sounds like I better stay with him just to save his life."

"I guess he could give us a lot of money," Esther suggested.

"He doesn't have it, Esther," Penny said.

Marilyn said, "He must have *some* money. He just bought a condo in downtown Lexington."

"That son of a bitch," Penny swore.

~ ~ ~

Kyle Becker spent the entire day moving what little he had of value into his new condo. It only took three runs of a box truck he'd rented, which came with two men to do the heavy lifting. Setting up the computer and stocking the kitchen took the most time, and once he was done, he went back to his house to give it a final cleaning. He intended to sell the property without a realtor.

By early Saturday morning, Kyle had the condo looking presentable. He wanted to impress Marilyn when she arrived for their hiking trip to Red River Gorge. Getting into his new digs from street level was a bit awkward. The walk-in entrance next to the garage accessed fire stairs leading up to the second floor where a vandal-proof door had been put in next to the elevator that did not have a button to summon it. Kyle heard Marilyn climbing the steps. He stepped out on the landing to greet her. "Good morning. Welcome to my castle." He threw his arms out, offering to embrace. She gave him a peck on the cheek and proceeded through the door.

"Pretty nice place you've got here. How's the noise at night?"

"A couple of sirens woke me, but other than that, it's pretty quiet."

Marilyn walked into the kitchen and poked around in the cabinets to see how things were arranged. Kyle felt a twinge of trepidation when she stared at the canisters of sugar and flour on the top shelf. "Are you going to show me the third floor?"

"Step in the elevator over there."

"Fancy," she commented as the doors opened smoothly. After she eyeballed everything on the inside of the top level, Kyle took her out onto the patio to check the view. There was a long shadow across the floor because the sun was low in the east. The only outdoor furniture he'd brought over from his old house was a round, wire-mesh table with two chairs. The pieces looked lonely and depressing in their new setting. "We might need to make a shopping run," Marilyn said as she went back inside.

"I knew you were going to say that."

"Let's get going. I want you to drive. There's a cooler in the back of my car that has sandwiches and a bottle of wine for us to enjoy when we're done hiking."

"Yes, ma'am." They were on the road to Appalachia by 9:20 a.m. and would make the trailhead a little after ten. Marilyn told Kyle to take Exit 33 off Mountain Parkway at Slade, onto KY 11 south, and continue a couple of miles to the parking area for the Whittleton Arch trail. He asked, "Is this where we're hiking?"

"Yes. It's the largest arch in the Daniel Boone National Forest. An easy two-and-a-half-mile hike. We'll drive over to a spectacular overlook for lunch after we're finished here."

"Lead the way."

The trail was rarely hiked because it was so short. What it lacked in distance, it had in stunning features—an awesome arch, waterfall, and breathtaking spring flowers. Marilyn pointed out each interesting attraction as they came upon it. Kyle felt inadequate, reflecting on the fact that he had no appreciation for the aesthetics of nature, or man-made objects of beauty for that matter. Marilyn McDonald was more than a bimbo. Something sinister crept into his mind. *What can she possibly see in me? She doesn't really like me. I'm being played.*

Kyle understood that a man living in a nice condo downtown, escorting a stunning erudite woman around, was expected to behave in a certain way and know certain things about art, literature, and music. He hadn't factored in being able to converse intelligently on any number of subjects as the price of admission to the elite class. He certainly wasn't going to drag her to the OTB, or other sporting events frequented by overweight, one-dimensional, obtuse bachelors.

After they got back to the car, Marilyn directed, 'Let's go find that good spot for lunch." She took a deep breath of fresh air and climbed in his roadster.

They set folding chairs along the edge of a remote, sheer cliff that looked over the massive gorge. Marilyn opened the cooler and asked, "What do you think of the view?"

"Unbelievable." He halfway meant it.

"Hold these cups while I pour some wine. When I see this splendor, it makes me think about the God who created it. Are you a religious person?"

"I probably would be if my mother had had her way. You see, my father was a bum. Still is a bum. He beat my mother down. She finally gave up. She loves me very much, and I love her. I remember her parents were churchgoing people."

Marilyn stared at Kyle and said nothing for a few seconds. "At least you have one good parent. Both of mine are bad."

"How so?"

"My father has hardly spoken to me his whole life. My mother has treated me like a red-headed stepchild."

"I'm sorry to hear that. I take it they aren't religious folks?"

"No." She looked down sadly and eventually fished the sandwiches out of the cooler for them to eat. "I think there's some skeletons in their closets that have messed both of them up."

Kyle offered an observation, "You know, sometimes we forget our parents are flawed people, damaged goods. I think in the end, we have to get past them and work out our own beliefs. I'm ashamed to say, I've spent little or no time thinking about who or what created something as beautiful as this." He swept his hand across the great chasm in a theatrical way.

"Yeah." She became mesmerized by the panoramic vista. Without averting her eyes, she said, "Pour me some more wine." Kyle got the bottle out of the icy water in the cooler to fill her glass. "Elijah Ashby was raised in the church. His parents were saintly people. Some of his good upbringing comes through occasionally."

"Sounds like you've still got a thing for him."

"I told you, I did have at one time." She looked at Becker again and said, "Then you came along. Now I've got a thing for you."

"And me for you." He raised his wine glass, and offered, "Cheers."

"Thanks for agreeing to go hiking."

On the way back to Lexington, as they rode in silence, Kyle resolved to watch the video another time. He hadn't paid close attention to what the drunk woman had said before Elijah Ashby shoved her into the fireplace.

Chapter 22

Maude walked into the cellar at Vigneron Winery late Monday morning to take a closer look at the inventory on hand. The temperature outside had reached seventy degrees, yet it was still under sixty inside the warehouse. Brock strolled in behind her and asked, "You want me to start dumping more barrels?"

"Yes. I'll write down the batches for you to pull."

"Good." His cell phone rang. Marcel's name came up. "City morgue," Brock answered.

"Ha-ha. A thought came to mind over the weekend. Why in the world would Elijah's father buy a ten-million-dollar life insurance policy on his son? I mean, that seems like an excessive amount, especially for a man making peanuts working as an assistant pastor at a church."

"I agree. What are you thinking?"

"Call Cheryl Welch and find out if she happens to know the name of the company that paid him out."

"Okay."

"If we can get it, I'll try to hack in to see if there's anything interesting in the policy file."

"I knew you'd start pulling your weight. I'll call her." Brock, excited about the possibility of a breakthrough, tapped in the number. "Cheryl, how's it going?"

"Fine, Brock. What's up?"

"Do you happen to know what insurance company paid Elijah the ten million?"

"That was a long time ago. He showed Marilyn and me the check when he got it."

"Who was it from?"

"I remember it being a funny name. I believe it was Argot Insurance. A-R-G-O-T. I think the T is silent."

"Good girl."

"Why do you want to know?"

"It doesn't make sense that his father would buy such a big policy."

"No, it doesn't. There's nobody still alive who could explain why he did."

"I'm not so sure. Maybe Ashby knows why, or possibly the agent who sold the policy to his father can tell me," Brock suggested.

"I doubt it. Just so you know, I made a deal with Elijah for Real Buy Louvers to purchase the stock of Gibbous Metals for fifteen million."

"That's a smart play. After you pay taxes, you'll have a tidy sum. I don't see how Marilyn can get that money away from you."

Tentatively, she replied, "You're right if Elijah pays her off in exchange for leaving us alone."

"He's got the money to do that off the books. See if you can find out if he's worked out something with her."

"When he hands me a fifteen-million-dollar check, I'll ask him."

"Good call. The only loose end will be Kyle Becker. If he's got the videos, he'll want to get paid for them."

"Where do you think he hid the jump drives?"

"They're either in his new condo or a safe deposit box."

"Elijah is going to visit him and try to buy them back," she said.

"Becker's no fool. He'll be patient like he is with the horses."

"Yeah. I still think you should play rough with him."

"Just get your money and keep quiet. I'll try to figure out how to neuter him. I take it your romance with Ashby has cooled?"

"Yes. Marilyn will have to choose between him and Becker, or she might take the money and dump both of them."

Brock concluded, "Which means one or both will get hurt."

"If she picks Becker, Elijah better not come groveling back to me," Cheryl replied with fervor, repulsed for the moment by the idea of Ashby putting his hands on her.

"I take it you're not in a forgiving mood?"

"Have a nice day, Mr. Skinner."

~ ~ ~

Kyle Becker spent most of Monday looking for a good race to bet on that week. Without Esther and Penny, he'd have to work a lot harder gathering intelligence on some dogs he thought might jump up and run well. There was a race set for Wednesday at Keeneland that had a horse in it by the name of Sir Berf, who had all the signs of being darkened. He knew the trainer and would hunt him down the next morning. Kyle turned off his computer just as the doorbell buzzed. He walked across the room to tug open the door. The man standing there, whom he recognized, asked, "Are you Kyle Becker?"

"At least for the moment," Kyle said sarcastically.

"I'm Elijah Ashby."

"How'd you know where I lived?"

"I saw you talking to Marilyn McDonald at Keeneland. She told me who you were and where I could find you. Are you going to invite me in?"

Becker stepped aside and asked, "Are you selling Girl Scout cookies?"

Elijah went to the middle of the room, surveyed it, and responded, "I'm here because I want to formally meet the man who stole my girlfriend."

"All's fair in love and war, they say. Somehow, I don't think that's the only reason you came around."

"You're right, of course. Actually, I'm here because I dropped something at Keeneland the day we were there and was wondering if you happened to pick it up?" Ashby thought he'd give him an easy way to sell the video back.

Becker shut the door, leaned up against the wall, and crossed one arm. "That's funny. I dropped something that day, too, and thought maybe you'd scooped it up."

"I did, in fact, but don't know exactly where it is now."

"Marilyn came here not long ago and asked me if I had a video. She insisted on looking on my computer to see if it was there. She came up empty. I signed a paper swearing I didn't have it."

Ashby put his hands out to the side like a charismatic preacher, and said, "I see your quandary. If she finds out you do have the video, you'll be branded a liar, and she'll dump you."

"There's plenty of lies to go around in this conversation we're having. If I happen to run across what you've lost, is there a finder's fee involved? If so, I'll put in a little effort to come up with what it is you're after."

"Did you have a figure in mind?"

"This condo is going to cost me three-hundred thousand. Do you think it's worth the money?"

"Seems like a bargain to me," Elijah said. "Look, if you happen to locate the video, I promise not to tell Marilyn that we've worked out an arrangement."

Kyle remarked, "Videos. I think I saw you drop two memory sticks." He figured Ashby would conclude that he had both copies.

"You know, you might be right. There were two."

"I bet they're together, and if I find them, you'll be the first person I call. Oh, by the way, if you do tell Marilyn we've had this conversation, those videos might turn up at the police station."

"Now, why would I tell her?" Ashby asked as he made his way back to where he came in.

"To win her back."

"Huh, I never thought of that." He opened the door and stepped through it, reflecting on the fact the condo needed better furniture.

Becker said, "Just to let you know, I'm going to call the Keeneland lost and found. I'll bet the cleaning crew found them. Maybe I can get them back for you that way."

"Sure. I hope you're right." Ashby bounded down the fire stairs and out onto the street. Becker went to the window and watched him walk hurriedly toward town.

~ ~ ~

The crowd at the winery late Monday afternoon was thick courtesy of the radiant blue sky that brightened the verdant plant life and limestone gray landscape prevalent in that part of the world. People had the urge to go places in April after being cooped up for the winter, and since the weather for the month had been relatively warm, they were on the move. Brock sat in a woven-wire chair at the front table on the winery's veranda, drinking a cup of coffee, perusing the craggy features of the Appalachian Mountains as far as the eye could see. He went back to studying the barrel numbers, and where they were in the warehouse, that were listed on the piece of paper Maude handed him an hour ago. Brock had given Marcel the name of the insurance company and was waiting for a callback.

"Breaking into Argot Life was ridiculously easy. I could have posted big insurance policies in our names, and they would have never known."

"I take it you found Isaiah Ashby's policy?"

"I did."

"Anything of interest?"

"The policy was taken out only days after Elijah was born. He was listed as the beneficiary. But get this: the backup beneficiary was Peter McDonald."

"What?"

"Yeah, and then after Marilyn was born, the backup was changed to her name."

"I thought the McDonalds and Ashbys weren't friendly."

Marcel offered a couple of explanations. "Either Ashby owed something to McDonald, or McDonald was blackmailing him. He was a policeman, so he may have found out some information old Isaiah wasn't proud of."

"No, it's something else. I'll think on it and ring you if I come up with anything."

"What are you doing tomorrow?" Marcel asked.

"Dumping barrels and bottling more wine for Maude. This business is getting too damned successful."

"Sorry to hear that," he added with sarcasm.

~ ~ ~

At eight thirty on Tuesday morning, Kyle Becker pulled close to the rolling, wrought iron gate that blocked the entrance to Shedwater Farm, a long and narrow tract of land straddling the Bourbon and Fayette County lines. He pressed the button and spoke to the speaker box, "Kyle Becker here to see Clifford Clay." The gate jiggled before sliding open. He drove through it up to the vinyl-sided, double-wide trailer serving as the farm office. Clay heard the car park and stepped out to greet Becker. Kyle said, "Long time, no see. What are you up to?"

"Oh, just picking shit with the chickens," he quipped with his hand out to shake.

Kyle was reminded of how soft he had become when he shook Clay's big, calloused hand. "I understand you have a horse running tomorrow in the fifth race at Keeneland."

"Sir Berf. One hell of a horse."

"I found a couple of works in his numbers suggesting that. Is the owner the one who darkened him?"

"Kyle, old buddy, you don't ask questions like that. Come on, let's run over and take a look at him." They got in the farm truck and drove down the access road to a dark-brown barn with red shutters. The mélange of leggy annuals along the barn walls were on the verge of flowering. Twelve horses in the stalls turned to see who was approaching. Several of them bobbed their heads and whinnied. Clay stopped at the second stall on the left and announced, "Here he is."

"Nice looking animal. Is he ready?"

"Tight as a drum," Clay confirmed. Sir Berf swung his head around to see if Becker had any food in his hand. Clay dug a carrot out of his pocket, and said, "Here, give him this." The horse daintily nibbled off the end and then tugged the rest of it out of Kyle's tentative fingers.

"Listen, I'm only going to play a superfecta. I'll leave the win pool for you and the connections," Kyle said.

"I appreciate that. You might want to take a hard look at a horse in the race by the name of Lendarcal. He won't catch the two favorites but is a sure thing for fourth place."

"I will."

"If you cash, it'd be nice if you paid the repair bill on my big mower. The crooks at that shop want twelve hundred dollars to replace the driveshaft on the bed."

Kyle remarked, "A farm like this needs a big mower to keep ahead of the grass."

"Anytime you want to come out and take a few laps, I'd be happy to have you."

"I wouldn't recommend that. I'm liable to run over something I shouldn't."

Clay looked back at the horse and reported, "I'm going to let him sleep here tonight. I'll take him over to the track in the morning to get settled in."

"What do you think he'll go off at?"

"Twenty-three or four to one."

"Clifford, I like your style."

The two men laughed and carried on for a while before Becker headed home. He threw his car keys on the kitchen counter when he got in and decided to call Marilyn. "Can you sneak away tomorrow afternoon for the fifth race at Keeneland?"

"That's nice of you to invite me instead of one of your other girlfriends."

"I'm hiding from them at the moment. They don't seem to be as broad-minded as you."

"Okay. I'll meet you in the second-floor paddock. I'll get us a two-top."

Kyle spent the rest of the day convincing himself that a thin bet on four horses was worth the gamble. He'd put Sir Berf on top, the two favorites second and third, and Lendarcal fourth. The two one-hundred-dollar tickets would read: 5-with-3,4-with-3,4-with-1. Tomorrow's weather forecast called for a 40 percent chance of drizzle. If the track got sloppy, he'd drop the bet amount, increase the number of horses for fourth, and buy some insurance at the top of the tickets.

The rain held off on Wednesday. The order of finish in the fifth race was 5-4-3-1. Kyle had it a hundred times. The pool of $68,886 was all his. The track wrote him a check for a little over fifty-five thousand after taxes. Marilyn followed Kyle out to the barns, where Clifford Clay was standing next to his winning horse, with a big smile on his face. He yelled, "Ah, it's Magi, bearing gifts!"

"Clifford, this is my friend, Marilyn McDonald." She smiled pleasantly at him.

"Nice to meet you," he said.

Becker had five thousand in one-hundred-dollar bills in an envelope in his sport coat. He hadn't intended on giving it all to Clay but decided to because of the tip he'd gotten on the fourth-place finisher, Lendarcal. Clay palmed the envelope and stuck it in the back pocket of his jeans.

Marilyn now completely understood what Esther Rice had meant when she branded Becker a user. It seemed every relationship he had was based on economics. Marilyn saw that in him but was blind to her own similar character flaw.

Chapter 23

Cheryl Welch sat in the conference room at Scales and Drumright on Friday morning beside her wizened, punctilious attorney, waiting for Elijah Ashby to arrive. When he walked in, she said, "You're looking sharp today." He had on a gray suit with a burnt-orange and Mediterranean-blue tie.

"Why, thank you. I don't think I've ever seen you more beautiful, Cheryl." He wanted to touch her on the shoulder but thought about what she'd told him recently, to never touch her again.

"That's what fifteen million dollars will do for you."

"I suppose."

It took ten minutes to sign all the papers transferring ownership of Gibbous Metals to Real Buy Louvers. Elijah handed Cheryl a cashier's check, and she dismissed the attorney once she'd tucked the money in her purse. "So, have you made a deal with Marilyn?"

"I have. The agreement states she has no future claim against you or me, and what she knows will remain confidential."

"But you have no collateral if she doesn't comply."

"I'll have her personal guarantee and can sue her for breach of contract."

"That sounds messy."

"It would be. That's precisely why she won't go that route. Most blackmailers like to get the money and disappear," he said. "About Gibbous, I would like you to stay on until I sell Real Buy, and I don't want to announce the purchase to anyone other than the board members."

"I figured as much. Have you tried to buy the video from Kyle Becker?"

"I have. I don't think he's in any hurry to sell."

"Has Marilyn officially dumped you for him?" she asked.

"I'm afraid so."

Cheryl stood and walked over to the conference room door. "That's justice for you. It wasn't long ago when you had two women pursuing you, and now you have none."

Elijah got up and turned to face her. "I'm still in love with you, Cheryl, but I can see it's hopeless."

"You had your chance." She disappeared from the conference room and left him standing there alone.

~ ~ ~

Ashby pulled into Marilyn McDonald's driveway instead of his own forty minutes later. She saw him get out of his car and went to the front porch to meet him. He was clutching a thin briefcase. "Come on in." She had all the lights on in the living room. The bright sunlight made them unnecessary. "Have a seat," she instructed.

He set the briefcase on the coffee table and flipped it open. "Here are the papers you need to sign. Did you get anything from your boyfriend on the video?"

She retrieved the paper he'd signed from the kitchen and handed it to him. "I'm not going to sign a release for you and Cheryl until I see the money. Where is it?"

"Marilyn, we need to be careful. Otherwise, the money you get will be taxed as a gift. We don't want that."

"What's the plan?"

"I'm going to ACH ten million dollars to a gold dealer, and then pick up five thousand gold coins that weigh three hundred pounds. You need to decide where you want to keep them. The government can't trace the transaction that way."

"I bought a big cabinet safe after my wall safe was broken into. When can you bring the gold here?"

"Tuesday morning."

"I'll be ready for it."

Elijah said, "Let me remind you of something. You shouldn't sell more than twenty-five ounces at a time, or the buyer will have to report it to the government."

"You mean I can only liquidate the coins in fifty-thousand-dollar chunks?"

"I'm afraid that's the long and short of it. Now that the deal's set, have you considered rekindling our romance?"

She looked at him dubiously. "I haven't made up my mind yet."

"Well, let me help you. I went to see your boyfriend Becker the other day. He's got the two videos and is willing to sell them to me for three-hundred thousand, which by the way, is the cost of his new digs downtown."

"That's hard to believe. He just won over fifty thousand at the track this week. He doesn't need the money."

"He must have gotten the second video from Cheryl. He also said he'd turn them over to the police if I told you he had them. The man's a liar. He's using you."

"I'll give you one thing, Elijah, I've never known you to lie."

"And I'm not now. You know we make beautiful music together."

"After I tuck the gold away Tuesday, we'll have a cup of coffee and talk about it," she said. He loaded the papers in the briefcase and drove across the street to his house.

~ ~ ~

Brock finished dumping several barrels of wine, filtering and bottling them by closing time at six o'clock on Friday. He joined Maude in her office. "Let's go home, sit on the back porch, and enjoy this weather," she suggested.

"Sounds good."

They grilled rainbow trout for supper and tried a bottle of the new white wine Brock had put in the freezer to get cold fast. He peered critically at his wine glass, and said, "This is really good."

"I know that look, Brock. You've got something on your mind. What is it?"

"Marilyn's boyfriend, who moved in next to us in Lexington, has the videos of the day Cheryl's mother died. Cheryl won't tell me what happened then other than to say Elijah pushed her mother into the fireplace, causing her death. I've got to get my hands on those jump drives."

"How are you going to do that?"

"Break into his place and see if he has them hidden there."

"What if you get caught?"

"He won't do anything."

"You sure about that?"

"No."

"See, this is what I was afraid of. You borrowing trouble. Can't you just let it go?" Maude gathered up the dishes and took them inside. He followed her.

"If I can get the videos, Marcel and I can help Elijah sell Real Buy Louvers with a clean conscience, and this thing will be over."

"It can be over now. Just play dumb."

"There's something rotten about the ten-million-dollar insurance policy that Elijah's father had on him."

"Like what?"

"Marilyn McDonald was listed as the backup beneficiary. Now, why would that be? The only way I can figure that out is to hear what Toni Carson had to say before she met her demise."

Maude stated, "So, you think all of this business is tied together?"

"It has to be."

"I see I'm not going to be able to stop you. When are you planning to drive to Lexington?"

"Tomorrow afternoon. He'll probably go out to dinner with Marilyn. I'll make my move then."

"Well, as I said before, there's one good thing."

"What's that?"

"No dead bodies yet."

Truman came to the back door. Brock let him in. "Maude, if you were going to hide a couple of memory sticks, where would you put them?"

"In a baggie, in the sugar or flour tin."

~ ~ ~

The Kentucky Derby was only a week away now, and the hype was building. Brock found a radio station previewing the race as he sped toward Lexington. A loaded Beretta pistol and the tools to pick a lock were lying in the passenger seat under a towel. He raised the garage door of the condo at four o'clock, and quietly eased the car in before putting the door back down. Brock took the elevator up to the second floor, got a can of soda, and pulled a chair over to the front window. The ringer was off on his phone. It began vibrating in his pocket. Cheryl Welch was calling. He spoke in a quiet voice, "Hello."

"I just wanted you to know I got the fifteen million yesterday," she said as she paced around in her kitchen.

"Good for you."

"Elijah tried to buy the videos, but Becker didn't seem all that anxious to sell."

"I think he's figured out once he sells them, Elijah will rat him out to Marilyn, and he might lose her. I'm guessing he'll wait as long as he can before he cashes in."

"Elijah wants me to stay on at Gibbous until he sells out."

Brock remarked, "And let me guess, he's not going to let anyone know he's bought the company."

"Right."

"What about Marilyn? You think he's bought her off?"

"Yes."

"If I can get the videos away from Becker, what do you think I should do with them?"

"Hold on to them until Real Buy gets sold," she said.

"Or I could sell them."

"You wouldn't."

"Just kidding. I like your idea." He saw a dark-blue roadster pull up next door and roll into the garage. "I've got to go. Stay out of trouble."

"You should talk." She hung up.

Skinner drug the chair back away from the window. He stretched out on the couch, expecting to be there for a while. Twenty minutes later, there was a muffled voice on the other side of the wall, talking on the phone. Shortly after the call ended, Brock heard movement. He went to the window and saw the roadster back out into the street and pull away.

Getting around the wire divider between patios on the third floor was a cinch. Brock had the pistol in his belt and tools to pick the lock in his pocket. Once he made it into Becker's condo, he hit the elevator button to ride down to the second floor of the three-level unit. The sugar and flour tins were where they should logically be. Skinner pulled them down. He dug in the flour with a knife blade first. No luck. The sugar tin had the baggie in it with the two jump drives. He shoved them in his pocket, put everything back, and got out of there. He was back on the road before six o'clock.

Brock stopped in Richmond to get a quick bite and call his brother-in-law. "I got the videos."

"Where were they?"

"Where Maude said they'd be, in Becker's sugar tin. You want to drive down to Hazard in the morning so we can watch it together?"

"I'll be there by ten o'clock."

~ ~ ~

At seven thirty, Kyle and Marilyn were finishing supper at Malone's Steakhouse on Tates Creek Road. She said, "Let's go back to your place and watch a movie."

"Excellent idea."

Marilyn parked her car on Market Street. Becker waited for her to join him in the garage. When they got to the elevator, he saw it wasn't on the ground floor where he left it. She noticed his dismay and said, "What's wrong?"

"Nothing." He pushed the button and gave her a cheerful smile. There was something wrong all right, and she knew it.

They rode the elevator up and stepped out on the second floor. He grabbed the remote to switch on the TV. "Do you know anything good we can watch?"

"How about *To Catch a Thief?*" she suggested to see if it rattled him.

"I've seen it. Let's watch the latest James Bond movie."

"Sounds good."

They queued up the show and nestled together on the couch. A few minutes later, Marilyn headed to the kitchen for a drink of water. She retrieved a tumbler from a cabinet and noticed traces of flour and sugar on the countertop. "What's this?"

"What's what?"

"This mess on the counter."

"I don't know." He went over to see what she was talking about.

"It's flour and sugar," she pronounced loudly. Kyle froze, not knowing what to say. She looked at him suspiciously and opened the cabinet above the mess. "Pull those containers down. I want to look in them." He complied, expecting to get caught red-handed. Marilyn took a knife and poked around in both tins. He stood there like a man waiting for a bomb to go off. The fuse went out. The memory sticks were gone. He was relieved for a moment, but the gravity of the situation soon consumed him. She said, "I'm going to head home. I'm feeling tired."

He asked, "Do you want me to drive you?"

"No. I'm okay." She gave him a perfunctory kiss. "I'll call you tomorrow."

When she got beyond the city limits on Harrodsburg Road, Marilyn called Ashby. "Elijah, do you happen to have Brock

Skinner's phone number handy? I want to call him and see if I can find out from his wife where she bought the dress that she wore to Keeneland. I'd like to get one like it in a different color."

"I don't believe you, but I'll text his number to you anyway."

"What happened to the trusting soul I once knew?"

There's that word trust, he thought. "After shelling out millions of dollars to my childhood friends, I'm running short on trust these days."

"Relax, everything's going to be okay," she reassured him.

~ ~ ~

Brock parked in the driveway of the log cabin in Hazard at eight thirty. He used a key to let himself in. Maude heard him and said, "You're back in a hurry."

"Quick trip." He felt the phone in his pocket vibrating. "This is Brock."

"Hi there. Marilyn McDonald."

"How's it going?"

"Great. Where are you?"

"At home, in Hazard."

"Say, I was calling to see if you could find out from your wife where she bought that beautiful dress she wore to the races."

"Let me ask her." He turned to face Maude, and said, "This is Marilyn. She would like to know where you bought the yellow dress with the little flowers on it."

"Serengeti."

"Did you hear that?"

"Yes. Tell her thank you. Have a good evening."

"We will." He glanced at Maude. She looked troubled.

CHAPTER 24

Becker awoke a little after six on Sunday morning. He quietly slipped on his sweat suit and went for an easy jog through the empty streets west of Broadway, north of downtown Lexington. The high, thin clouds turned smoky blue as the light of day emerged. After returning home, he showered, dressed, rode the elevator down to the second floor, and fixed a cup of coffee. As he opened the refrigerator, a knock on the door startled him. He yelled, "Who is it?"

"Open up." When he did, Esther Rice and Penny Gaines were standing there looking catty. Esther spoke, "I bet you weren't expecting your jilted girlfriends to pay you a visit." The women brushed him aside and came into the room. Esther had on navy jeans and a gray, high-collared top. Penny wore khaki cargo pants and a green, zip-up sweatshirt with a decorative hood.

"Are you two friends now?" he asked.

"We are," Penny confirmed. She flopped on the couch, and Esther sat in the side chair closest to the window. "Have you got anything for breakfast?"

"Yes. What can I fix you?"

Esther said, "Eggs, bacon, and toast for me."

Penny added, "I'll have Greek yogurt and fruit. What are you going to have?"

"A bagel. Is this my last meal?"

"Come on, Kyle, you don't actually believe we fell that hard for you, do you? There are other fish in the sea," Penny replied.

"I decided to chase after the guy you met at my brother's church," Esther reported.

Penny tagged on, "And I'm going to give the guy at work who's in love me a chance."

"That's a relief," he said. "To what do I owe this pleasure?"

"We're trying to figure out whose team we're on," Esther proclaimed.

"Are we playing pickup basketball?" Kyle cracked and whisked the eggs, put bacon in the microwave, and wheat bread in the toaster.

"No, it's a lot more serious game than that."

"How so?" He scooped a dollop of yogurt, put molasses on it, and rinsed some blueberries to throw on top.

Penny remarked, "We've come to the conclusion that this Marilyn McDonald woman is a bigger user than you are. We're trying to figure out what game she's playing. We need to hear your side of the story."

Kyle spread butter on the toast and assembled Esther's plate of food. He set places for them at the counter, and asked Penny, "Do you want anything else besides the yogurt and fruit?"

"I'll take a bagel, if you've got an extra."

"Esther, come and eat while it's hot."

She asked, "Do you have any coffee made?" He went over to the pot and poured her a cup.

Penny said, "I'll have some too."

Kyle buttered the bagel for Penny and dropped it on her plate. He gave her the last of the made coffee. "Here we go with that user business again."

"You've used us for information to win a lot of money at the track. Now you've got a fancy condo downtown, and we're living in the country like peasants. That's our beef," Esther said.

"Ah, I'm starting to see where this is going. You want me to buy your loyalty."

Penny shot back, "That sounds rather crass. I think of it as an equitable settlement for services rendered in the past."

"Did you have a figure in mind?"

"What do you think, Esther? Say, fifteen thousand for each of us?"

"That's too cheap, but I'll throw in with the group at that price."

Kyle said, "Enjoy your breakfast. I'll be right back." He took the elevator to the third floor to retrieve his checkbook in the nightstand next to the bed. He made out checks to each for the suggested amount, and handed them over when he returned to the kitchen. "Are we square now?"

Esther declared, "We are. So, let's hear it. What's going on with Ms. McDonald?"

"What makes you think she doesn't like me for who I am?"

"Kyle, part of your brain works pretty good, and part of it has no clue. You've taken no interest in the finer things in life. You're what a person would call one dimensional. Classy women don't settle for a lug head like that. You were right to go after a bimbo. Marilyn McDonald ain't one of them. Ergo, she's using you."

"The situation is rather complicated. She enlisted me to retrieve something that belonged to her. I did, but didn't give it to her. I claimed I didn't find it. My curiosity got the best of me."

"What was it?"

"A smartphone video of her boyfriend shoving a woman to her death."

"Did she take the video?"

"Yes."

Penny inquired, "Where did you retrieve it from?"

"Her boyfriend's place. She enticed me to break into his house because he'd scooped up my winning superfecta ticket off the floor at Keeneland. I wanted to get it back."

"I see. You found it. That's why you came by my office with the fifteen-thousand-dollar peace offering."

"Was there anything else on the video?" Esther asked.

"Yes. I didn't pay much attention to what was said. I was going to look at the video again, but somebody stole the two versions I had from me yesterday."

"What do you mean, two versions?"

"Marilyn told me a woman by the name of Cheryl Welch also had a copy, so I broke into her house and got that one too."

"You were planning to sell them to the highest bidder?" Penny quizzed.

"To the guy who shoved the woman to her death, Marilyn's boy-friend."

"I see the setup now. She was blackmailing him. He must have gotten the video away from her, and she needed to steal it back to have any leverage on him."

"Did Marilyn know you had it?"

"She thought I did but wasn't sure until last night."

"What happened?"

"When we got back here after dinner, Marilyn noticed I was confused about something in the garage. She remembered later that we had to wait for the elevator to come down from the third floor, which meant someone had been in here, and must have departed by the third floor without riding the elevator back down."

"Did something else clench it for her?"

"She saw some flour and sugar on the kitchen counter."

Esther surmised, "So, you had the videos hidden there. Someone broke in and took them. She saw the sugar and flour, and put it together."

"Yes. She walked out on me, and now I've got nothing to sell."

"Who stole the videos?"

"I don't know."

"I do," Penny said.

"Who?"

"The guy who owns the condo next door. His name is Brock Skinner."

Esther blurted, "Hey, he came to see me. He was asking questions about Kyle."

"The realtor who sold me this unit said the owners were a rich couple from Hazard," Kyle confirmed.

Penny added, "I remember they were with Marilyn McDonald's group at Keeneland a couple of weeks ago."

Esther stood with a start. "I just had a sickening feeling."

"What?"

"Penny, do you remember when we went to Marilyn McDonald's house? When she came in, she plugged her phone in to charge it, and set it on a stand."

"I remember."

"What if she was recording our conversation?"

"What for?"

"To capture anything interesting we said."

"Oh, no. You told her we were going to kill Kyle, and I confirmed it." They both had frightened looks on their faces. Penny turned to Kyle and muttered, "You'll have a target on your back now."

Esther commented, "I told Brock Skinner something similar."

Penny walked over to stand next to Esther. "I did too."

~ ~ ~

Marilyn called Elijah at nine o'clock and said, "I've got some bad news. I'm coming over." She ran across the street and knocked on his door within seconds. He let her in.

"What bad news?"

"Somebody stole the videos from Becker."

"Who?"

"I thought it was Brock Skinner. After I got his number from you last night, I called him. He said he was in Hazard. I heard his wife in the background. If he was there, he couldn't have stolen them."

"Are you sure about the timeline?"

"I guess he could have been waiting in his condo for Kyle to leave for dinner with me, and then found the videos quickly before hightailing it back to Hazard. Seems unlikely. Call Cheryl and find out if she knows anything."

Ashby got her on the line. "Cheryl, Marilyn's new boyfriend had the videos stolen from his house yesterday. Do you have any idea who might have taken them?"

"I don't know what you're talking about. I've got the videos." Cheryl thought it was the right time to bluff.

"You mean you have them now?" Marilyn squawked, hearing Cheryl's voice over the speaker.

"Yes. They're where nobody can get them. You needn't worry. I'm going to destroy them once I see the agreement you signed promising to keep your mouth shut."

Elijah spoke in a truculent manner, "You'd better be telling the truth, or so help me, I'll make you pay."

"How? I've got my money and the only copies of the videos in existence. And I also know what crooked things the two of you have been involved in the last several years."

"You've been right there with us, Cheryl," Marilyn retorted.

"Elijah killed my mother, and you've been blackmailing him and me for years. When you get your money, you'd better crawl in a hole somewhere."

"Why, you little bitch. Just because I stole Elijah from you, you're resorting to this?"

"Damn right." She hung up.

Elijah growled, "Get in the car."

"What?"

"We're driving over to her place. Now!"

"What are you going to do?"

"Get those videos back. Even if I have to threaten to kill her."

"I don't want any part of that. You can go by yourself."

Elijah said nothing and ran out of the room. Marilyn heard him burn rubber as she closed his front door to head back to her house.

Cheryl Welch, back at home, called Brock. "Hey, I need your advice again. I just told Elijah and Marilyn I had the videos and planned to keep them until Marilyn was hogtied."

"That was a bad move. He'll be coming for you. You've got no more than ten minutes to pack a bag and get out of your house. When he arrives, he'll ransack the place, searching for the videos. Look, you need to come down to Hazard and stay with us until this thing settles down. Bring your computer so you can work and answer emails." He gave her the address to put in the GPS on her phone.

"Okay."

"Leave the front door of your house unlocked so he won't have to kick it in. After he runs through the place, he'll try to call you. Don't answer. Don't tell anyone you're coming to Hazard."

"Got it."

Brock called the realtor who sold the condo in Lexington to Kyle Becker. "Good morning. Brock Skinner calling. I hope I'm not disturbing you?"

"Realtors never sleep. What can I do for you?" she asked.

"Can you give me the phone number of my new neighbor? I want to call and make arrangements to meet him."

"Sure." She went silent for a few seconds and then called out the digits.

"Thanks." Skinner deftly punched in what he'd written down.

"Hello."

"Is this Kyle Becker?"

"Yes."

"Brock Skinner."

"Ah, the man who owns the condo next door to me, and the person who stole the memory sticks out of my sugar tin."

"I've got a suggestion for you. Call your girlfriend and tell her you don't have, and never did have, the videos. She'll believe you."

"Why do you think that?"

"Because Cheryl Welch just told her that she has them. You stole her copy. A turnabout is fair play. I suggest you lie to Marilyn and claim you never had them."

"Yeah, I heard you the first time. That'll just be another lie. I've told several already. What's one more?"

"If I were you, I'd do everything possible to hang on to her. She's about to come into a lot of money. Being a horseplayer and all, I'm sure you understand what I mean."

"Does this Cheryl woman have the videos?"

"As far as you're concerned, she does."

Becker said, "It sounds like you're on the level. This may be helpful information. My other two girlfriends have forgiven me. They've made a bit of a misstep, though, which has placed me in jeopardy."

"How so?"

"They went to see Marilyn. Esther and Penny believe she took a video of what was discussed."

Brock interrupted, "Let me guess, they said they were going to kill you. Each of them told me the same thing."

"So, if I turn up dead, when the police come around, she can point the finger in their direction."

"Who wants you dead?"

"I can think of one person, her ex-boyfriend, Elijah Ashby."

"That just reinforces what you should be saying about the video—that you've never had it, or saw what's on it."

"I see where you're coming from. If he believes I could testify in court that he killed a woman, he'd be motivated to make me disappear."

"It's probably best you don't tell anybody we've had this discussion. Watch your back. If there's anything you need to know, I'll call you again."

"I look forward to meeting you and your wife. I love my new condo. I'm not sure how I'm going to pay for it yet, but I've got plenty of time to figure that out."

As the call was ending, Marcel walked through the door of the log cabin. Brock greeted him. "Cheryl Welch is on her way here. She told Elijah and Marilyn she had the videos."

Maude came into the room and heard what Brock said. Her response was, "Marcel, I'm going to get you for dragging Mr. Bull here into your China shop." All he could do was shrug.

CHAPTER 25

Brock had his laptop sitting on the coffee table with a cord running to the side of the TV mounted on the wall in the family room of the log cabin. Marcel, perched on the lounge chair, was leaning forward, hands clasped, arms on his thighs. Maude was standing behind him. The video burst on abruptly with a rustling sound and the camera panning around the room. It settled on who, ostensibly, was Toni Welch, wearing a floral moo-moo, holding a cocktail. She proclaimed in a drunken voice, "You'd drink too if you had a worthless daughter like mine, and your husband was dead. I'm stuck here all alone."

"That's your choice, a bad one." It was Marilyn's voice, and she, apparently, was the person holding the smartphone.

Toni Welch staggered toward the camera and roared ferociously, "Why, you little whore. Your father'd whip you if he heard you talking to me that way."

Marilyn crowed, "Hah! That's a laugh. My father hasn't said two words to me his whole life."

"Why should he? A sleep-around like you." Toni regained her balance and backed away with an ugly expression on her face.

Elijah Ashby began speaking. The camera moved to him. "Stop, Mrs. Welch. Cheryl's wonderful. You mustn't say bad things about her."

"What do you know?"

"The three of us have been friends as long as we can remember. We like her very much."

"Well, she's not my daughter. She's nothing like me. Not anything like her father either. More like somebody else. There's something wrong with her."

Marilyn got in another shot, "Thank goodness she's not like you."

The cocktail Toni was holding slipped out of her hand, hitting the floor with a ringing thud. The small amount of liquid in the glass slopped onto the bottom of her moo-moo. She said nothing at first, as tears welled up in her eyes. Finally, she said meekly, "Cheryl's out of my will."

"Now, why'd you do that?" Elijah asked.

"Because I don't want her to inherit the company!" Toni screamed. She turned away and shuffled toward the fireplace. The camera followed her.

"Why not?"

"You wouldn't understand," she uttered bitterly.

"Who are you going to give it to, then?"

Toni Welch gathered herself, looked around the room, and replied, "I knew for sure until a few minutes ago."

"What happened?" asked Elijah.

She ignored his question and went on the attack. "You always thought your parents were goody two shoes, didn't you, Elijah? Well, they weren't. Your father had a problem, and your mother was a religious hypocrite. She had an affair with another man."

Ashby hollered, "Stop it!" He lunged at her, lost his balance, and hit her in the sternum with his head. She gasped and fell backward. Toni Welch twisted awkwardly as she fell, hitting the side of her head on a jagged fireplace stone. Blood poured from the wound when she settled on the floor, face up.

Cheryl Welch punched three digits in her phone, waited for the call to be answered, and then emoted, "Please send an ambulance to Saratoga Estates! My mother has fallen and hit her head." The screen went black.

Brock stood in front of the TV to face his wife and brother-in-law. "First question is, why did Marilyn feel the need to provoke Toni Welch?"

Maude said, "That's fairly obvious. She thought the drunken woman was a pathetic human being."

Marcel leaned back in the lounge chair. "I think there's more to it than that."

"Here's what I think. Marilyn either knew or suspected Toni Welch had had an affair with her father. Even though she didn't care much for dear old dad, she could still have been angry about it," Brock said. "And then Elijah felt like he needed to be the peacemaker, which caused Cheryl's mother to lash out at him."

"But what about Mrs. Welch disowning Cheryl and saying something was wrong with her?" Maude asked.

"Wrong enough to take her out of the will. So, that's what Marilyn has on Cheryl, proof that Toni Welch intended to or had dumped her as an heir. Cheryl was young when this happened. The lawyers would have settled the estate, and she ended up with the company, anyway, meaning the will might not have gotten changed. Or maybe it did. I'm sure Marilyn told Cheryl that she expected something in return for keeping quiet, namely a job at Gibbous Metals."

Marcel asked, "Wonder who Beatrice Ashby had an affair with, and what was wrong with her husband?"

"The only people I can think of who might know are Mindy and Peter McDonald," Brock said.

Maude piped up, "Didn't you say Mindy McDonald told the neighbor that her husband wasn't the father of her child? Maybe Isaiah Ashby's problem was philandering. Could he be the father?"

"That doesn't square with what Cheryl told me. She confirmed that Peter McDonald was Marilyn's dad. There's a striking resemblance between father and daughter. I could see that from the driver's license picture."

"What if Mindy McDonald isn't Marilyn's mother?" Marcel speculated.

"I'm going to have to take some chances to find out," Brock said. He avoided Maude's eyes.

~ ~ ~

Elijah Ashby viciously cranked the knob on the front door of Cheryl's house and stormed in without knocking. He went room to room, looking for memory sticks. When he couldn't find any, he rang up Cheryl. The call went to voicemail. "Cheryl, call me. It's important." He dialed Marilyn next. "She's not here, nor are the videos."

"That's not surprising."

"Where do you think she went?"

"Hiding somewhere. My guess is Hazard, Kentucky. She's gone to see her consigliere, Brock Skinner."

"How much do you think he knows by now?"

"If she shows him the video, he'll be able to piece most if not all of it together."

"Why does he care?"

"He doesn't want to get caught up in anything illegal," she replied emphatically.

"After I deliver your gold on Tuesday, we should have a board meeting to put Humpty Dumpty back together again."

"Then send out an email calling the meeting for Thursday afternoon in a private room at Shaker Village."

"I like that idea. I'll do it," Elijah said.

"I'd also send an email to Cheryl asking her to meet you before that to swap the videos for my agreement to keep quiet. You should do it in a public place where she won't feel threatened. Take a laptop along, and let her know you'll hand her the paperwork before she hands you the two jump drives. Put them in the laptop to confirm the videos are on there."

"What exactly could Skinner point to as being illegal?"

"The fact you gave me ten million dollars."

"That's none of his business. I don't even know why I'm paying you the money now that I'm sure you don't have a copy of the video."

"Because you'll want me to keep quiet and disappear if anything goes wrong. Don't underestimate Skinner. He's the white-knight sort. He may want to punish us for sport."

"Why do you say that?"

"I know his type. He's got balls," she said. "I've got another call. Talk to you later." Marilyn switched lines. "Hi, Kyle. How are you?"

"Good. I was worried about you when you left last night. Is there anything wrong?"

"No, not really."

"Do you still think I have your video?"

"No."

"I want to say one more time that I don't have it, and never did. When do you want to get together again?"

"Your call. Let me know," she said.

"Okay. I'll think of something fun to do. You'll hear from me when I have a plan."

~ ~ ~

Truman popped his head up when he heard a hard knock on the front door of the log cabin. Brock shuffled down the hall to fetch Cheryl Welch, who was standing on the porch. She looked harried and unsettled, holding a designer, soft-sided piece of luggage.

"Come on in." Brock led her to the family room where Maude and Marcel had gotten to their feet to greet her. "Honey, would you show Cheryl the guest bedroom?"

"Sure. Follow me."

When the two women returned, Brock asked Cheryl, "Can I get you anything?"

"No, thanks. I'm fine."

"Let's sit down. We've just finished watching the video and have a few questions for you. Better yet, why don't you just tell us what happened after the death of your mother."

"She was cremated, and I called the attorney who had her will. He said I was her heir, and that he would close out her estate and get everything conveyed to me. I asked him if she had made any changes to the will recently. He said she had made a minor change, but it hadn't affected anything."

"Did he tell you what the change was?"

"No. I asked him. He wouldn't tell me. I was too young to challenge him on it."

"But when I met you at the attorney's office recently, you were there to look at the language in the will, weren't you?"

"Yes."

"What did you see?"

"Nothing really. The heir was listed as her child."

"Okay, tell us what Marilyn did."

"The first thing she told me was that she wouldn't go into court and show them the video she had taken of my mother disinheriting me if I would give her a job at Gibbous Metals when we graduated from college. I saw no harm in that, so I did. Our friendship got stronger for a while, until Elijah's father died. When Marilyn saw he got the ten million in life insurance, she decided to put the squeeze on him too."

Brock leaned forward on the sofa and rubbed his face. "Hence, the louver company. She also told him to give you and her an option to buy one-third of the company for thirty-three thousand each, exercisable only if the company was to be sold. Otherwise, she'd send the video to the police."

"I've already told you that."

"Then she was the one who cooked up the scheme to push all the profits over to Real Buy, while Gibbous Metals got bled dry. The end game from the beginning was to sell the louver company, and you and Marilyn would exercise your options right before the sale. Gibbous Metals would close and sell off what little assets were left shortly afterward."

Marcel interjected, "And everything was going according to plan until Elijah got the bright idea to steal the video from Marilyn. When he did that, she lost her leverage, and he could keep Real Buy if he wanted to."

"There's one little twist," Cheryl revealed. "Elijah started thinking that Marilyn might try to prove I wasn't the biological daughter of Toni Welch."

Maude asked, "Why would she think that?"

"Because my mother said something of the sort just before she died. You saw it on the video."

"You are her daughter, right?"

Cheryl stood, shrugged her shoulders, and remarked, "My birth certificate says I am."

Brock commented, "That information could have been altered by Peter McDonald since he worked for the police. Can you tell me this . . . do you think Marilyn will stick with the dog player, Kyle Becker, or will she go back to Elijah?"

"She'll go back to him."

"What makes you so sure?"

"She knows he wants her, and she'll get more blood out of him after she gets the first payoff. And besides, she'll move heaven and earth to keep him from coming back to me."

Marcel asked, "What's this business about Isaiah Ashby having some sort of problem your mother talked about?"

"I didn't know anything about that, and I'm sure it was the first time Elijah had heard of it."

"The bigger question is whether Beatrice really did have an affair. If she did, was it related to her husband's problem? And who did she have an affair with?"

Brock jumped up from the sofa. "Now you've got me wondering if Isaiah Ashby was killed for the insurance money."

"By whom?"

"Hell, I don't know. Cheryl, did Elijah try to call you?"

"Yes. I didn't answer, like you said. He wants me to call him back."

"Okay. I say you give him the two jump drives in exchange for an agreement from Marilyn not to come after you or your assets. Call and tell him you want the document to include that language. And be sure you make the swap in public."

"I can do that. What are you going to do now?"

"Go to Lexington tomorrow to meet Kyle Becker. There's one way to bust this thing wide open."

"How's that?" Maude asked.

"Convince Mr. Becker that he should find out if he's being played by Marilyn McDonald."

"What good will that do?"

"Give us some leverage." Brock went over and petted Truman, and suggested, "Let's head to the winery for a little lunch. What's on the menu today, Maude?"

"Crab Louie."

Marcel grinned and proclaimed, "You don't say? I'm in." Truman went to the back door to be let out. He was going to shoot through the vineyard and beat them over there.

CHAPTER 26

Early on Monday morning, Elijah Ashby sent an email to Cheryl Welch asking her to meet for lunch at Shaker Village on Tuesday and to bring the memory sticks with the videos. He promised to have the hold harmless and release of all claims from Marilyn. Cheryl asked him to send a draft of the document for her approval. He did so, and she was satisfied with the language in it. Next, he called the precious metals company in Louisville, where he had purchased the ten million in gold, to confirm the coins would be ready for pickup at nine o'clock on Tuesday morning.

Brock Skinner, at the same time, was pulling into the parking lot of the boxing gym in Lexington. He dressed and warmed up on both bags before stepping into the ring to have a go with a smaller fighter trying to learn how to throw good body punches. Skinner swatted them off, frustrating the fighter, returning a few blows selectively. The second pugilist he took on was an up-and-coming heavyweight—a bigger, faster, and younger man than Brock, but not as smart. The young fighter left the ring all beat up, muttering to himself. Skinner showered off and drove to Market Street. He had an eleven o'clock appointment to meet the infamous Kyle Becker, dog player.

Becker ushered Brock into his place and offered him a cup of coffee, which he accepted. Skinner said, "Well, neighbor, how do you like your new digs?"

"Love them."

"People tell me you're a professional gambler."

"Try not to spread that around," Becker replied coyly. He rested his straight arms on the kitchen countertop.

"I grew up on a horse farm east of town. I've known a few plungers and high rollers in my day," Brock admitted.

"Any of them worth a damn?"

"I can't say for sure."

"I'm guessing you'd rather talk business than gambling." Kyle flashed a fake smile.

"I would. How did Ms. McDonald react when you told her about the video?"

"I think she believed me. I pretty much inferred there were two videos when her ex-boyfriend, Elijah Ashby, tried to buy them from me. He may have told her that."

"Since you don't have them now, you should be in the clear."

"What about Marilyn's latest video of Esther and Penny threatening to kill me?" Kyle asked. He picked up the pot and refreshed Brock's coffee.

"If you meet an untimely demise, Marilyn will be in the blackmail business again."

"I'm afraid Ashby wants me bumped off, so I won't be a threat."

"That is a possibility. Did you watch the video you stole from him?"

"I did. He shoved a woman to her death."

"Did you pay attention to anything else?"

"Not really."

"Cheryl Welch is in it."

"I didn't notice."

Brock got up from his seat in the kitchen and went to the front window to clear his thoughts. "When are you planning to see Marilyn again?"

"I'm going to ask her to meet me at Red River Gorge on Wednesday for lunch. We went hiking there recently. She showed me a secluded spot on the edge of a cliff that had a spectacular view of the gorge. I want her to join me so I can find out where we stand."

"I've got some bad news on that front. I'm pretty sure she's using you and is planning to go back to Ashby."

"How do you know?" Becker's face sagged.

"It's complicated. Let's just say you're trade bait."

"I guess I'm not surprised. She's the most beautiful woman I've ever seen. I've had it in the back of my mind she's been using me all along."

"You're not a bad catch, Becker, but as a dog player, she wouldn't know what to do with you long term."

"Unless she really loves me."

"Take it from me, the woman is incapable of love. I thought you had a chance with her for a while, but I heard something yesterday that snuffed that out."

"What?"

"Elijah Ashby is willing to give her anything for her to come back."

"I see what you mean. He has a lot more to offer her than I do."

"Yes, I'm afraid that's the cold, hard reality."

"Well, if she dumps me, I'll have to be looking over my shoulder all the time and find some way to pay for this condo."

Brock went to the door, preparing to leave. "Look, go ahead, see if you can have Marilyn join you Wednesday at Red River Gorge.

Make up some excuse to go in separate cars. Also, would it be possible for you to get Esther Rice and Penny Gaines over here at five o'clock today?"

"Probably so. What do you have in mind?"

"I promised Penny a favor when I saw her. I want to make good on that promise. Esther might also like what I have in mind."

~ ~ ~

Marilyn left Real Buy Louvers at eleven thirty to go into downtown Harrodsburg. She worked out at the gym and got an Asian salad for lunch. After returning to the company, she went directly to Ashby's office. He saw her come through the door, and asked, "What's it going to take to win you back?"

"I told you we'd talk about it after you filled my safe with gold." She had on a black, crepe pantsuit with draped décolleté and slits in the sleeves.

"Let's talk about it now." He raised his shoulders and stuck out his hands, pleadingly.

"No," she harped, and turned away.

"Why not?"

"Because I have a nice boyfriend already and see no reason to leave him."

"There must be something that could pull you away."

Marilyn pivoted to face him again, and said, "I'm sure there is, but it would have to be pretty enticing."

"You mean having me isn't enough?"

"Listen to you, Elijah, you're acting childish. There is one thing that would interest me. Getting Brock Skinner by the short hairs."

"How can I do that?"

"Think on it. You'll come up with a way." She left his office swinging her hips. Her cell phone rang as she sat down behind her own desk. She recognized the number. "What kind of fun do you have planned for us, Kyle?"

"We had such a good time at Red River Gorge, so I thought we should try a longer hike."

"When?"

"If you can get off work, let's have lunch on Wednesday at the overlook you took us to last time. We can study the map and pick out a good trail. I'll bring the food. I hope you don't mind if we drive separately since I'm going on to Ashland late in the day to have dinner with a trainer who has some information on a couple of horses I want to bet on."

"I'm always up for a hike. Do you remember how to get to the overlook?" Marilyn asked.

"I do."

"Okay, I'll meet you there at noon on Wednesday." Marilyn opened her email and began reading, moving, and deleting Inbox items. She read the one from Ashby addressed to the board, announcing a meeting to be held at four o'clock on Thursday at Shaker Village. *With any luck, things will turn in my favor after the meeting*, she thought.

~ ~ ~

At five o'clock, Skinner left his condo and walked around to bang on Becker's door. Penny Gaines opened it and said, "Here's hunk number two, Esther." Brock stepped into the room.

Esther Rice came over and gave him a big kiss on the cheek. "Penny, which one of them is sexiest?"

"That one." Penny pointed at Skinner. "He's rich."

Kyle said, "I've heard his wife knows how to use a gun."

"So do I," Penny said with glee.

"This party is starting off with a bang," Becker commented dryly.

"Thanks for coming, ladies," Brock said obsequiously. "Penny, I promised to do you a favor, and since you haven't called in your marker yet, I decided to take action."

"What is it?"

"I have tickets to the Kentucky Derby on Saturday for you, Esther, and your dates in the clubhouse at the finish line."

"You paying for it?" Penny asked.

"Yes. And for the limo to and from the track."

Esther addressed Becker, "You need to keep this guy as a friend."

Penny acted possessed. "All right! Thank you! Esther, we've got to figure out what to wear." Something registered in Penny's mind, and she turned serious. "What's the catch?"

"Does anybody have a nice camera with a good lens and time stamp?" Brock asked.

"I do," said Becker.

"Good. I'd like you girls to snap a few pictures for me, if you can take a day off work on Wednesday."

Esther coasted into the side chair by the window, and remarked, "We can. That doesn't sound too tough. Where and when?"

For the next forty-five minutes, Skinner laid everything out. When he'd finished talking, somebody knocked on the door. "Ah, that'll be the pizzas I ordered."

"He thinks of everything," Penny said.

Brock went back to his condo after they finished eating. He closed the unit and pointed the Lamborghini toward Hazard. On the drive into Appalachia, he called a friend in Louisville to arrange for the Derby tickets.

~ ~ ~

Elijah Ashby sat in his car outside the gold dealer's place of business at 8:50 a.m. on Tuesday. The little stucco building looked like a bail-bond operation with one main difference: there were massive bars on the windows and a steel-bar overlay on the entrance door. At nine sharp, a fellow who looked like a mortician, wearing a black tie, opened the joint for business. Elijah got out of his car and went in. The man inside asked to see Ashby's identification before saying, "Pull your car around to the back of the building and park next to the door. I'll have the security guard load the coins in your trunk. He'll follow you to wherever you're going to make sure you don't get ambushed or robbed."

"I appreciate that."

Elijah pulled into Marilyn McDonald's driveway an hour later. He got out to release the man who had tailed him all the way there. Marilyn appeared on the front porch with a grin on her face. She said, "Bring your car around back. Park in the garage." They carried the twenty bundles of coins to the safe, stacking them neatly in the open space. She shut the safe door, turned the latch, and slapped her hands together several times to signal the job was all finished. "Come in. I'll give you the signed document."

The paper he was after was on the kitchen counter. When he reached to pick it up, she put her hand on it. "Let's have that cup of coffee now and talk about the future." She lifted her hand to let him have the document.

Elijah spoke, "I've been thinking on what you said about Skinner. The best way to get him by the short hairs, as you called it, is to release him and his brother-in-law from the board."

"What kind of excuse will you use to do that?"

"I'll tell them I've decided not to sell the company. Since I'll be keeping it, their services won't be needed."

"Is that true?"

"Yes. There's no reason to anymore. You and Cheryl have been paid off, and I'll have the videos."

"You know I'm interested in marrying you, Elijah. We could sell this house, and I could move into yours. I've never liked this place."

"Are you ready to say yes?"

"I am. All you have to do is make me president of Real Buy Louvers."

"What am I going to do?"

"Run Gibbous Metals. Build it into something as good as the louver business, maybe better."

"Why don't you do that instead of me?"

"I've worked there before. It's more of a man's operation."

"I don't know if I like that," Ashby thought out loud.

Marilyn walked up to him and put her arms around his neck. "Let me give it to you straight. It's not a good thing when a married couple tries to run a business. The people working there won't like it, and we won't either."

"But I own the business. I should run it."

"Did I mention I want to buy half of it?"

He grimaced and stepped away from her. "For how much?"

"Half of what's in my safe back there."

"Five million dollars?"

"You're good at math."

"That's not a fair price," he said.

"Okay, then I'll sell this house and move into Kyle Becker's condo in downtown Lexington. He's smart, good looking, and treats me really well. Now that I think of it, I'm not sure I want to dump him for you after all."

"I'm sure Cheryl will take me back. We might be a better fit for each other," Elijah countered weakly.

Marilyn laughed uproariously. "She's not going to take you back. You've insulted her too many times."

"One thing's for sure, Marilyn, if you stick with the dog player, I'll fire you."

"Go ahead. I'll go to work for a competitor and clean your clock," she threatened stridently.

"You think that scares me?"

"Elijah, do you know what they call people who go around picking up discarded tickets at the racetrack? Scoopers. You'll end up as one full time if you fire me. You should reconsider that five-million-dollar deal I'm offering."

"Before I consider marrying you, I'm going to call your parents and ask for their blessing. If they give it to me, I'll consider meeting your terms. I could use the five million right about now, and sometimes it's smart to change management at the top of a company. After all, I've been in charge there for ten years. A change might do me good."

Chapter 27

Brock stood at Cheryl's car window as she was getting ready to leave Hazard for Shaker Village. He said, "You want me to follow you there to make sure everything goes all right?"

"No. It'll be okay."

"Remember, haul your butt back here after you get the signed document. Don't go to your house or the company. Once the papers are locked away, you can get back into circulation. I'd like you to stay here until we go to the board meeting on Thursday afternoon."

"Yes, boss." The weather on the next to last day of April, although sunny, was coolish. A gentle breeze made it even more so. She rolled up her car window to block the wind and stepped on the gas.

Brock watched her drive away before tapping the phone number of Kyle Becker. "How's it going?"

"I'm sealing the envelopes now."

"Be sure to take them to the main post office and drop them in the slot around eleven o'clock."

"Will do."

Cheryl, when she reached Shaker Village, saw Ashby standing on the porch of the gift shop as she pulled in to park. He had on a green business suit and silver laptop tucked under his arm. He yelled out, "Hello, Cheryl!"

"Hi. You're all dressed up."

"It's a special occasion. I'm having lunch with an old, trusted friend."

"Who's that?"

"You," he said with conviction.

"Oh, yes, I see." She couldn't help but smile, even though she was still angry and frustrated with him.

"Let's get a seat before the crowd." Ashby led the way to the table they were given. He opened the laptop and put it off to the side. "Do you want to take care of business before we eat?" She reached in her purse for the two jump drives and held them in her hand where he could see them. He retrieved the papers from his suit coat and handed them to her. She scanned the wording to confirm it was the same as the draft she'd seen. Once satisfied, she studied the notarized signature of Marilyn McDonald and then tossed the jump drives in Elijah's direction as she stuck the paperwork in her purse. He put both memory sticks in the laptop and checked the dates the files were saved, to make sure they weren't copies. One file was dated several years ago, which would be the one that languished in Marilyn's safe for a long time, and the other coincided with the time someone pulled the file off his computer. "All done," he said, "What shall we have for lunch?"

"I like the shrimp salad."

"We'll make it two." The server brought them sooner than expected, cutting off the small talk they were having, almost like old times.

Once they'd finished eating and ordered coffee, Elijah leaned on the brick wall that the table abutted, and looked away. He said, "I should have married you when I had the chance."

"And have Marilyn follow you around night and day, trying to seduce you?"

"You've got a point there."

"Well, let me hear it . . . is she going to take you back or stick with that dog player?"

"She says she'll marry me if I make her president of Real Buy and sell her half the company."

Cheryl stiffened and chortled. "Tell her no way!"

"You would say that. She says she'll go to work for a competitor and ruin my business otherwise."

"I don't know why I care. I've got my money."

"Just to let you know, on Thursday, I'm going to remove Skinner and Sutherland from the board. I'll share with them that I plan to keep the company instead of selling it, and their services won't be needed anymore."

She said, "Skinner's not going to go away quietly."

"I haven't done anything to him."

"I wonder if Marilyn will stay on the crusade to prove Toni wasn't my mother?"

"I doubt it. She's just signed over her rights to hurt you. No, I think she's going to focus on being top dog at a louver company: Real Buy or somewhere else."

"What are you going to do if she runs the louver business?"

"Manage Gibbous Metals. Grow it."

"Ask for the check, Elijah, I want to get out of here." Cheryl clutched her purse. She put her hand over her mouth as though she wanted to stifle her own speech, which she did, as well as his.

~ ~ ~

A few days before the Kentucky Derby, the "pill pull" was held to determine the post positions for the contestants. The eighteen horses in this year's race had the makings of a raucous donnybrook in the two most exciting minutes in sports, based purely on the number of rambunctious three-year-old colts in the field. Kyle made it a point to read what all the touts were saying. He was always trying to learn. After the race went off, he'd loop back to the prognostications to see which ones had called certain aspects correctly. He scanned the post positions and noticed the favorite drew the number twelve hole. Becker rarely bet the Kentucky Derby because, with that many horses, it was hard to hit an exotic. He became intrigued by a couple of dogs in the race, numbers 5 and 14, and began to believe there was money to be made.

Kyle, his brain muddled with worthless horse minutiae, left his condo at nine thirty on Wednesday morning to pick up Esther and Penny in the lot near I-64 where their cars were parked. The sun seemed newer and fresher than usual as the three of them sped toward Red River Gorge in Kyle's vehicle.

Marilyn McDonald eased her car across the bumpy dirt path leading to the turnaround near the secluded escarpment where she was to meet her boyfriend in five minutes. His Mercedes was parked there, so she pulled off in front of his vehicle. The uneven sandstone path through the trees, gaining elevation, widened at the clearing by the cliff. She saw two folding chairs and a cooler between them right near the edge, but Becker was nowhere to be found. She stepped in front of the seats and looked down into the massive gorge. Kyle Becker's contorted body could be seen lying in a clearing that would be very hard to reach on foot. He must have jumped or was pushed, she surmised before panicking.

Marilyn panned around to make sure no one had seen, or could see her. She folded up the chairs and scampered back to her car to put them in the trunk. She circled back to get the cooler and made sure no other evidence of her being there had been left behind. Once she stowed the cooler, she drove slowly back to the main highway. It took her nearly two hours to return to her house in Saratoga Estates, where she took everything out of the trunk and stored it. Marilyn knew when Kyle's car got spotted, finding him wouldn't be far behind. She dressed for work and got to Real Buy at three thirty.

Ashby visited her office at four o'clock and said, "Where have you been? I was looking for you after lunch."

"Working from home. I just came in to get out of the house. What did you need?"

"I wanted to make you a counteroffer. Why don't you give me all the gold in your safe and let me keep the stock in Gibbous Metals, and you can have 100 percent of Real Buy."

"I might go for that. After all, if we marry, the gold's a moot point. When are you going to call my parents?"

"Tomorrow after the board meeting, and if they give me their blessing, I want to get hitched as soon as possible."

~ ~ ~

Penny Gaines, though she'd taken the day off, went to the office of the horse farm where she worked at four thirty. She plugged the camera into her computer to download and print out the pictures she'd taken earlier in the day. She also sent the folder to Brock Skinner.

Cheryl sat in the leather chair in Brock's home office in Hazard, working on the laptop she'd brought along. Brock heard the ding of an incoming email. He saw it was from Penny Gaines and opened it. "Look at this, Cheryl." She walked over and stood behind him. He opened the file of pictures. The first shot, dated 11:59 a.m., was a picture of Marilyn McDonald standing in front of a cooler and chairs at the edge of a cliff, looking down. The second one showed her folding up the chairs at 12:01 p.m. The next five photos were her carrying the chairs and cooler away from the cliff. The last shot, dated 12:06 p.m., was taken from the edge of the rock shelf, down into the expanse of the gorge. It was a shot of Kyle Becker's body lying in a clearing.

"What's this all about?" Cheryl asked.

"It appears that someone has photographed Marilyn pushing Kyle Becker to his death."

"But none of the pictures show her actually pushing him."

"If she didn't, then why is she packing up and leaving instead of calling 911?"

"She might have panicked, thinking someone was trying to frame her."

"Huh."

"Don't huh me. You're behind this, aren't you?" She stood erect and put her hands on her hips.

Skinner got up from the computer and said, "Can I get you a glass of wine? Maude has whipped up a fabulous supper."

"No, thank you. I can't say she doesn't deserve to get played."

Maude served a fabulous fettuccine Bolognese with salad and hot-and-sour soup. Cheryl said, "I don't cook much, or very well, and this has been a real treat for me. Thank you."

"We're glad you enjoyed it," Maude replied. "Would anyone like a decaf coffee?" Brock and Cheryl both raised their hands.

"I'm still trying to process what your mother said before she died," Brock commented. "I'd like to understand why your parents became alcoholics."

"I think they tried to escape something painful in their marriage."

"Could it be that Carson was your father, but Toni wasn't your mother?"

"Marilyn had that idea too. Elijah believed she wanted to prove it."

"Didn't you say your mother's heir was her child?"

"Yes."

"Maybe she changed her will by replacing your name with the wording 'her child.' The attorney might not have caught the significance of that."

"No one stepped forward claiming to be related to her," Cheryl stated.

"Could it be that someone out there doesn't know Toni was her mother?"

"Seems farfetched, but I'm sure it's possible."

Maude remarked, "It's water under the bridge at this point."

Brock said, "I'm not so sure. This business with Ashby's parents might figure into it. I need to find out what was going on with them."

"Good luck on that. Regardless, I've sold Gibbous Metals to Real Buy and can start a new life away from this madness."

"And you'll have a line of two-bit suitors if word gets out that you're loaded," Maude warned.

"I could use some interest from men right about now," Cheryl said.

"I know one quality candidate. Marilyn's old boyfriend, Kyle Becker."

"I don't know him, and besides, according to you, he got pushed off a cliff." She knew then then that Becker's death was a setup, and that he was still alive.

Maude stared at Brock, and said, "Ah, a dead body. What do you know?"

~ ~ ~

Marilyn got in her car after dark on Wednesday night, drove out to Harrodsburg Road, and turned toward Lexington. She took a right on Vine Street in less than an hour, down the hill in the valley of town. She parked across from Columbia Steak House and walked west in the direction of Market Street. After loping up the stairs of Becker's condo, she rapped nervously on the locked door. Nothing. She had to find a way in. Marilyn tried to envision the superfecta results in her mind's eye on the day she met him when he won the one hundred fifty thousand. It came to her: 6-5-2-3. She went down to street level and punched the numbers in the keypad to actuate the garage door. It worked. His car was gone. She hit the elevator button, and the doors opened immediately.

Marilyn remembered the password to Kyle's computer. She found a word file dated yesterday.

> *Esther and Penny,*
>
> *I love you both. I'm sending you this letter in case I go missing at the hands of my girlfriend, Marilyn, or her ex-boyfriend, Elijah Ashby. I know she provoked a woman to rage, and he killed her. I fear they won't trust me to keep quiet. I suspect there's something rotten in their business dealings. Since they've killed before, they'll do it again. If something happens to me, take this letter to the police.*

There was no name shown at the bottom, so she figured Kyle printed the documents out and signed the copies. The question was . . . how did he get it to them, and when?

She sent the letter to the trash bin, and then permanently deleted it from the computer.

Once back home, Marilyn went to the old wall safe in the bedroom closet to find her passport. She wanted to make sure it hadn't expired. Elijah Ashby saw a light on in the McDonald house. He called Marilyn and said, "Why don't you come over?"

"I'll be right there." When Elijah opened the door to let her in, he saw a look on her face that he'd never seen before.

CHAPTER 28

Maude left for the winery before breakfast on Thursday in a nasty morning fog. Cheryl came into the kitchen soon after, dressed for the board meeting in an olive-green business suit, and proclaimed, "I'm going to the plant until the meeting this afternoon. I'll see you there." Brock raised his coffee cup and nodded.

~ ~ ~

Penny Gaines was standing in the front room of her house, waiting impatiently for the mailman to come. She kept looking at her watch and wondering what was keeping him. Finally, he whizzed up, chucked a haphazard stack of mail in the box, and slammed the door. She ran out to see if Kyle's letter had arrived, flashed a grin, and waggled her head. She scurried over to her phone when she got back in the house. "Esther, your mail come yet?"

"Yes. The letter's here."

"Good. I'll pick you up, and we can head to the louver plant." Penny threw the pictures and letter in the backseat of her car.

Esther watched Penny pull up to the front door of her apartment. She ran out, got in, and said, "Brock told us to open one of them and keep the other one sealed." She tore her envelope and read the letter aloud.

They arrived at Real Buy Louvers at one thirty, expecting Marilyn McDonald to be back from lunch. She was and looked cheerful when she came down to fetch her visitors. She had on a plain, gray dress with a thin waist belt and scalloped sleeves. "Come on up."

The slick, refined, polished feel of Marilyn's office intimidated Penny and Esther as they inspected it carefully. Penny asked, "Have you seen or heard from Kyle Becker lately? We've been trying to call him since yesterday afternoon."

"No." Marilyn maintained a pleasant expression as she glanced at what each girl had in her hand.

Esther said, "That's funny. I got the darnedest thing in the mail today." She gave Marilyn the letter.

"Who's behind this charade?" Marilyn asked.

"Well, frankly, you are," Penny said.

"What do you mean?"

"You pushed Kyle off a cliff in Red River Gorge."

"I did not."

"How do you explain this?" Penny handed the pictures to her.

She scanned the photos and asked, "Who took these?"

"Smokey the Bear, I suppose," Esther volunteered.

Marilyn walked around her desk and eased into the rolling chair. She deftly opened the small desk drawer on the right and pulled out a pistol that wasn't loaded. "I'll keep these if you don't mind. And, Esther, I'll take that unopened letter in your hand." She aimed the gun at Esther's stomach.

"No, you won't. If you shoot me, you'll have to shoot her, and one of us will get to you before we go down."

Marilyn kept the gun pointed at Esther. "Is Kyle dead?"

"How do we know? You're the one who should have called 911."

"Brock Skinner's behind this, isn't he?"

"I don't know what you're talking about."

"What is it you want?"

"For you to leave us alone. We know you recorded us saying we were going to kill Kyle. That better not see the light of day, or we'll go to the police."

"If Kyle happens to reappear, you've lost your hole card."

Penny rebutted, "Not quite. That letter incriminates you and your lover boy as the couple who provoked and killed a woman. It also questions your business practices. Have anything to hide there?"

Marilyn stood slowly and bellowed, "Nobody threatens me!" Her face became contorted in anger.

"We just did. We'll find our way out." Penny and Esther left the building post haste. They called Brock to report how things went down. He told Penny to put the unopened letter in a safe deposit box as soon as she could.

Marilyn stormed into Elijah's office, seething. He was wearing a navy suit, white shirt, and solid red tie. "I'm going to hire a hitman to kill Brock Skinner." She shifted from one foot to the other in disgust.

"You'll do no such thing," Ashby said. "Once in a while, Marilyn, you'll run into people who've been around more than we have. Forget about him. Calm yourself. Think pleasant thoughts."

"I hate being bested by anybody. If he makes a mistake, I'll get him."

"Wasted energy. Look at it this way, he hasn't gone to the police, which is a good thing for us, and I don't think he will if we keep smiles on our faces. And besides, he may have already rigged it to bring us down if we push him too hard."

"I know he's been helping Cheryl."

"So?"

"You know something, Elijah? You have no balls."

"Uh-huh. Where were yours when it was time to get the videos from Cheryl? You better gain your composure before our meeting later today," he warned.

~ ~ ~

Ashby had arranged the four o'clock board meeting to be held in a spartan conference room set up for eight people, in one of the outbuildings at Shaker Village. Marcel found the room first, followed by Cheryl Welch. Soon thereafter, Brock came through the door, and Marilyn and Elijah were the last to arrive. A lighthearted, informal discussion about the upcoming Kentucky Derby ensued before everyone sat down. Finally, Elijah said formally, "This meeting is called to order." He shifted in his seat as he looked down at the table, and then raised his eyes and smiled. "A lot has happened since our last meeting. I'll be giving you a full report today." He opened the folder he'd brought along and checked the first subject on the outline. "Does anyone want to make any comments before we get started?"

Cheryl murmured, "None from me." Her countenance was subdued. The other board members sat motionless.

"Okay. First, I would like to announce that Real Buy Louvers has purchased the common stock of Gibbous Metals from Cheryl Welch for fifteen million dollars cash. Cheryl has agreed to stay on as long as we want her to. Congratulations, Cheryl. You've helped us grow Real Buy with the good quality service and prices for materials Gibbous has provided over the years." She nodded curtly.

Brock asked, "Does that mean you'll be combining the historical financial statements of both companies before showing any numbers to a prospective buyer?"

"We would do that, of course."

"If I may ask, what impact will that have on the performance of Real Buy? Are the earnings of Gibbous accretive?" Brock knew they weren't but wanted to smoke Ashby out.

"No. Gibbous Metals has been losing money."

"Why is that?" Marcel asked.

Cheryl answered, "Because we underpriced the material Real Buy purchased over the years."

"Why was that done?"

"Some of the die weights were wrong, and we weren't charging enough. Once I found the error, I asked Elijah to cover the substantial underpayment over the years. Instead, he offered to buy the company from me as is. I thought it was a good solution to the problem."

Marcel commented, "That means Real Buy likely isn't worth fifty million dollars. Have you considered that in your planning?"

"We have, Marcel. You'll hear about our proposed direction later in the meeting."

"Sorry to keep asking questions. Do you have to disclose the accounting irregularities, go back and restate the profits for both companies, and amend the tax returns?" Skinner quizzed.

"I suppose we'll have to do that," Elijah agreed.

"Have the attorneys you hired in Chicago to discreetly reach out to prospective buyers of the company advertised the sales and profits of the business? If so, I would suggest you recall them and correct the numbers. Otherwise, there might be action against the company for racketeering. I'm sure none of us want to be accused of that."

"Again, Brock, I think you'll see where the point is moot as we go forward in the meeting. Now, the next thing I'd like to announce is that Marilyn McDonald will be named president of Real Buy in about sixty days. I've run the business for ten years and believe she has earned the opportunity to take the company to new heights."

Cheryl remarked pleasantly but with a hint of sarcasm, "Congratulations, Marilyn. I'm sure you'll do a great job."

"Thank you," Marilyn replied in a self-deprecating, coquettish manner.

"What are you going to do, Elijah?" asked Marcel.

"Take the reins at Gibbous Metals and grow sales if I can."

"Sounds like a challenge you'd enjoy," Brock offered. "But what about the suitors of Real Buy? They might insist you give them three years as the top man. Ms. McDonald running the business might be seen as a risk to them."

"Well, that happens to be the next thing on the agenda. I've decided not to sell the company. My two best friends will be in good positions, and I'll be able to recharge my batteries doing something different."

Skinner added, "Good for you. I presume you'll have no desire to retain Marcel and me on the board."

"Sadly, we won't. I hope that doesn't come as a disappointment. You guys have been great to work with."

"I think I can speak for Brock. We want what you want. That's what's important to us."

"I second that." Brock put his head back and splayed his fingers.

"Oh, there's one more item on the agenda. I'll be negotiating with Marilyn to sell her Real Buy sometime in the future, without Gibbous Metals. I'll keep the stock in that company. We'll all have the chance to go about our business without any entanglements."

Brock dropped a bomb. "Would you ever consider selling the louver company to Marcel and me? We'd pay you a fair price, in cash."

Ashby rested his chin on his hand in thought. "There's one out of left field for you. I'd have to think about it. I'm trying to take care of Marilyn because she's done such a nice job for us. Would you give her a favorable employment contract?"

"Yes. Whatever she wants, for as long as she wants." Marcel looked at Brock, stunned after he said that.

"I would suggest you speak directly to her to gauge her interest in such an arrangement. I'll negotiate with her first and try to put a nice deal together if I can. If no agreement can be reached, I'd consider a deal with you if she blesses it."

Brock closed the subject by saying, "You've got a nice company here, and as Marcel said: we want what you want. I just thought you might be trying to cash out and wanted to give you another option to do that."

Marilyn was steaming. She knew immediately that Elijah would use Skinner to run the price up on her. *Maybe I should quit and go to work for a competitor after all*, she mused. *But wait, Elijah would go back to Cheryl instead of marrying me*, she reflected in disgust.

"If there's no further business, the meeting is adjourned." Elijah started to stand up.

Brock said, "If I may, my wife sent a bottle with me of the best red wine from her winery, for us to try after this meeting. Would it be okay if I retrieved the bottle and some glasses from my car? After all, Marcel and I may not see you folks again anytime soon."

"By all means. Bring it in."

Marcel fell in behind Brock, walking out to the parking lot. "Are you crazy? We don't want to own that louver company."

Brock ignored his pestering. "I think I've figured out what happened."

"What happened when?"

"Before Elijah, Marilyn, and Cheryl were born."

"What difference does it make now? We're out of this deal."

"Cheryl. I want to help her," Brock stated as he reached in the passenger seat of the Lamborghini for the bottle of wine and plastic cups.

"Haven't you done enough?" Marcel pleaded.

Skinner shut the car door and stared at his brother-in-law. "Look, Marcel, she had alcoholic parents, isn't as good looking or as smart as the girl next door, got shafted in a blackmail scheme because of the boy next door, and worst of all, isn't sure who her mother is. No, I haven't done enough." They marched through the Shaker Village grounds, back to the room where the board meeting had just ended.

Elijah and Marilyn were standing outside in the grass, away from the door. He said, "Your father absolutely insisted I come see him in person before he'd approve our marriage. I'll rent a plane in the morning and fly to Jacksonville. Do you want to come along?"

"No," Marilyn replied. "I don't know what his problem is. He never cared much about what I did, and he's always liked you."

"I want to see your parents again, anyway. It's been a long time."

Brock overheard what Ashby said through the cracked window behind the head of the table. He opened the bottle of wine, lined up five plastic cups, and filled them. Marcel tried to hand one to Cheryl, but she declined. When Marilyn and Elijah came back in, Elijah also passed, so Marilyn poured what was in his cup into hers. She took a sip and reported, "This is very nice. Maude is certainly an accomplished vintner."

Brock said, "As far as I'm concerned, she's accomplished at everything."

Elijah smiled and put his hands in his pockets. "Give her our best."

"I will. Thank you."

The three musketeers from Saratoga Estates departed one by one, leaving Brock and Marcel sitting at the table. Marcel asked, "What is it you've figured out?"

"The first domino."

"What would that be?"

"Isaiah Ashby."

"Yeah, what about him?"

"His problem."

"And?"

"He was sterile."

CHAPTER 29

Skinner, all wound up from the meeting, arrived home in the dark, dank air. He had decided not to call Maude on the way, to report what happened, because he wanted to tell her in person.

Maude asked, "Have you had anything to eat?"

"No."

"I'll nuke last night's Bolognese." She warmed the dish and set it in front of him. "So, how did things go?"

"Marcel and I got removed from the board." Brock laid into the pasta.

"That's the best news I've heard all week," she remarked. "Is everything done then?"

"No. It will be by Sunday, though. Would you like to run over and watch the Derby on the big screen at Keeneland on Saturday? We can leave here around two o'clock, drop Truman off at the condo, and make it in plenty of time to see the race at six thirty. We can ask Marcel to join us for dinner downtown afterward."

"Sounds like fun."

"Great. Now the bad news. I'll be leaving to drive through the night to Jacksonville in a couple of hours." Maude rolled her eyes.

Brock spent the next fifteen minutes unpacking what he thought to be the sordid tale of the people from Saratoga Estates. Maude went into the family room, flopped on the couch, put her head back, and exhaled. "Just don't get hurt, Brock. When will you be back?"

"With any luck, right after you close the winery tomorrow evening."

"That's a lot of driving in twenty-four hours."

"Yeah." He put his dishes in the dishwasher, packed a bag with a loaded pistol, and took a quick nap. He got on the road at ten o'clock, stopping for a tank of gas near the on-ramp at I-75.

The stretch from Macon, Georgia, to the Florida state line was wide open. He pushed the Lamborghini up to 140 mph for about twenty seconds. It wouldn't do, he thought, to be jailed for reckless driving while carrying a loaded firearm, so he ran mostly at 85 mph, which was like pushing a baby pram around the neighborhood.

Brock found a Waffle House near where the McDonalds lived and joined the locals for breakfast at eight o'clock on Friday morning, before going to the lobby of a nearby hotel to have a second cup of coffee. He drove to the high-rise next to Bamboo Dunes, parked his car out of sight, and tucked the pistol in his belt, under the gray-patterned Hawaiian shirt he had on. The two-hundred-yard walk through blustery wind, under fast-scudding gray clouds, heightened his manufactured alertness fueled by a coffee buzz. Once inside the building, at the end of the second-floor hall, Brock knocked on the door of the McDonald unit, hoping they weren't still at breakfast. Marilyn McDonald had similar facial features as the man who whisked open the door. He said, "Yes?" His bone structure would rate in Hollywood, along with the broad shoulders and thin, sinewy body.

"My name's Brock Skinner. I'm on the board of Real Buy Louvers, the company managed by Elijah Ashby and your daughter."

A woman's voice inside could be heard, "Who is it, Peter?"

He didn't respond to her immediately, and said, "Come in." After Peter McDonald closed the door, he said, "Mindy, this is Brock Skinner, an acquaintance of Elijah and Marilyn."

"What are you doing here?" Mindy McDonald had a dyed-blonde pageboy, weak chin, and sallow face, creased with worry lines. The apartment had been done in buttercream walls and white wainscoting. There was nothing personal, no photos of family on the walls or parked in picture frames on the side tables.

"I wanted to speak to both of you before Elijah arrived. He's on his way here on a private jet."

"How do you know that?" Mindy stood and crossed her arms.

"I heard him tell Marilyn at the company board meeting yesterday afternoon."

Peter said, "Elijah called me last night, Mindy. What is it you wanted to talk about?"

"Your son and daughter," Brock replied to Peter, and then addressed Mindy, "And your daughter."

Peter took on a supercilious air, and pronounced, "Frankly, it's none of your business. It's a family affair."

Skinner slipped that punch. He responded, "I'm trying to keep anybody from getting hurt when the truth comes out."

"What truth?" Mindy asked.

Brock looked at Peter again. "Does she know the truth?"

"Oh, yes. We've lived with it for thirty-five years." He turned his back.

"Now that Elijah wants your approval to marry Marilyn, you folks are in a pickle," Brock warned.

"Peter, you didn't tell me that." She walked over and glared at him.

For the next twenty minutes, Skinner told the McDonalds the many things that had transpired since Toni Welch's death. He suggested what Elijah should be told when he arrived, and what should be left unsaid, at least for the time being. They reluctantly agreed. Brock also convinced them to allow him to hide in the bedroom to listen in on the conversation and be ready to intervene if Ashby got physical. While the three of them waited for a knock on the door, Brock asked a few more questions he wanted answered to fill in the gaps.

Peter ushered Elijah Ashby in and said, "You remember Mindy, don't you?"

"Yes. How are you, Mrs. McDonald?" He walked over and held her hand in his.

"Fine, Elijah. Nice to see you again."

"I'm sure your husband has told you that I want his and your approval to marry Marilyn." She pulled her hand away.

Peter intervened, "Sit down, Elijah. I have some things to share with you that you should know."

"Like what?" Ashby sat on a leather banquette against the wall and leaned forward.

"It's about your parents."

"What about them?"

"Your father asked me to do him a favor before you were born."

"What was that?"

"Your mother wanted to have children, but your father, shall we say, was shooting blanks."

Elijah straightened his arms and spoke in a high-pitched voice, "What are you saying?"

Peter broke eye contact. "He asked me to impregnate your mother, so she could have a child, a family."

"What are you talking about?" Ashby looked as though an electric shock had run through him. "That's a lie. My father would never have done that!" He blinked his eyes, trying to control his rage.

"Believe me, I kept telling him no. Then your mother pleaded with me, and Isaiah offered to buy a ten-million-dollar life insurance policy with you, the child, as the beneficiary."

Elijah jumped up and asked, "Is this true, Mrs. McDonald?"

"Well, that's his version. Mine is that he had an affair with your mother and spun that yarn to cover his tracks."

"Mindy, we've been over this a thousand times. Isaiah was a man of the church. He didn't want anyone to know about his problem. I should have never told you what I'd done."

"No, you shouldn't have. Then I'd have never seduced Carson Welch to get back at you." She sat down and slammed her elbows into the cushions of the sofa.

"Look at it this way, Elijah, if I hadn't agreed, you wouldn't be here, and you would have never ended up with ten million dollars."

"That's sick," he lashed back.

"Since Marilyn's your half sister, I suggest you tell her the truth, and break it off with her. Surely you know by now that Marilyn's evil. You should chase after a nice girl like Cheryl Welch."

"I can't believe you people. You're warped." Brock heard movement and thought Ashby intended to strangle his father. Skinner drew his gun and went to the bedroom door to see if he needed to stop him. Instead, Elijah left the apartment without looking back.

Brock went to the door, turned to face the McDonalds, and said, "I'll talk to Cheryl Welch. She deserves to know who her mother is." On the way home, he called Marcel and blurted out the whole story in one long sentence.

~ ~ ~

Elijah Ashby got back to Real Buy Louvers midafternoon on Friday. He went to his office, organized his mind, and used the company phone to ring Marilyn. "Could you come in here?"

She arrived, looking relaxed, and asked, "How did it go?"

He was standing at the window, gazing at the wispy clouds in the pearl-gray sky. "Not exactly how I expected. Your parents told me some bizarre things."

"Like what?"

"That my father was sterile, and my mother had sex with your father so she could have a family."

Marilyn rushed over to the window and grabbed Elijah by the elbow. "You mean my father is your father?"

"So, they say." Ashby pulled away from her and sat down behind his desk.

She dumped herself in the chair across from him, and said, "That son of a bitch. You're my half brother."

"Which means we ain't getting married."

Marilyn reviewed her options quickly, stood, and proclaimed, "I'm quitting, effective five o'clock today. I'll clean out my desk and leave any company property I have at home on your porch." She pivoted and made a beeline for the door.

"Wait. What will you do now?" Elijah asked.

She didn't turn as she barked on the way out, "Find another job."

~ ~ ~

Brock slinked into the house, bedraggled from over twenty hours behind the wheel, just after Maude got home from the winery. She seemed relieved that he'd returned in one piece. "Learn anything new?" she asked.

"Not really. If you don't mind, I'm going to invite Cheryl Welch and Elijah Ashby to join us at Keeneland tomorrow. I want to put a bow on this mess Marcel got us into."

"Go ahead. They'll be good company. I'm not very hungry, Brock. Would it be okay if we had a salad and beef consommé for supper?"

"Sounds wonderful."

After they ate, Skinner called Kyle Becker's cell number. He didn't answer. "Brock here, Kyle. You can come out of hiding now. Marilyn McDonald will keep her nose clean from here on out. My wife and I will be in Lexington tomorrow night and Sunday morning if you want to stop by. More importantly, I'd sure like to know how to bet the Derby. Text me your recommendation if you get a chance. Thanks." The plan had been for Becker to stay in Louisville, handicapping horses, until the coast was clear.

Cheryl Welch, who Brock called next, answered with, "Hello there."

"Hi. You doing all right?"

"Pretty well."

"Listen, I would like you to join Maude and me at Keeneland tomorrow to watch the Derby on the big-screen TV. Also, I have something very important to tell you."

"What is it?"

"I finally figured out why your parents became alcoholics. I'd like to share what I've learned when we're together."

"Okay. What time?"

"I'll meet you under the canopy of the clubhouse at four o'clock."

The last call Skinner made was to Ashby, who sounded forlorn when he came on, "Yes, Brock?"

"Is everything okay?"

"I'm just sad because Marilyn McDonald resigned this afternoon. She's going to get a job with a competitor."

"Sorry to hear that. Not unexpected, though, right?"

"What do you mean?"

"The ten-million-dollar insurance policy your father couldn't afford. Marilyn McDonald was the secondary beneficiary. That would suggest Isaiah Ashby couldn't have children, and Peter McDonald is your real father, which means Marilyn's your half sister."

"I can see now that having you and Marcel join the board of my company was a tragic mistake."

"I'm not so sure about that. I'd like you to come to Keeneland tomorrow at five o'clock to watch the Derby with Maude and me. Cheryl Welch will be there."

"She hates me because I went for Marilyn."

"Then you better convince her that Marilyn's out of the picture."

"That'll be a tall task."

After lunch, on Derby Day, Maude returned home from the winery to get ready to go to Keeneland. She made sure the help was prepared for the large crowd that would roll through that afternoon while she was gone. Brock loaded a few things for the trip in the SUV. He had on a sport coat and tie. Maude put on the other dress she had bought that didn't make the cut the last time they went to the races. Truman jumped in the back seat.

When the Skinner family arrived at their condo on Market Street in downtown Lexington, they went to the third-floor patio for a few minutes to take in the magnificent, blue sky. Brock said, "Come on, Truman. Let's take a walk over to the park." The two of them returned in a half hour. It was three o'clock by the time the SUV left for Keeneland. At three thirty, Maude and Brock were seated at the four-top they'd reserved for the event. He took out his phone and placed a call to Esther Rice. "Hey, have you heard from Kyle?"

"No, but he texted me how to bet the Derby," she replied.

"Care to share that with me?"

"Okay. Superfecta part-wheel. Five with the three twelve with the three twelve with the four six thirteen fourteen."

"How do you like the seats I got you?"

"Out of this world. Penny and I want to be your friend forever."

"Enjoy yourself."

At four o'clock, Brock told Maude, "I'm going to get Cheryl." She was standing under the canopy wearing a solid periwinkle dress, squinting up at the sun. "Nice seeing you again, Ms. Welch." They proceeded to the table. Maude offered pleasantries.

Cheryl had a serious look on her face. "I tossed and turned all night wondering what you know about my parents."

"I suspect it will come as no surprise. Before I tell you, let's talk about how we're going to bet the Derby. I got a tip from Marilyn's boyfriend."

"You mean ex-boyfriend."

"I'm not so sure about that. Elijah told me last night that Marilyn had resigned from the company, and she intends to get a job with a competitor."

"Ha! That's rich," Cheryl spewed.

Chapter 30

The hubbub at Churchill Downs had reached a fevered pitch by four thirty. Half-drunk men were staggering around, talking loudly, making disparaging comments about the clownishly dressed women who strolled by. Penny Gaines sat in the upstairs clubhouse, next to the man who loved her, the one from work with the Van Dyke beard. Esther Rice had her beau planted in a chair at the table where he couldn't easily see the track. She said to him privately, with her hand guarding her mouth, "If we're going to get along, you'll have to stop talking about yourself and pay more attention to me. I figured I better make that clear to you, so there'd be no misunderstanding."

All the poor man could do was smile. When the waiter came over to check the table, the two girls from Woodford County High School treated him like they owned the place.

At Keeneland, Skinner ran through the thoughts in his mind before proceeding to spill the beans Cheryl was waiting to hear. He nibbled around the edges at first. "I'm pretty sure Marilyn McDonald doubted Toni Welch was your mother."

"Why do you say that?" Cheryl asked.

"Because she was always looking for a blackmail angle. She picked up on what Toni said right before she died."

"Well, Elijah and I have shared the same doubts."

"I found out what happened. I hope it comes as a relief to you," Brock said. Maude watched Cheryl's expression to make sure she could handle what was coming next. The voice of the track announcer blaring through the speaker on the wall distracted the three of them momentarily.

"Let's hear it."

"Peter McDonald worked in the police department when you were born. He bribed someone in state records to alter the birth certificates of you and Marilyn."

"How so?"

"Switch the names of the mothers on each. You see, your mother is Mindy McDonald, and hers was Toni Welch."

Cheryl's mouth fell open as she leaned back in her chair. "Oh, my God. How did that happen?"

"Peter McDonald told Mindy about an affair he'd had with another woman, and she seduced your father to get back at him."

"And let me guess, Toni seduced Peter McDonald to get back at her husband, my father."

"That's about the size of it, and why your parents became alcoholics."

"Are you telling me Mindy and Toni swapped children after we were born?"

"Yes. Peter and Carson must have gotten together and told their wives they weren't going to raise a child who wasn't their own. They forced the women to make the switch."

"Luckily, Marilyn didn't find out Toni had changed her will to read 'her child' as the heir instead of me. My name was shown originally," Cheryl revealed.

"That's one of the few tricks she missed. Probably because she couldn't find a way to get a copy of Toni's will." Brock replied.

Cheryl turned her attention to the small TV overhead broadcasting a race from Churchill Downs leading up to the Derby. After the race ended and the successful horse wheeled back to the winner's circle, she said, "I guess it doesn't matter now. I just wish things were like they used to be, when the three of us were at Transy, before Toni died."

Maude asked, "What was so good about those days?"

"We were friends. We helped each other, liked each other. Look at us now. Rancor and distrust. Disappointment."

Brock said, "Money will do that. It would have been best if your parents hadn't done what they did. Sins of the fathers visited upon the children." He got up from the table and announced, "I'll be right back."

He returned a few minutes later with Elijah in tow. Cheryl saw Ashby and caught her breath. She looked away when he made eye contact. "Hello, Cheryl."

She asked Maude rhetorically, "What's he doing here?"

Brock cut in, "We invited him. He's got something interesting to tell you."

"What's that?"

Elijah said, "I told Marilyn I will never marry her, and that I loved you."

Cheryl shot back, "A little late for that now, don't you think?"

"Frankly, no. I do love you, Cheryl. How many times will I have to tell you?"

"Probably every day for the rest of your life," she answered derisively.

Ashby added, "Just think about it. I'll be waiting. Oh, by the way, Marilyn quit Real Buy today. She's going to try to ruin my business."

"I heard," Cheryl said.

~ ~ ~

The eighteen Thoroughbreds were in the starting gate for the running of the Kentucky Derby. Penny, Esther, and their dates were out on the veranda, by the handrail, gazing up the homestretch. The bell rang, the crowd cheered, and the horses leapt from the gate, banging into each other, jockeying for position. The animals were bunched up in the front and strung out in the back by the time they hit the first turn. Inertia caused several of them to veer wide as the pace slowed.

The panoply of tired horses barreling down the homestretch was an exciting moment, even for those disinterested in the sport of kings. The favored twelve horse, leading with a mere furlong to go, was no longer gamboling, but laboring to reach pay dirt. Horse five rolled way wide, out of view of the three contestants along the rail. Horse number three pulled within a neck of the favorite at the finish line, followed closely by the fourteen, but the win belonged to the sneaky horse number five running by himself in the middle of the track.

The order of finish was listed as 5-12-3-14. Brock and Maude waited for the results to be official. The superfecta paid $2,404.60 on a one-dollar ticket. They had it forty times, which was good for ninety-six thousand dollars before taxes were taken out. Penny and Esther each had twenty-dollar winning tickets, and there was no telling how many times Kyle Becker had it. Brock wondered where Becker was, and why he hadn't called or surfaced.

After the excitement of the Derby had finally died down, Elijah said to Cheryl, "Let's you and me meet at our favorite bar in downtown Danville for dinner."

"I don't know why I should say okay, but okay." The two of them thanked the Skinners and left Keeneland at the same time.

Maude commented to Brock, "You've helped Cheryl now. Is this thing over?"

"Almost. There's one more loose end to tie up."

"What's that?"

"It's who. Marilyn McDonald."

~ ~ ~

Le Deauville Bistro, two blocks from the Skinner condo, on North Limestone, occupied the corner of the first floor of a hundred-year-old brick building. The windows were painted hunter green. The band above them, in black, advertised the name of the restaurant in white, script letters. The double doors on a chamfer led right into the front corner of a bar that had been placed on a small section of tessellated flooring. Most of the seating was set up in the room to the back left. It's possible the place could be characterized as anti-feng shui, but the French had their own views on how to live life.

Marcel heralded, "You'll be buying dinner, I suppose, after winning so much at the track. Why is it I'm never that lucky?"

"It ain't luck, pal. It's information," Brock reminded him.

"Yeah, yeah. Maude, I'm sorry I introduced you to this guy. He's more trouble than he's worth sometimes."

All she could think to say was, "But he's so loveable."

"So, what's happened to the dog player?" Marcel questioned.

"I don't know, and I want to find out. After all, he's our neighbor, living at or near the center of the universe," Brock replied, half in jest.

Maude went for the salmon, Brock the Bouillabaisse, and Marcel the duck leg. The Skinners paid and left the restaurant after coffee, returned to their condo to take Truman for a walk, while Marcel took a stroll around downtown before heading home. Maude turned on the TV to watch the news. Brock, who heard nothing, was preoccupied with his own thoughts and unanswered questions. The couple turned in a little before eleven.

The digital clock beside the bed that had big, square red letters read 5:06 when Truman whimpered and pawed Brock. He snapped awake, pulled on his clothes, and grabbed the pistol. There was noise down on the street, like the sound of a garage door going down. A few seconds later, the light went on in Becker's bedroom for less than a minute. Brock took the elevator down to the first floor and raised his own garage door. When he stepped out onto the street, he saw Kyle Becker running toward a waiting cab. He closed up and went to the kitchen to try Becker's phone again. No answer. He placed another call. "Cheryl, it's Brock. Sorry to call you at this hour."

"It's all right. What's the matter?"

"I don't think Marilyn McDonald is home. Do you have any idea where she could have gone?" Brock asked. She told him without hesitation. He began searching on the computer.

The noise of the elevator going up to the third floor signaled that Maude was up. She came down to the second floor and wanted to know, "Why are you up so early?"

"Truman heard noises. It was Kyle Becker. It looks like he parked his car, retrieved something from his bedroom, and hightailed it out of here in a cab."

"Where's he going?"

"That's what I'm trying to find out." He kept scrolling through information on the computer, and then said, "Aha. I should be back by noon. Why don't you walk over to church this morning and tell me about the sermon when we head back to Hazard after lunch."

"On one condition. You promise to never mention Real Buy Louvers or its board members ever again."

"Cross my heart." Brock pocketed his phone, fixed a cup of coffee, put it in a traveler, and backed the SUV out onto the street. He was on I-75 north ten minutes later.

The dingy parking deck at the Cincinnati airport was quiet when he arrived. The security lines that cleared passage to the gates were notoriously long inside the terminal. Brock banked on that fact. He took the escalator and jogged to where the train out to the security area boarded. There was a long, hollow-metal wall with bullet-proof glass separating the lines from the onlookers. Skinner began searching for Becker and Marilyn McDonald. He found them the same time they saw him, so he called Becker on the phone, and said, "I won a pile of money on the Derby, thanks to you. Now I know why you dropped out of sight. Marilyn must've rekindled your romance and talked you into taking a trip with her. I hope you're planning on coming back from Lisbon." He could see that Marilyn was agitated.

"How did you find us?"

"I heard you park your car and go in to get your passport. A little birdy told me you were headed for Portugal."

"Skinner, I like you. I hope you're not here to cause any trouble." Kyle raised his hands and shrugged.

"Quite the contrary. I'm here to end trouble. Let me speak to Ms. McDonald." He handed her the phone.

"What do you want?" she growled.

"It's a pretty long list, but I don't think you'll object."

"I told Elijah he should have gotten rid of you."

Brock didn't respond and began stating demands, "First, I want you to promise to treat the dog player well. He's a decent guy. The type of person who might get you to change your wicked ways. Second, you must promise to leave his ex-girlfriends alone, as well as Elijah and Cheryl, who'll soon be an item."

"And what do I get in return for being so righteous?"

"Me on your team."

"I don't need you on my team," she remarked caustically.

"Yes, you do. Otherwise, I'll prove you killed Isaiah Ashby with the intent of blackmailing Elijah when he got the ten million dollars."

"I knew nothing about that insurance policy."

"You're lying. Your father had Ashby list you as the secondary beneficiary after you were born, and you learned about it when you got older. Probably the only good thing he ever did for you."

Marilyn McDonald raised her arms, and said, "I give." Then she cut the line and handed the phone back to Becker. One thing was for sure. She was the finest looking woman he, or anyone, had ever seen. With those looks, the big question was whether Kyle Becker could hold on to her. Everybody, even his ex-girl-friends, would be rooting for him.

CHAPTER 31

Marcel Sutherland loaded golf clubs in the trunk of his Mercedes and left the house at four fifteen on the Friday before Memorial Day. His brother-in-law had agreed to a big-money game, arranged by a couple of shills for Saturday afternoon at a course near Hazard, and wanted to head down early to visit his sister's winery on Saturday morning. He looked in the rearview mirror and saw Elijah Ashby's Audi turning into Saratoga Estates as he sped away from the neighborhood. He arrived at the log cabin just before supper. After wolfing down the delicious Indian food Maude had prepared, the three of them played gin until bedtime.

The Appalachian weather on Saturday morning was sensational, warm sun, low humidity, and a light breeze. Brock and Marcel went for an easy two-mile jog before breakfast. They drove to the winery at eleven thirty. Maude had been there for a couple of hours, bracing for what was sure to be a record crowd for the day. The men sat out on the veranda, watching her scurry in and out, attending to customers. Brock recognized George Pelham from Harlan, escorting a woman sure to be his wife, approaching on foot from the parking lot. He yelled in their direction, "George, over here!"

"Mr. Skinner, I want you to meet my wife, Constance." She was a tall, attractive lady who wore no makeup and had an innocent-looking face.

"Nice to meet you. This is my wife's brother, Marcel." He bowed slightly to her and shook George's hand.

"What brings you here on this fine day?"

"Have you heard?" he asked.

"Heard what?"

"About Marilyn McDonald. It was on the evening news."

"No, what?"

"Someone broke into her house last night around dark. Robbed and killed her." Marcel froze, and Brock looked skyward. "Reports said her boyfriend found her at home on the floor. Head had been bashed in. The door to her safe was open, and the contents gone."

Brock waved his wife over and introduced the couple. "Maude, George just told me that Marilyn McDonald has been murdered."

"No, that's terrible." She shivered, put her hand on her forehead, and looked down.

Brock said, "Well, that comes as a shock." He spoke to Maude, "Honey, Marcel and I are going to run over to the house to see if we can find any details on her death. We may be gone for a while," he said to the Pelhams. "I hope you folks don't mind."

"Not at all. We understand."

As they were moving off, Skinner said, "Next time we see you, hopefully, it'll be under better circumstances." When he reached the parking lot, Brock started running toward the Lamborghini. Marcel picked up the pace to stay with him, and Truman, looking nonplussed, watched them go. "I need to stop at the house for a minute. Then we can take off."

"Where're we going?"

"I'll tell you on the way. I'm not going to take a gun. We'll have to call and cancel our golf game." Skinner hurried into the house. He quickly saved a copy of the video of Toni's death on a memory stick and put it in his pocket.

~ ~ ~

Elijah Ashby's car was parked as close as possible to the front door of Cheryl Welch's house in Danville. He was sitting inside at her kitchen table, tapping his foot, fidgeting. She was standing in the hall, closing up an overnight bag she'd just finished packing. The front door flew open, surprising them. In stormed Brock Skinner and Marcel Sutherland. Ashby could tell they were loaded for bear. He stood and asked, "What do you want?"

Brock didn't answer. "Cheryl, when did he show up here?"

"I met him last night at our favorite bar downtown, at about eight thirty. We had dinner, came here, and he stayed over last night."

"Are you guys headed somewhere?"

"Yes. We're taking an overnight trip to Nashville. We're leaving now."

"No, you're not."

Ashby asked indignantly, "Who's going to stop us?"

"I am."

Cheryl, confused, wanted to know, "What's happening here?"

"Haven't you heard? Marilyn McDonald was murdered last night."

"What? No! How did it happen?"

"Elijah killed her."

She looked at Ashby. "What's he saying?"

Marcel fueled her disillusionment, "He's not going to tell you."

In a split second, Ashby bull-rushed Skinner. Brock turned and squatted slightly, hitting Elijah in the chest with his left shoulder, stopping his advance. Then he landed a right uppercut that knocked the man cold. Cheryl screamed and fell back on the couch. Brock straightened up, took a breath, and dug in his pocket for the memory stick. "Get his car keys and put this in the console between the front seats. Don't leave any fingerprints." Marcel took the jump drive, got Elijah's keys, and started for the front door. Brock added, "And see what's in the trunk."

Cheryl, now scared out of her wits, stood and demanded from Skinner, "You better have a good explanation for this."

"I do. Elijah must have seen Marilyn come home last night after being in Portugal for three weeks. He went over to see her, and she asked him to help her load the contents of her safe in the trunk of her car. I'm not sure what happened next, but she probably started needling him, like she did your stepmother fifteen years ago, and that's when she told him."

"Told him what?"

"That she'd killed his stepfather, Isaiah Ashby, so he could collect the ten million dollars in insurance. He must have become enraged and hit her in the head. It gave him a chance to avenge Isaiah's death and get back the money she'd taken from him."

Ashby began to moan and come to. Marcel came back in the house and announced, "The trunk is packed to the gills with gold coins."

Brock told Cheryl, "Call the Danville police. I'll hold him down until they get here. Hurry!"

Marcel asked Brock, "Do you think he'll confess?"

"I'm betting he does. He was raised right by his parents."

Cheryl called 911, like she had done when Ashby killed her stepmother.

While they were waiting for the police to arrive, Brock said, "When this is over, I hope you'll get to know that dog player, Kyle Becker. He's a better match for you than the scooper here." Elijah Ashby groaned, sat up, rubbed his chin, and said nothing.